STILL FALLING

A TROUBLED SPIRITS NOVEL

J.R. ERICKSON

DEDICATION

For my aunt Debbie who is likely looking out at sandy beaches while I gaze at drifts of snow.

AUTHOR'S NOTE

Still Falling is inspired by a true story. To avoid spoilers, that story is briefly retold at the end of this book.

1

Iris gripped the wheel, blinked into the fuzzy darkness. She hated night driving. The unfamiliar corner of the Upper Peninsula in northern Michigan coupled with three cocktails at Nina's house celebrating the case Marv had won that day ensured an anxious journey back to her grandmother's house.

It was all made worse by the landscape itself, slick snow and ice below, masses of black pines surrounding her, and a dark sky above. In this part of the world, no streetlights illuminated the road. Few if any cars shared it with her.

Ephemeral gray clouds periodically blotted the half-moon, thickening the shadows below. Iris had never enjoyed driving—period. She'd managed during undergraduate and then law school to live walking distance to all the necessities and to take the bus to those places too far to walk. Vehicles, despite their prevalence in modern society, struck Iris as alien spaceships. Complex engines, oil and tire pressure gauges, dashboards lit with a hundred different lights and warnings.

Her mother had died in a car accident when Iris had been thirteen. An accident on a night not so different from the one Iris drove in now: snow, trees, and slick roads. Her mother had struck a tree going sixty. Iris still couldn't piece together how. Hadn't she hit the brakes, let off the accelerator? Questions she'd posed to her dad and gotten only the blank, haunted stares he'd been known for in those days.

Iris gripped the wheel and squinted at the dark world beyond the windshield, concentrating on the sinuous white line that ran the edge of the winding forest road.

As she came around a curve, she glanced toward a gated seasonal road. A young man sprinted down the road, face twisted in terror beneath a brightly colored ski cap. Something was behind him, tall and dark in the shadows. Iris gaped at the two figures, lingered too long with her head turned.

She missed the curve in the road.

Iris grabbed the wheel and jerked hard, overcorrecting, but it was too late. The car launched off the snowy embankment toward the wall of trees. Iris screamed as the car went airborne. It catapulted into a tree, releasing a metallic shriek as the hood crushed in.

The force flung Iris forward, but the airbags on the driver's and passenger's sides exploded, punching her back in her seat.

The forward propulsion and riot of sound extinguished in an instant when the momentum of the car finally stopped. The tree had won.

Iris's heart hammered in her chest and her forehead throbbed. Dust from the airbags drifted in the still air. Her hands that had clutched the wheel lay curled at her sides, one wrist aching from the force of the airbag.

Broken glass lay scattered across the dashboard. Her headlights illuminated the dark trees, flecks of glass sparkling in the snow.

She had to move, unbuckle her seat belt, climb from the wreckage, but she couldn't will her fingers to move.

Stunned, she gazed into the dark trees, naked save the snow that clung to their leafless branches.

Minutes passed, and she smelled the scent of gasoline, oil, other engine things. Iris imagined some tick in the engine causing the car to burst into flames as she sat paralyzed inside.

"Three... two... one," Iris murmured, mustering her courage.

She unfurled her fingers, winced at the pain in her joints, and jammed a thumb against her seatbelt until it clicked. Gripping the door handle, she slumped sideways and pushed. The door stuck, the frame likely bent from the collision. Dizzy, warmth spreading down her face, which she suspected was blood, Iris tried again to push open the door.

Every part of her cried out as she shoved. The hinges screeched and the door opened an inch. Gritting her teeth, Iris turned and kicked the door open with both feet. Her body trembled as she eased out of the car and immediately sank into a thigh-high drift of snow.

She waded forward, snow filling her leather boots and seeping through her thin black leggings. She scrambled up the embankment and fell to her knees at the edge of the road, touching her forehead. Her fingers came away smeared with blood.

"Oh, no… no…" She murmured the words vacantly, trying to get her head straight.

She'd had three drinks at Nina's and might blow above the legal limit. The thought disturbed her, but not nearly as much as the one whispering on its heels. It was freezing cold, December in Sault Ste Marie, Michigan. She was stranded on a frozen road miles away from town.

Iris stood shakily and fumbled her phone from her coat pocket. Her fingers, already numb, grew more useless in the cold. She struggled to turn the phone on, to type in her passcode. Twice she punched it in wrong and swore. Would it lock her out if she typed it in wrong a third time?

"Focus," she whispered, swallowing the saliva thickening in her throat. Nausea was creeping in. Her head ached and the blood from her forehead had begun to leak beneath the collar of her coat.

Another feeling invaded her as well, a sense of something amiss, as if she'd crashed not merely in the woods, but on another planet, an alien place filled with hostile entities. A twig cracked in the woods behind her and she spun around, stumbling sideways when the pain of her abrupt movement tore across her head.

A breeze picked up, hissed through the trees. *Irisss…*

It brought a scent-campfire smoke tinged with something putrid like soured meat.

Swallowing, helpless to deny the rising panic seizing her, Iris squinted into the forest. Her headlights cast a pocket of light, flimsy, serving more to highlight all that she could not see.

But something was out there… watching her.

Despite the state of her car, she wanted to climb back inside, scrunch herself into a little ball and hide from whatever lurked in the forest.

"Stop it," she snapped, furious at her own fear, wanting to reach inside and yank it out, bury it in the snow.

She returned her attention to her phone. After two more tries, Iris entered the correct password and the home screen lit with an image of a quote she'd added to keep her motivated during law school. It read 'Pain is temporary, but a law degree lasts forever.'

Why had she drunk the third martini? She'd known better, even said as much to Nina before proceeding to gulp it down.

"It's done," she muttered, scrolling to her contacts, "no changing it now."

Her only friends in Sault Ste Marie were Nina and Marv, her co-worker and boss. Her only family was her grandma Lola, eighty-eight years old, who didn't drive at night because of cataracts.

She'd call Marv. He was heading back into town that night as well. He could pick her up, help her figure out what to do.

Behind her, lights lit the night, the flashing red and blue of a police car.

2

———

"Shit," she whispered, glancing at her wrecked car.

The fear of what lurked in the woods fled, replaced by a fresh fear, a drunk-driving citation. In an instant everything she'd worked for could be gone. A DUI wouldn't get her disbarred, but in a small town like Sault Ste Marie word would travel fast. She might lose her position at the Fraser Firm.

A state police cruiser pulled onto the shoulder and a man stepped out. He was tall, shadowy in the dark, and Iris stiffened. She'd never been one to trust people simply because they held positions of power. If anything, just the opposite. This man might have sworn to serve and protect, but what would he do on a dark, lonely forest road with no one the wiser?

The trooper moved into the beams of his headlights, spotted Iris, and jogged over. She took a faltering step back. He appeared to be in his thirties, tall and broad, with light hair and eyes.

"Hey, are you all right?" He stopped close to her, scanning her from head to foot. "Nasty scrape on the side of your forehead. Anything else hurt?"

Iris shook her head, willing her brain to switch on. "I… umm, lost control on some ice, I think."

"Yeah, that curve is dangerous, especially this time of year. Let me call it in and we'll get a tow truck out here. Do you think you need an ambulance?"

"No." Iris wrapped her arms across her chest, teeth chattering.

"Here, come on, get in the cruiser, warm up."

She followed him, guard lowering, though still ready to defend herself if he started asking questions. He hadn't mentioned a breathalyzer, sobriety tests. She'd never felt more sober in her life, but she wasn't sure her blood-alcohol level would say as much.

She sat in the cruiser, listened as he called the accident in, requested a towing service.

When he pulled into Lola's driveway, his high beams swept over the large pink house. Snow capped the points of the roof and icicles hung from the eaves, making it look less like its usual dollhouse and now oddly like a wedding cake.

"Thanks for the ride," Iris mumbled, shoved open the door and hurried through the swirling snow.

Iris stepped into the house and sagged against the wall. The warmth, the smell of the pecan pie her grandma Lola had made earlier that day, even the twinkling of the Christmas lights from the living room made her want to cry.

"Poppet?" Lola called.

"Yeah, it's me, Grandma." Iris slipped off her boots and hung her coat. Little red fireworks burst behind her eyes with each movement, sending streaks of pain across her head.

Iris trudged into the living room. She'd wiped the blood away from her face in the cruiser, but it had stained the neck of her gray blouse. She saw red beneath her fingernails and imbedded in the cuticles of her hands.

"My goodness me, what happened?" Lola struggled up from her chair and hurried to Iris, brushed the hair from her face and tilted her chin up.

"I crashed my car. I'm okay."

Lola gently touched the side of Iris's head and moved down her neck and shoulders and along her arm. "Are you sure nothing is broken? Do you have pain in your neck?"

"No, my face bore the brunt of the damage."

"Oh, honey." Lola pulled her close. "Thank God you're okay. Come on, come in the kitchen. I'll fix you something to eat and we'll whip up an ice pack for your head."

Iris didn't argue. Her grandma Lola was the only person she'd ever felt comfortable letting care for her.

She sat heavily at the table. The headache that had started after the crash took root and grew branches in her head.

Lola took a bag of frozen corn from the freezer and slapped it on the counter to loosen it. She put it in a towel and disappeared from the room, returned a moment later with a wool scarf. "Here. It's not perfect, but it will do. Tomorrow you're going into the health clinic and getting a proper bandage."

Iris adjusted the frozen corn on her head, and Lola tied the scarf behind her scalp.

Her grandma opened a drawer and held up two plastic bottles. "Aspirin or ibuprofen?"

"Ibuprofen."

Lola shook two pills on the table and handed Iris a glass of water. After Iris swallowed the pills, Lola set to fixing her dinner. She ladled white bean chili into a bowl and added a hunk of homemade bread to the side.

"There," she said, hands on her bony hips. "That will fix you right up."

Iris smiled and spooned the hot chili into her mouth. It warmed her as she swallowed. "Thanks, Grandma. I really appreciate it."

"Nothing gives me more pleasure than having you here with me, poppet. What happened? Slippery roads?"

Iris thought of the man she'd seen running, the shadowy thing behind him. Had she imagined it?

As if sensing her thoughts, Lola pulled a chair close to her. "Was it a spirit, honey? Did you see something that startled you?"

Iris shut her eyes. Lola talked of spirits and otherworldly things as if she were asking whether Iris had seen an opossum in the road. She didn't want to mention the shadowy thing, didn't want to acknowledge she'd seen anything at all.

"I'm not sure. It was dark..." Iris's head drooped forward. The adrenaline of the previous hour had worn off and exhaustion fell over her like a sudden rain. "I think I need to go to bed."

Lola patted her hand. "Yes, that's a good idea. Sleep is the greatest healer, after all."

Iris stood. Her feet and legs ached in protest.

"Thanks, Grandma. Good night," she murmured, leaning heavily on the banister as she made her way up the stairs to her bedroom.

Iris sat on the bed and switched the heated blanket on high. She lay back and pulled the covers up. Her head still pounded, but the pain had lessened with the cold of the corn and the first relief from the pain medicine.

Her mind plodded back over the crash, the seconds before when she'd looked down that stretch of deserted road. Had there been a sign there? Marking the entrance to something? She thought so, but it had all happened so fast she hadn't read it, or even registered it really. Had the man been real? Or had he been, as Lola suggested, a spirit? And what of the thing behind him? Dark, shaped like a man, but much taller.

It didn't matter. Iris had no intention of telling anyone about it, whatever it was.

3

———

The following morning, Iris found her grandmother standing in the kitchen wearing her usual pink bunny slippers and a long pink nightgown.

"Bacon and eggs? Pancakes? Let Grandma make you a big hearty breakfast." Lola gave Iris a hug and kissed her cheek before examining Iris's forehead. "A little goose egg and a cut, but not too bad."

Iris touched the bump. "It feels better, that's for sure. No breakfast though. Coffee is the only thing I'm interested in." Iris yawned and beelined for the coffee pot, filled a mug and sat at the table, wrapping her hands around the cup and shivering.

"It's cold in here," Iris murmured, pulling her knees into her chest and wishing she'd put on socks.

"Is it? Well, let me turn up the heat."

Her grandmother shuffled out of the room before Iris could insist she'd do it. Frankly, she didn't want to do it because it meant she had to put her bare feet back on the cold floor.

Through the kitchen window fat snowflakes fell.

"Great... more snow," she muttered.

She wondered yet again why she'd thought moving to the Upper Peninsula in Michigan was a good idea. Who escaped to a frozen tundra? Miserable people were supposed to choose tropical locations, so they could sip frozen margaritas and glare at happy couples while hiding behind a chunk of pineapple and a paper umbrella.

Despite Iris's protestations, Lola made pancakes and eggs and insisted Iris take a few bites so her pain medicine didn't make her sick.

Iris ate her breakfast and watched the minutes of the clock tick closer to the time she should have been showering, gathering her briefcase, starting her car. Oh wait, she didn't have a car-starting Lola's car. She needed to get moving or she'd be late, but the pulsing behind her eyes zapped her motivation to get her butt in gear.

"Why don't you call in, poppet?" Lola asked, her pale blue eyes regarding Iris with concern. "Surely they'd understand that you were in an accident last night."

"No, I don't feel comfortable doing that. New associates are held to certain standards and I'm not about to show them I'm unreliable. I think I'll go in late, though." She dialed the number for the law firm.

"You've reached the Fraser Firm, this is Candace. How may I help you?"

"Hey, Candace, it's Iris. How are you?"

"I'm just dandy. I spent ten minutes chipping ice off my windshield this morning and walked in to two voice messages. One from an angry divorcée—I'll be directing her to Paul—and a man calling to seek defense counsel for assault and battery. Lucky Marv. Another glorious morning."

Iris closed her eyes and willed the throbbing in her head to calm down. "That's life, I guess. Can you let Marv and Nina know I'll be in at ten? I crashed my car last night and need a bit of extra time."

"Oh, no, that's terrible. Are you okay?"

"Yeah, just bumped my head. My car's in rough shape, but I can drive Lola's."

"Maybe you should take the day. I'm sure Marv wouldn't mind."

"No, it's okay. I'll be there."

She'd barely set down her phone when it rang. Marv's name popped up on the screen.

"Hey," she answered, standing from the table and walking the hall toward the front door.

"Candace said you wrecked your car last night?" he demanded.

"Pretty much. I doubt it will be salvageable, but I'm fine, just a lingering headache."

"Jesus. Did you get a concussion?"

"No. I don't think so anyway." Though the drumming behind Iris's eyes told another story.

"You don't think so? Didn't you go to the hospital?"

"No. In case you forgot, I had a few martinis last night. I wasn't trying to get a DUI."

"They wouldn't have done blood work just because you smacked your head. Anyway, I'd have gotten you out of a DUI if they tried," Marv said. "Well, forget about coming in. We don't need a new associate collapsing on the job. Take the day, go see a doctor, and get some rest. I expect you bright-eyed and bushy-tailed tomorrow, Walsh."

"Thanks, Marv. I really appreciate it."

He barked a laugh. "I love the gratitude of new fish." He hung up the phone before she could respond.

Snow swirled beyond the frosted glass in the front door and Iris sighed, thankful she wouldn't have to trek into it that day. She started back toward the kitchen and paused at the table of photographs in the hall. In several of the images, her brother looked back at her—forever frozen in childhood.

There'd been few photos of Frankie in Iris's childhood home after his death. It was her mother who'd stashed them away, unable to endure the reminder that she'd once had a son. But then her mother had died too, and unlike his wife, Iris's father hadn't taken down any photos. He'd done just the opposite. Left everything where it was. The photos had slowly gathered dust.

Only the photos in Iris's room had changed. She'd replaced elementary dance class photos with the high-school volleyball team. Her high-school graduation picture became photos of her graduation from law school. Each year, she'd removed the photos from the year before and put new ones in their place.

The pictures Lola kept of Frankie were many and varied, scattered throughout the house as if they were no different than the others. Iris picked up a frame decorated in red and blue rhinestones. In the photo, Frankie and Iris stood on Lola's front lawn, each holding sparklers. Iris wore red and blue ribbons in her ponytail. It must have been the Fourth of July weekend. Iris returned it to the table and picked up another picture. This one depicted Frankie straddling a bike in Lola's driveway. Iris didn't remember the bike.

"Frankie picked that out at a garage sale," Lola said, startling Iris.

Frankie grinned his gap-toothed smile. His coppery hair, almost identical in color to Iris's, fell across his forehead. She tried to remember his voice, his laugh, but the memories of those sounds had been eroded by the sands of time.

"Was this the summer he died?"

"Yes. He was so excited about that bicycle." Tears filled Lola's eyes.

Iris turned away, not wanting to watch the grief and perhaps guilt that often appeared on Lola's face when they spoke of Frankie.

Lola put a hand on Iris's shoulder and squeezed. "Here, let's sit you down in the living room and I'll brush your hair."

Iris thought of arguing, reminding her grandma she was twenty-eight years old, but she kept her mouth closed and allowed Lola to guide her into the warm room lit by the Christmas tree. Iris sat in a well-worn pink and gray striped chair.

Lola stood behind her and ran the soft bristle brush she'd used on Iris in childhood through her long, copper-colored hair. Iris closed her eyes and leaned back. It brought back a hundred memories of sitting on her grandmother's bed as Lola brushed her damp hair and told her folk stories about fairies and mischievous little men and haunted places.

Iris had believed the stories in childhood, but as she'd transitioned to a teenager, she'd grown leery of anything she hadn't seen with her own two eyes. Any talk of faith, church, or miracles caused her to inwardly cringe. She'd become deeply cynical about the far-fetched stories people told themselves regarding the nature of reality.

After Frankie passed and then her mother died just three years later, Iris's visits to Lola grew few and far between. Her father hadn't had the time as a single father to drive Iris four-plus hours from Haslett to Sault Ste Marie to visit her grandmother. Iris too had filled her time with extracurriculars, getting lost, much like her father, in busyness.

During her final years in law school, Iris hadn't seen her grandmother a single time. Those magic childhood days of summer had faded further from her mind. She'd thought little of Lola until the great implosion, the disturbing night when the voice of her long-dead brother spirited to her from the darkness.

Tears gathered behind Iris's eyes. She wanted to ask about Frankie's final summer alive, tell her grandmother about the shadow man from the night before, talk about how deeply she resented her mother for dying and leaving her behind.

It wasn't only that her mother had abandoned Iris, it was that she'd never been there fully to begin with. Not for Iris. She'd been there for Frankie. He'd been her clear favorite and his death had destroyed her.

Several weeks after her mother's accident, Iris had overheard the woman who babysat for her talking to a neighbor. 'She gave up,' the woman had said. 'After she lost her son, she gave up on life. I wouldn't be surprised if she steered right into that tree.'

It might not have been true. Iris's father more than once had called the woman meddlesome and gossipy, but the words had planted themselves like a poisonous flower in Iris's heart. It bloomed and grew thorny. It stripped Iris of any good memories she'd had of her mother and painted their life together in shades of black and gray. Her mother had favored Frankie and when Frankie was gone, she'd had no reason to live.

Lola stopped brushing and kissed Iris on the head. "I'm going to get a vegetable stew started in the crockpot. How does that sound for dinner tonight?"

"Sure, thanks, Grandma." Iris drew the blanket further onto her lap.

I ris must have dozed off because when she woke, she discovered her grandmother had heaped another blanket on top of her and set a glass of water on the coffee table. Her skin felt damp and clammy, her throat dry. Iris leaned forward and grabbed the water, gulped half of it down. The sudden movement caused a slice of pain through her head, and she leaned back against the couch and gritted her teeth.

Maybe her grandmother and Marv were right, and she needed to see a doctor. Then again, what could they do for a concussion anyhow?

Iris shifted her gaze to the picture window and froze.

A man watched her through the crystalizing glass, as if his breath were icing the window pane rather than warming it.

Except he had no breath. The pallor of his skin was as gray as the sky above, his eyes sightless and cloudy.

He had a face and shoulders and the start of a torso and then nothing. Iris could see the porch, the snow-heavy yard beyond where his legs should have been.

4

"Poppet," Lola said.

Iris jumped and twisted around to face her grandma.

"Sshh… it's all right," Lola murmured, resting a hand on Iris's shoulder. She squeezed gently and Iris tried to relax, but her heart thundered behind her ribs. "That's Morris Flannery, just an old neighbor stopping for a visit." Lola walked closer to the window and pressed a palm against the glass. "Hi, Morris, I see you, darlin'. Go on now. Go back home."

The man stood in place, but slowly he grew transparent until Iris could see the house across the street, the snow-capped roof, the glittering icicles hanging from the eaves.

Iris let out an unsteady breath.

Lola turned back to her. "See, poppet? It's not so bad. Most of 'em are just peeking in, lookin' in on things. They don't do any harm. The real trouble happens in our own heads when we start gettin' scared."

Iris pushed her hands through her hair, tangling her fingers in it and jerking them free. "I just… I don't want to see them." She looked at Lola as tears pricked the backs of her eyes.

Great, more tears. She'd cried more in the previous six months than in the past decade. What had happened to her cool, collected self? The woman who'd graduated valedictorian in high school, had top marks in law school, passed the bar on her first try?

Lola ambled across the room and sat in her easy chair. She propped her slippered feet on the stool in front of her. She studied Iris, but Iris didn't meet her eyes. Lola had always had the kind of penetrating gaze that made Iris feel as if she could puzzle out exactly what lived in her granddaughter's mind.

"It's okay to talk about it, poppet. You need to talk about it. Staying hush about the things that scare us is bad for the soul. Those secrets will get hold of you like a cancer, eat you from the inside out."

Iris shuddered and tugged a pillow to her chest as if it might act as a shield against the apparitions who'd invaded her life like a plague. "Maybe… maybe I should go to the doctor again. See about some kind of prescription."

Lola put a hand on her chest as if Iris's statement made her heart ache. "Oh, poppet, there's no pill that makes this go away. The sight is as tethered to you as the ears attached to the sides of your head."

"Surgery could remove those," Iris mumbled.

Lola smiled and leaned back in her chair, interlacing her fingers on legs that looked especially bony beneath her flimsy nightgown.

"I was seven years old when I first started seeing the dead," Lola told her. "In those days, us kids went to the blue schoolhouse on Aspen Lane. A few times I noticed a little girl in the play yard swinging alone on the swing set. I'd watch her and wonder why she wasn't getting lessons like the rest of us. Except in those days, a lot of families schooled their kids at home, if they schooled them at all. Some of them worked on the farm and around the house and the children couldn't be spared for an education.

"One day I pointed the girl out to the teacher, Mrs. Swanson. Mrs. Swanson said she didn't see a little girl. I described her. I said, 'She's right there on the swing. She has white-blonde hair braided in pigtails and she's wearing a yellow smock with a navy-blue ribbon around the waist.' For some reason, this really bothered my teacher. She kept saying she didn't see her, but getting more and more upset until she dragged me by the hand right out there to the swing, demanding I show her where this girl was. Then she just started wailing and shaking me.

"We had another teacher who worked with the older kids who ran out and stopped her. That teacher sent me back inside, and we all watched through the window as Mrs. Swanson cried and tugged on the swing. Finally, she just ran off down the road. She never came back to teach us and the next day the upper teacher, Mrs. Dempsey, slapped my fingers with a ruler for making up lies about the little girl to tease Mrs.

Swanson. Oh, how I cried. There are few lashings that compare to a ruler across the knuckles. Later, an older boy who walked to and from school with me told me that Mrs. Swanson's daughter had died years before at the schoolhouse. She'd fallen out of a tree and broken her neck. I'd been seeing that little girl all year."

Iris picked at the blanket in her lap, her usual skepticism buzzing in the back of her mind. Despite having seen things herself, she continued to question their validity, to think it was more likely she and Lola shared a common neurological disease, some hereditary trait explained away as an intuitive gift when really it was plain old hallucinations.

Still, Iris was curious about the story her grandmother had shared. "Did you ever see her again? Mrs. Swanson?"

Lola nodded. "I surely did. The following summer, she paid a visit to our farm. She asked my mother if she could speak to me privately. I wasn't scared. I knew why she'd come. Her daughter had told me that very morning. I'd woken to find the girl in my room sitting on the floor looking in my dollhouse. She said, 'My mama's going to come see you today,' and then she just disappeared.

"Mrs. Swanson wanted to know if it was true. If I'd really seen her little girl. I told her it was and then I told her that sometimes Ellen—that was her daughter—talked about somebody named Bernard and how she missed cuddling him. Mrs. Swanson said Bernard was their dog. I also told her that Ellen loved to sing *London Bridge is Falling Down* and her favorite food was stuffed celery. Mrs. Swanson cried because she knew I couldn't have known those things. It brought her peace, Iris. Knowing that her little girl was still around, even if she couldn't see her.

"I was able to ease this woman's grief, little old me, Lola Imogen Walsh. That was the beginning for me. So I was never afraid when they came calling. Now and then they wanted me to pass on a message so I would, but most of the time they just drift through. It's not a curse, poppet. I know sometimes it feels like that to you, but I promise you it's not. In some ways it's the greatest contribution I've brought to this world. That gift has been bestowed upon you as well."

Iris tried to digest her grandmother's words, but they ignited a deep inner turmoil. Accomplished attorneys didn't talk to spirits on the side, spend their weekends at psychic fairs connecting people to their dead relatives. Iris simply could not imagine how such a gift could ever fit into the life she wanted, the life she'd worked for.

"Did your mother know what you were seeing?" Iris asked.

"She did. She'd not gotten the sight, but her mother had it. My grandma, Leona. Leona died when my mother was a girl, but she told me about the strange ability my grandmother had to see family members they'd already buried. I'm not sure she truly believed in it until I started telling her what I saw. It took time, but eventually she believed. They just want to be seen, poppet. Be part of the world again, even if just for a breath. They aren't bothering nobody, so don't let 'em bother you."

Iris sighed. "I appreciate the story, Grandma. I think I'll have a little nap and then get some work done."

Lola cupped her cheek. "You do that, honey. And trust me, someday you'll look back on this time and all you'll remember is the magic."

Marv had asked Iris days before to review and highlight witness depositions in a burglary case he was defending the following week. She highlighted several inconsistent statements given by the only eyewitness, an elderly man who lived nearly half a block away from the home that had been burglarized.

Iris clicked the red button on her voice recorder: "Gordon Huck," she recorded, "witness for the prosecution, stated in his deposition that the man he saw running from 382 Perry Avenue was a white male, approximately six feet tall with sandy-colored hair. In his original statement given to police, he described the man as five feet eight inches tall and said it was too dark to see hair color."

She ended the recording and returned to the typed deposition, making notes in the margins. The typed words seemed to have grown smaller, blurrier in the previous hour.

The headache had crept back in. She glanced at her watch. It was nearly five p.m. She was due for more pain pills.

In the living room, she heard the voices of Lola and her two friends Minnie and Jan as they sat playing a game of Monopoly.

"Park Place with hotels," Minnie announced loudly. "Lola, you are about to sell off those houses you just bought."

"Darn it, Minnie. How do you get those properties every time?"

"I've got the Midas touch." Minnie laughed.

"Hmph," Lola said.

"I think she's bringing weighted dice," Jan cut in.

"Pish-posh," Minnie said.

Iris rubbed her eyes. It was strange at times living in a house full of sounds. Her own home had been quiet, her father gone at work or watching the television on mute, preferring to read the subtitles rather than hear the voices and music. Sometimes, when Iris had been home alone, she'd cranked her stereo or the television on loud, but it rarely comforted her.

Iris stood and made her way to the hall, poked her head into the living room. "I'm going to lie down," she called to her grandmother and her friends.

"Do you need anything, poppet?" Lola asked.

"Nope, I'm good." Iris waved and retreated.

Pain pills in hand, she trudged up the stairs into her room. She sat on the edge of the bed, popped the pills in her mouth and took a sip from the glass of water she kept at the side of the bed.

Iris lay back and drew the covers up, turning on her side. From the corner of the room, something moved. The closet was open a crack. As she watched, the door creaked open further. Iris felt eyes on her, and the dark crevice looked not merely like an unlit space, but more like the inky black of the shadowy figure from the night before.

She blinked at it, trying to will the feelings away, but they only loomed larger as the closet door crept further open. A scent spilled out like smoke and burned meat.

Iris jumped out of bed and strode for the doorway leading out of the room. She was halfway down the stairs when anger at her cowardice erupted. She turned and stalked back to the room, jerked the closet door open.

Her clothes, arranged on her hangers, occupied the space. On the floor sat a row of shoes and her suitcase.

Nothing else.

No shadowy beast crouched within the closet, and the smell too had dissipated. Still, Iris pulled the string that illuminated the single bulb in the space. She opened the curtains to let in the dull afternoon light.

The darkness banished from the room, she climbed back into bed and slept.

5

"My vote's on meth," Marv told Nina as Iris walked into the law office the following day. "Look how he's running, like something's chasing him when there's not a soul in sight. He went out there, got high on a bad stash and thinks there's a machete-wielding clown behind him."

Iris stopped, staring at the news broadcast playing a video clip of a young man running down a dark road, illuminated only by a single floodlight pointed toward the snowy path. Several feet behind him, a dark silhouette followed, too tall to be a man, but in the shape of a man.

A touch of panic gripped Iris as she watched the scene she'd witnessed two nights before. For several seconds she relived it all: the fleeing young man, the terror of the accident, and finally the dead quiet when she'd stepped from her car.

Something had been watching her.

Nina leaned closer to the screen. "Yeah, there's no one following him. Miles Fincher released a statement that no one was on the grounds that night. I'd say you're right. Either drugs or mental illness."

Iris wanted to point out the shadowy figure, but she bit her teeth together, woozy. The young man had been running, chased by the same figure in the video—a figure Marv and Nina couldn't see.

"Iris, hey, you okay?" Nina turned and stepped toward her, putting a steadying hand on her arm.

Iris swallowed. "Yeah, just a dizzy spell."

"Because you shouldn't be working," Marv said. "Who comes to work right after they wreck their car and smash their head into the windshield?"

"I didn't smash my head into the windshield. The airbag got me."

"Well, it looks like someone took a baseball bat to your face."

"Thank you. That's very reassuring, Marv."

Nina waved him away. "Marv, did anyone ever tell you you're kind of an ass?"

He ticked off his fingers. "My brother, my last three ex-girlfriends, my mom once or twice."

"Come on, Iris, let's get you a donut from the break room."

Iris allowed Nina to lead her away. In the break room, Iris selected a glazed donut, though she really wasn't hungry. Nina went for powdered sugar.

The cornflower-colored walls were peppered with framed quotes, what Marv liked to call lawyer humor.

'A lawyer is a person who writes a ten-thousand-word document and calls it a "brief."' —Franz Kafka

'He who is his own lawyer has a fool for a client.' —Proverb

"What's the story on that guy who's missing?" Iris asked.

Nina took a bite and blotted her sugary lips with a napkin. She chewed and swallowed before answering. "Brett Stephens, nineteen, was doing some work at Skelling Hall and no one has seen him since."

"What's Skelling Hall?"

"It's this big old mansion out on the Skelling Peninsula. It's a historic site now, open three days a week for tours, and they do a few big events every year. I don't know much about it, but Brett's family owns a lawn company and I think they do snow removal in the winter. I'm assuming he was out there doing that. It's unclear what exactly happened.

"His mom reported him missing yesterday, but it sounds like she told the police he probably took off. Drug problems run in the family. Marv has defended the guy's brother and dad. The caretaker at Skelling Hall, Miles Fincher, reported to police that Brett's plow truck was parked out there. Miles checked surveillance. The hall only has one camera on that stretch of road that runs up the peninsula. Around seven o'clock Brett's truck drove in and then who knows what he did for the next three hours. Just after ten the camera catches him running like hell down that road—nothing chasing him."

"Could there have been something in the woods? You can't see into the woods on either side of the road in that video."

Nina raised an eyebrow. "Something? Like a bear?"

"Or someone?"

Nina nodded and took another bite, thoughtful. "Could be, but why wouldn't he run back to the hall or get into his truck? He's running toward the main road and I can tell you that place is deserted at night. You're not flagging anybody down out there."

Iris's donut grew dry in her mouth. She struggled to swallow it. It had been deserted out there, but she'd crashed just yards away from the guy. Why hadn't he fled to where she was climbing dazed from her car? Why hadn't Brett flagged down the cop who drove her back into town? Where had Brett gone in the moments after her wreck?

"Do you know him personally?" Iris asked. "Brett?"

Nina shook her head. "No, but like I said, Marv's dealt with his family. Brett's older brother, Parker has been arrested a few times for possession. Marv thinks the kid is probably high in that video, experiencing delusions or something."

Iris only half listened. The haunting image of the fleeing man played on a reel in her head. It wasn't drugs that had had him on the run. Something had been chasing him. "Has there been a search of the grounds? It's so cold. If he ran off, got lost…"

"He's dead then," Nina said matter-of-factly. "I doubt anyone could survive two nights in this weather, and in the video he wasn't exactly in survival gear."

"That's a disturbing thought," Iris murmured. "They must be searching for him, right? The police?"

"I doubt they're dedicating a lot of manpower to a nineteen-year-old who got stoned and took off. The sheriff can be a hardass about certain folks in this town. He has that tough-love, teach-'em-a-lesson personality. He's expecting this kid to appear at home with a story of passing out on somebody's couch for a week. I'd imagine they've looked around a bit, but…" Nina shrugged. "I'm guessing he'll show back up."

"Yeah, maybe," Iris said.

~

"Anything jump out in those depositions?" Marv asked, poking his head into the office Iris and Nina shared.

Iris rubbed her eyes, the words before her merging into a stream of nonsense. It was after noon and she'd been reading depositions for nearly four hours.

"Yeah," Iris admitted. "This guy gave two different descriptions of the perp he saw running from the house."

"I thought so." Marv laughed, slapping his thigh. "I couldn't remember what he'd said in the original report, but when I took that deposition, I swore it didn't line up."

"It doesn't," Iris agreed.

"Well, there goes the prosecution's eyewitness testimony. Anyway, I'm running out to Skelling Hall to grab some documents for Don. I can pick up lunch. What does everyone want?" Marv's gaze shifted from Iris to Nina.

"I need a salad. I totally overdid it last weekend," Nina said. "My boyfriend's family equates the month of December with a holiday every weekend. I think I ate five pounds of mashed potatoes and apple pie."

Marv wrinkled his nose. "Not together, I hope. Okay, salad. How about Tony's? They've got salad and those really good sandwiches."

"You're going to Skelling Hall?" Iris sat up straighter.

"Yep. Don Fraser handles the estate stuff and Beatrice Skelling insists on dropping all the documents related to the estate at the hall and then having one of us go out there to pick them up. I'm the gopher this time."

"You could just send one of us minions," Nina said.

"It has to be a senior associate," Marv groused. "She's particular."

"Can I come with you?" Iris asked.

Marv cocked an eyebrow. "You trying to get me alone, Walsh?"

Iris rolled her eyes. "Hardly. I've never seen the place. I'm curious."

"You've never seen Skelling Hall? I thought you spent summers up here? I can't believe your grandma Lola never dragged you out there."

"She didn't." Iris frowned. "Not that I remember, anyway."

"Well, shake a leg then. Get your coat. This train is pulling out."

6

Marv slowed his car as they came toward the road that led up the isolated peninsula to Skelling Hall.

Iris twitched as her eyes drifted over the shards of glass glittering in the ditch from her accident. Bits of green fiberglass flecked the snowbank where her car had landed. Bark hung in peels from the tree she'd smashed into. Marv didn't seem to notice the debris as he turned onto the snowy road.

The road was flanked by trees. As they neared the end of the long driveway, the trees bent toward one another, creating a snowy canopy over the entrance to Skelling Hall.

"Wow," Iris breathed as the enormous house slid into view.

"Welcome, Miss Walsh, to Skelling Hall. Once the most magnificent mansion in all the land and also one of the most obnoxious displays of wealth a man could mar the otherwise perfectly wild shoreline with."

Iris turned and peered back down the long, wooded driveway. From the road, she'd never have imagined such a house lay tucked behind the trees, yet here it was, huge and hulking against the glacial blue sky. "What is it, though? This was someone's home."

"Felix and Angelique Skelling. French Canadians. Felix was a lumber baron. They amassed a fortune in Canada and then moved to America in the early 1900s. I've done the tour, but the facts elude me. I think it took three years to build this place—Renaissance Revival, obviously. I guess he wanted to show off for the freighters passing because you sure can't see this abomination from the road.

"They had a few kids, two of whom disappeared. Angelique passed, Felix ended up in a mental hospital, blah, blah, blah. If you've heard one of these stories you've heard them all. What is it with rich people and going mad? Not that it stops me from chasing the almighty dollar, mind you. I'm putting my hopes in the stock market. Churns out far fewer wackos."

Iris only half listened as he parked in a line of cars. She pushed open the door and climbed out, shivering. It wasn't the cold exactly. Something icy emanated from the house and the surrounding property. That alien sense that Iris wanted to build a wall against, but couldn't seem to block.

As they walked the paved path toward the grand entrance, Iris glanced up. The faces of two pale children loomed in an upstairs window. Tourists? The windows went black as if someone had poured tar down the glass. Iris stopped abruptly and Marv walked into the back of her.

"Christ, Walsh. Walk much?" He stepped around her. "What?" He tilted his head to look up at the house, but the black had faded. The windows reflected the blue sky. Marv put a hand up to shield his eyes.

"Nothing, I just... never mind." She continued on, pausing as the front door opened and two old women, arms linked, burst from the interior. They were talking excitedly.

"Welcome to Skelling Hall," Marv told Iris as they stepped through the doorway into a grand foyer with marble floors and soaring ceilings.

Oil paintings of pastoral settings, churches and poised families hung on the walls. A high archway opened into a large room across the foyer and Marv took her hand and dragged Iris through it.

"In here, madame, we have the grand ball room. Magnifique! And also the location of La Fête de Noël."

"La what?"

"La what?" He made a horrified face. "Were you born in a barn? It's the fabulous Skelling Hall Christmas party—only the premier social event of the season."

Iris gazed over the expansive room. An enormous brick fireplace stood at the opposite end. A crystal chandelier hung from the patterned tin ceiling. A gold and maroon rug covered the length of the floor. Tall narrow windows were slated along one wall and revealed the St. Mary's River beyond.

"There's a Christmas party here?" Iris asked Marv.

"Oh yeah, the Skelling Hall Christmas Gala. Anybody who's anybody will be here." Marv chuckled. "They deck this place out. Early in the day there's a Santa and sleigh rides on a trail along the water. At dark the kids are shuffled off to their nannies and the champagne flutes come out. It's all right. I've never missed one because inevitably someone will get drunk, strip naked and go do a polar plunge in the river. It's worth it for that show alone."

He drew Iris out of the ballroom and toward a room that might have once been a parlor, but was now an enormous gift shop.

"Sault Ste Marie coffee mug? Skelling Hall Christmas ornament? How about a Petoskey stone magnet? Anything your little tourist heart desires is right here in this room."

An attractive woman in navy yoga pants stood at a wall of glass shelves trying to reach a Skelling Hall champagne flute.

"Duty calls," he murmured to Iris with a wink. Marv swaggered over to help her, but had to stand on tiptoes to get hold of the flute.

A man providing a guided tour spoke loudly to a group on the opposite side of the room. "In his prime," the man boomed, "Felix Skelling hosted captains of industry between these walls. As you see, this room boasts vaulted ceilings and striking period features, including ornate cornicing and the decorative hearth. This was also the grand dining room. The Skellings threw lavish parties. It is rumored that for one such party they had crates of oysters shipped from New York."

Iris walked closer, pausing at the edge of the group.

"Our waterway here is St. Mary's River, which is fed by Lake Superior. Lake Superior, despite her name, is largely considered an inland sea. Superior holds more water than Lake Michigan, Erie, Huron and Ontario combined.

"In the 1600s the fur trade was the primary commerce in these parts and ruled largely by Native Americans, though French explorers soon followed. The economic windfall arrived in the form of deposits of iron ore and copper. These minerals were originally moved by boat and by horse and buggy—grueling work, I can only imagine. That all changed in 1853 with the construction of the Soo Locks. The locks changed the industry forever and turned Lake Superior into a major shipping highway. More than eight million tons of cargo pass through the locks every year.

"Skelling Hall is built on a peninsula, though it is vast and densely wooded, as you saw on your drive in. Many have gotten lost in the forest here, however, if you walk far enough in any direction, you'll surely run into water. Still, it is inadvisable that you venture into the trees more than a few steps.

"Felix was particular about building the house with all these windows facing the St. Mary's River in a northwesterly direction so he could catch the sunset each evening. It is a glorious view, is it not?" The guide paused and stared as if in awe at the sparkling water that could be seen through the enormous windows. "This may only appear to be a river, but this is an extension of Lake Superior and that body of water is no friend. Called Gichigami by the Ojibwe tribe, which means big water,' Lake Superior has sunk some of the strongest ships ever built. Some of you might have heard of one particularly grievous disaster—the sinking of the SS *Edmund Fitzgerald*."

As if on cue, and surely it had been orchestrated that way, the song about the wreck began to play from speakers tucked in the corners of the room.

"The *Fitzgerald* set out on November ninth, 1975, from Superior, Wisconsin, en route to Detroit, Michigan, carrying a massive twenty-nine-thousand-ton load of iron ore. A day later the *Fitzgerald* became ensnared in one of the worst storms ever to hit Lake Superior."

The man's voice had grown quiet, but now he raised it and lifted his arms above his head. "Waves more than thirty feet high! Imagine it." He looked up as if he could see that great bleak wave rolling to a crescendo. "Then boom!" He slapped his hands together.

Iris, along with a few others in the group, jumped. The story itself was riveting, but Iris was equally mesmerized by the previously impassive man suddenly exploding with emotion.

"Straight to the bottom the *Fitzgerald* went, more than five hundred feet down into those black depths." Again, he looked toward the window. "The entire crew of twenty-nine men still lie in the wreckage."

Overhead the song played on, the ominous message that Lake Superior never gives up her dead bringing the tune to a close.

Iris shuddered. She'd always hated the song. In high school, her social studies teacher had played it during class when they'd been learning about the disastrous shipwreck. It was eerie in itself but for her, it was personal. Frankie had drowned in St. Mary's River, a river fed by Lake Superior, and like Lake Superior the river had not given up her dead.

Iris followed the guide's gaze and the river, which had seemed perfectly peaceful a moment before, now appeared menacing. A little boy clutched his mother's hand as he too looked at the water.

"Why didn't they recover the bodies of the crew?" the mother asked, patting her child's dark hair.

"The water is too deep and too cold. It's simply too dangerous. The Skelling family themselves were similarly affected by the cruelty of the water. In 1931, the two Skelling sons Andre and Phillippe disappeared without a trace. It's believed the boys went swimming and drowned. Their bodies were never recovered. You'll see a painting of the Skelling boys in the foyer on the west wall if you're so inclined."

"Does the river ever freeze?" a man, wearing a Detroit Lions jacket and matching knit hat, asked.

The tour guide slowly turned from the window and eyed the man. After a pause, he nodded. "Yes. If you walk out to the shore, you'll see the ice shelves starting to build on the shoreline. Another few weeks and that ice will spread towards the opposite shore."

Iris turned to see Marv had abandoned the attractive woman and stood chatting with a tall, slender man with white hair combed back from his forehead. The man wore a maroon suit with a black bowtie. He handed Marv a large tan envelope. They shook hands and Marv started across the room to where Iris stood.

"Is that a Skelling?" Iris asked.

Marv looked back at the man. "Nope. That's Miles Fincher. The overseer here. He's been looking after this place for a long time. Rumor has it he met Felix Skelling at the Northern Michigan Asylum. That was the mental institution Felix died in." Marv dropped his voice. "I think Fincher was even a patient there, or so people say."

Iris glanced at Fincher and realized he was watching her with vague curiosity, almost as if they knew one another. She stared back at him, trying to place his face in her memories, but found no recollection of the man.

As they walked back through the foyer, Iris peered at a curved marble staircase that led to a second level. A velvet rope blocked visitors from entering. Children's laughter floated down from the upper level.

"Do they allow tourists on the second floor?" Iris asked.

Marv glanced at the stairs. "I've never seen anyone go up there. Probably full of old stuff they don't want broken."

The laughter came again and Iris glimpsed a child darting across the landing at the top of the stairs and down the opposite hallway. "Did you see that?" she asked Marv.

"What?" He scrunched his forehead and peered up the stairs.

Iris started to say more, but closed her mouth as she picked up on the voice of the tour guide who'd moved his group into the large foyer.

"The Skelling boys vanished in 1932. These are their pictures here behind me. Andre, the eldest, was fourteen years old and Phillippe, the youngest of the Skelling children, was ten."

Iris strode across the room, paused at the edge of the group to look at the oil painting of two boys. Though she'd barely seen the boy at the top of the stairs, she sensed that she'd just caught a glimpse of the long-dead Phillippe Skelling.

"Walsh, let's make tracks," Marv called.

Iris studied the boys' faces for another moment and then hurried across the room.

A young man pushed through the doorway, stopped abruptly when he saw Marv. The scowl melted from his face.

"Marv, hi, how are you, man?" He thrust a hand out and Marv shook it.

"I'm good, Parker. Any word on Brett?"

The man shook his head and looked angrily toward Miles Fincher, who'd stepped into the foyer. "No. Nothing, not a word. I brought a buddy to get his truck outta here yesterday and me and a few guys wanted to do a search, but Faggot Fincher is throwing walls in front of us. He said the police already did a search, but I'm calling bullshit."

"Any chance someone picked him up?"

"Who'd be drivin' all the way out here to pick his ass up? Nah, something weird went down."

"What makes you say that?" Iris cut in, knowing the question was totally out of line. She hadn't even been introduced to the man and she was asking questions about his missing brother.

Parker leaned forward, bloodshot eyes weaving between Marv and Iris. "I came out here yesterday morning when Brett never came home. I drove up to the hall, parked, saw his truck and did a little walk-around. I noticed his footprints in the snow heading down the road that leads out of here. I followed 'em down. He ran almost that whole road, a mile at least, right down the center, so I could see 'em clear as water. Then his tracks just disappeared like some giant bird swooped out'ta the sky and snatched him up."

"Mr. Stephens, I'm assuming you're here to speak to me?" Miles Fincher asked, an expression of displeasure on his narrow features.

Parker grunted. "Good seein' ya, Marv." He stomped off towards Miles Fincher.

"Let's get out of here before all hell breaks loose," Marv said, grabbing Iris's elbow and steering her away. Marv opened the heavy entrance door and a flurry of snow gusted into their faces.

As they walked back to Marv's car, Iris scanned the forest surrounding the great house. She shifted her eyes to the snowy ground. Any evidence of the footprints Parker had described had been obliterated by the day's visitors to the hall.

"What do you think of his story?" Iris asked after they climbed into Marv's car.

"Parker's? I think he and Brett have been getting high on the same bad stash."

Iris watched the dense trees of the peninsula pass by. She imagined the shadowy figure she'd seen chasing Brett Stephens, the thing she'd seen again in the surveillance video released on the news.

Nothing stirred in the forest.

So where then was Brett Stephens?

7
____

The rest of the day, Iris had little time to think of Brett Stephens or Skelling Hall. When she left the office with Marv a quarter after six, she longed to take off her nylons and stiff suit and drink a cocktail.

"Happy hour at Bitters tonight. Don't try to blow it off because you nearly died," Marv told her as Iris made her way across the slippery parking lot.

"I'll be there," she told him.

~

Lola's Victorian house shone like a pink bauble against the glittering snowscape.

Iris arrived pulled into the driveway just after six-thirty pm. As she turned off the engine, her cell phone rang.

"This is Iris."

"Hi, Iris, this is Joel from the Soo Auto Shop."

"Hey. How's it looking?" Iris climbed from Lola's car, slung her briefcase over her shoulder and hurried up the porch steps.

"Not good. It's a total loss."

Iris slumped through the doorway and dropped her briefcase on the interior bench. "Damn, really?"

"Yeah."

"All right, I'll call my insurance company tomorrow. Do I need to get it towed or something?"

"Nope, we can take care of that."

"Thanks." Iris ended the call and sighed, stuffing her phone in her pocket.

"How was your day, poppet? Head feeling better?" Lola asked, coming down the hall wearing two pink reindeer oven mitts.

"Good, until I found out my car was totaled."

Lola's face fell. "Darn it. Well, don't you worry. My car is your car. I never drive it anyhow. Minnie does the driving whenever we go shopping." Lola walked to Iris and wrapped her arms around her.

Iris hugged her back. "Thanks, Grandma. I'm going to get changed. I'm meeting Marv at Bitters for a drink."

Lola nodded. "I reheated the vegetable stew. Better have a quick bite before you go."

"I'll just grab something at the bar. Thanks though."

Iris hurried upstairs and stripped out of her slacks and blouse. She pulled on dark jeans and a black sweater. She washed her face, scrubbed away the residue of the day and put on lotion and fresh makeup, adding extra concealer to the bruising and cut on her forehead.

"I'll be home in a few hours," she called to Lola, wrapping a scarf around her neck and pulling on thick knit gloves.

Bitters Bar was only five blocks from Lola's house. Iris intended to walk, having no interest in getting behind the wheel after another night of martinis.

I ris took a seat at the bar next to Marv, who was typing furiously on his cell phone. She unzipped her coat, but didn't take it off. The chill had followed her in.

The bar, which she visited with Marv and sometimes Nina weekly, was filled with the usual faces—Sault Ste Marie's professionals, many of them still in their suits and blazers, not having bothered to go home and change after a day at the office.

It wasn't a dive bar. A fire crackled in a stone hearth. Leather club chairs were arranged in a semi-circle facing it. Sturdy, but scarred tables gleamed as if they received a regular polish.

"Goddamn divorcées. I'm your lawyer, not your daddy," Marv

grumbled. He set the phone down and grinned at Iris. "Finally, a fellow shark to swim with me. Dandy," he said to the bartender, "get us a couple of shots of whiskey."

"No." Iris shook her head. "I'll take a dirty martini."

"Ooh, I forgot, the big city girl drinks martinis. You watch *Sex and the City*, don't you? Tell me, are you a Carrie or a Samantha?"

"How much whiskey have you had, Marv?"

"This is my first," he said, playing offended. "What are you implying?"

"Here you go, city girl," the bartender told her.

"Thanks." Iris pulled the martini closer and took a sip. "Did you call her Dandy?" Iris asked as she watched the bartender grab two bottles of beer and slide them to a pair of men in suits several stools away.

The bartender—mid-fifties, Iris thought—appeared to have gotten trapped in the eighties. Her hair was a pouf of fluffy curls that barely moved, implying copious amounts of hairspray. Blue eyeshadow coated her lids from lash to eyebrow. She wore a blue and black leopard-print blouse cinched at the waist with a black shiny belt over dark blue leggings. Despite her appearance, Iris suspected she didn't take shit, and had either a baseball bat or a shotgun tucked behind the mahogany bar.

"Yep, Dandy, who is oh-so-dandy," Marv confirmed.

"Is that a nickname?"

Marv wrinkled his brow and shrugged. "I don't know. I've never asked her."

The double doors pushed in and a man blew into the bar, followed by a billow of snow and wind. It tousled his dark hair and coat. Piercing blue eyes roved through the room. Behind him, more shadow than person, stood a woman with sunken eyes and translucent skin. The snow churned around her and, as it settled, it took the girl with it, all disappearing into the warmth of the bar.

Iris swallowed thickly and looked away, silently repeating Lola's reminder about the spirits.

'They just want to be seen, poppet. Be part of the world again, even if just for a breath. They aren't bothering nobody, so don't let 'em bother you.'

But they *did* bother her. They bothered her because her version of reality didn't include apparitions, fleeting glimpses of non-persons, there and then gone.

"Who's that?" Iris asked, tilting her head toward the door where the dimpled man stood talking to a group that had snagged him when he walked in.

"The golden boy? That's Jack Skelling. He's the chief assistant prosecuting attorney—and only thirty-five, mind you. I can't believe you don't recognize him on sight. His face gets splashed across the paper every time the county has a case, even if he's not the one prosecuting it." Marv rolled his eyes. "Half the city treats him like a movie star."

"If the shoe fits. He's a Skelling as in Skelling Hall?"

"Yep, descended from the original Skellings. Most of the people in the D.A.'s office seem to like him, but I find the perfection to be nauseating. Graduated from the University of Michigan Law School summa cum laude, track star in college, started some victims' rights program. He's the rising star in these parts."

"His backstory sounds like it was written by a PR guy."

"Maybe it was," Marv chuckled. "Lord knows his parents had the money to hire a whole firm to make that kid look good."

"What was his story before college? All-American kid? Quarterback, cheerleader girlfriend?"

Marv drained his whiskey. "Most likely. A story that will turn you off your drink. His grandpa was a judge, so he was a shoo-in for the D.A.s office. Not to mention his family has a lot of money and a lot of pull in these parts. He's one of those guys who's so squeaky clean, you wonder if he pisses sitting down."

Iris, like Marv, was instantly skeptical of anyone with such a perfect reputation. Still, she watched Jack Skelling covertly throughout the night. He was handsome and charismatic. That was enough to draw the eye of most of the women in the bar, but for Iris it was the ghost that had followed him in, there and gone. Who was she? A sister, a girlfriend who'd died, or merely an apparition that had nothing to do with the man at all?

"Hey, looks like that bruising is getting better."

Iris looked up to see the trooper who'd helped her after her crash. She touched her face where the purple bruise had yellowed. "Yeah, thanks. I appreciate the help."

"That's my job. I'm Andy Bale, by the way. We didn't exactly get a proper introduction."

Iris shook his hand. "Iris Walsh. Though since you looked at my driver's license, you're probably aware of that."

"Andy, you're up," a man called from the back of the bar, where two pool tables sat beneath hanging burgundy lamps.

"Good to see you, Iris," Andy told her, nodded and headed for the pool table.

"Hmm... that's an interesting development," Marv said.

"What does that mean?"

"Oh, I saw the way he looked at you. Dashing state trooper, up-and-coming attorney, a match made in heaven."

"Hardly," she grumbled.

"What gives? You got burned, is that it?" Marv asked, grabbing two of her discarded olives and popping them in his mouth.

"I got doused in gasoline and set aflame by a blowtorch," she told him, downed the last of her martini and stood to use the bathroom. She wobbled and sat back down before she crashed sideways and took the table with her. "Shit," she muttered, imagining how much worse she'd feel at eight the next morning.

She'd eaten nothing since lunch. Iris grabbed the menu and glanced at it.

"Get you something, city girl?" Dandy asked.

"Yeah, a club sandwich and chips, please."

"Marv?" Dandy asked.

Marv held up his glass. "I've got all the sustenance I need right here." He turned his attention back to Iris. "So, tell me about getting scorched. Your guy cheated on you?"

Iris shook her head. "I don't want to talk about it."

And she didn't. She'd never talked about it with anyone. She'd had a few friends in law school who'd asked, but Iris had brushed them off and thankfully Cody hadn't spilled either.

It hadn't been he who'd cheated on her, but the other way around. Iris had cheated on him with his best friend. Cody had been out of town. Iris, lamenting a tough week in law school, had started with wine, segued into tequila and woken the following morning with the worst hangover of her life and her boyfriend's best friend naked in the bed beside her.

She'd never learned how Cody had found out, but she suspected the friend had spilled his guts, proving himself to be more honorable than Iris, who would have gone to her grave without ever mentioning her infidelity. Two weeks later she'd returned from a day in class to find Cody's half of the closet empty, the couches gone—his mother had bought them. He'd even taken his fish out of the fish tank. They'd had three. Two had been his, one was Iris's. He'd taken his two fish and within a month Iris had discovered her own fish, Duke, floating belly up at the top of the tank.

Iris tilted her head back, and the room swam. She quickly righted it, focusing on the bar and gripping it with both hands.

"Mum's the word, huh?" Marv asked. "Well, let me throw some salve on the wound, Walsh. They come and go, the lot of 'em. I've dumped. I've been dumped. It's all in a day's work."

Iris grabbed pretzels from the bowl on the counter and stuffed a few in her mouth. She'd tried to tell herself something similar after Cody had left. There were plenty of fish in the sea, when one door closes another opens, but Iris didn't like losing and that was what Cody leaving had felt like. As if she'd failed some critical test.

He'd ghosted her after he moved out. He wouldn't answer her calls, emails. She'd kept telling herself they both needed closure. What a bullshit word, but it had been the constant refrain in her mind as she tried again and again to make contact with no luck.

Iris had finally cornered him one night at a bar downtown. She'd had way too much to drink and when she'd tried to talk to him, he'd refused to acknowledge her at all. In her fury, she'd thrown a punch, missed, and ended up careening into a table of bridesmaids on a bachelorette outing. The bouncer had escorted her out and then supervised her at the curb like an insolent child until her Uber had arrived to take her home.

That had been it, the end of the only serious relationship she'd ever had, the first man who'd, for a time, rooted for her, believed in her. She'd ruined it. Cody had been collateral damage, part of the great implosion, not an explosion. Those happened outward and for Iris it had been entirely internal. Anyone looking at her from the outside would have been unaware of the total meltdown occurring in Iris's internal world.

"Another whiskey," Marv called out to Dandy, jerking Iris out of her reverie. He turned to face her. "My best advice to you, Iris, is to brush off the seat of your pants, hop back on the horse and take a ride."

Iris looked at him sidelong. "What the hell are you even talking about, Marv?"

"Love. I'm talking about love, or lust. Whatever gets your pony prancing."

She groaned. "I'm a first-year associate. I don't have time for love."

Marv smirked. "There's always time for lovin' in Marv Booker's life."

"We have different priorities."

"You don't say? Although for a woman turning a cold shoulder to love, you've got an admirer hanging around." He did a way-too-obvious nod in the direction of the state trooper, Andy.

"He helped me when I was stranded and my car was totaled. End of story," she muttered.

"That's what romantic comedies are made of."

"And serial killer documentaries."

"Hey, Dandy, two more over here," Marv shouted to the bartender, pointing at their empty glasses.

Iris pushed her plate away and shook her head. "No... no more. I need to go home."

"I'll take you home."

"Uh-uh. I walked here; I'm walking home. The fresh air will..." She closed her eyes, watched the inky world swim by and opened them. The food had helped absorb the alcohol, but not enough to offset the additional two martinis she'd ordered.

Her eyes drifted away from Marv, and she noticed Andy on the opposite side of the room. He glanced up and caught her eye. He blurred, and she snapped her head back to Marv too fast. She nearly toppled out of her chair, but Marv caught her by the elbow.

"She's done," Dandy said, appearing with a tray that held one whiskey and a glass of water.

"What?" Marv demanded. "Ain't that some sexist shit? Dandy, I've had one more than her and you're cutting her off? Do you know who this is? Attorney Iris Walsh. She's going to sue your ass to the wall for this sexist behavior."

Dandy rolled her eyes. "The only sexist around here is you, Marv." The bartender stooped to face level with Iris, holding up the glass of water. "Drink this and then I'll call you a cab."

"There are cabs here?" Iris asked, dreading the icy darkness that lay outside the cozy bar.

"Two, and I have them both on call."

"I only live just..." She pointed a wobbly figure in the opposite direction of her grandmother's house.

"Yeah, exactly," Dandy said.

Marv grinned. "I've got to hit the john. Save my seat, Walsh." Marv stood and disappeared down the dark hall to the restroom.

"Can I have a coffee as well?" Iris asked the bartender.

"Club soda with a lime," a man said beside her.

Iris turned to see Jack Skelling sliding onto the stool next to hers.

"Coming right up, Jack," Dandy said, handing Iris her coffee.

Iris wrapped her hands around the mug. It was warm in the bar, but never warm enough for her. Ever since the first snowfall, she'd felt perpetually cold.

"I'd be awake all night if I had a cup of coffee right now," Jack told her.

"I'm betting on the vodka to counteract it," Iris said, sipping her coffee. It tasted strong, but not good—several levels beneath Folgers, the kind of coffee sold in jumbo tins at surplus stores.

Jack laughed. "It's an effective numbing agent."

"No vodka for you?"

He smiled and shook his head. "I rarely drink."

"Then why come to the bar?"

He grinned and rubbed the back of his neck. "The curse of being a public servant. Most of my colleagues like to do business here. I'd prefer the office, but..." He shrugged. "Got to go where the people are." He extended his hand. "I'm Jack Skelling."

"Iris Walsh." She gave his hand a quick shake. "I'm working at the Fraser Firm."

"You're a lawyer? I should have recognized one of my own. You've got that defense attorney gleam in your eye. Am I right?"

"That's the plan, though I've yet to try a case. I just passed the bar a few months ago." She took another drink of her coffee.

"Well, if you decide to play for the good guys, we always need young blood at the D.A.'s office."

She scoffed. "I won't be staying up here. I've waited my whole life to move south. I want to be somewhere where it never gets below fifty degrees."

"Heading for the equator, are you?"

"In the general direction."

He eyed her for a moment, his expression pensive.

"What?" she demanded.

He shook his head. "I hate to dash your dreams, but you won't make it. You're a northerner, through and through. If you pack and head south, make sure you buy a round-trip ticket."

"That's a pretty big assumption."

"I'm an excellent reader of people. Comes with the job." He winked at her and revealed those ridiculous dimples again.

She rolled her eyes at him. "I don't think people who look like you can be excellent readers of people. You're too good-looking. People put their best foot forward around you, they snap on the mask."

"True enough, not about the good-looking part, but the masks I agree with. Though I'd say everyone does that all the time. Who among us isn't wearing a mask?"

"Not the good-looking part?" she jeered. "False modesty. How does that work out for you?"

He sipped his drink and watched her, eyes sparkling. "You are ferocious, aren't you? I'd love to offer some more traits for you to tear me down on, but I have a friend over there who's looking annoyed at my absence. It was interesting, Ms. Walsh. I'm sure I'll see you around the courthouse."

He stood and walked away. For a moment, the spirit of the young woman was there again, drifting behind him, her back to Iris. Lank blonde hair fell over her shoulders. She was barely a whisper, as if the dust motes in the room had assembled for an instant to form her shape and then dissipated as quickly.

Iris grimaced and rubbed her eyes.

When she turned back to the bar, another image flashed in the mirror behind the illuminated liquor bottles. The shadow man she'd seen chasing Brett Stephens was there, standing just behind her. Faceless, which made it all the more menacing.

Iris gasped and stood too quickly from her stool, nearly knocking it over. She steadied it with her hand. The tender spot on her head throbbed from the sudden movement. She winced and touched it.

"Iris, can I give you a ride?" Andy, the state trooper, asked. He offered a smile. Kind eyes.

She didn't need a ride, but suddenly Iris wanted a man, a night in a stranger's bed, to snuff out the plague of thoughts crowding her mind.

"Let's go to your place," she said, grabbed her purse and pushed him toward the door.

A ndy's house was a cedar shingle Cape Cod on a big tree-lined corner lot only a few blocks from her grandmother's house. Iris barely registered the interior as they pushed into the dark living room.

She grabbed him and kissed him, kicked off her boots and yanked so hard on the zipper of his coat it got stuck.

"Wait, hold on." He stilled her hands. "Are you sure?"

"I'm sure," she muttered, jerked the coat all the way off and flung it to the floor.

8

____

"There's some interesting talk around the water cooler this morning," Marv said, adding a grotesque amount of powdered cream to his cup of coffee.

"What's that?" Iris asked, slipped two aspirin between her teeth and took a swig of coffee, realizing too late it was scalding hot. She choked and spit the coffee out, splattering Marv's cup and the counter.

"Jesus, Iris," he muttered, dumped his coffee into the sink and tossed the cup into the trash. He grabbed a fresh cup and filled it. "The gossip is a few folks saw you leave the bar last night with the handsome trooper."

"Sorry," she mumbled, wiping the counter with a wad of napkins.

"Sorry for going home with the cop?"

"No," she snapped. "Sorry for spewing all over your coffee." She started out of the break room.

"You can't fill the void by filling your bed, Walsh. But there's no better distraction," Marv called behind her.

"Mind your own business, Marv," she told him, taking her coffee back to her chair. She had a stack of folders on her desk. Just looking at them caused her eyes to pulse in her head.

Nina perched on the edge of her desk and handed her a bottle of water. "You need this," she said. "Not that." She pointed at Iris's cup of coffee. "So how was he?"

"How was who?"

Nina narrowed her eyes. "Come off it, Iris."

Iris grimaced, attempting her aspirin for a second time, swallowing them successfully with water. "I'd tell you if I remembered."

In truth, she did remember, and Andy had been good. Slow and attentive, not the typical sweaty fumbling of a one-night stand, which had been pleasurable but also mildly annoying. He'd asked her to stay the night, had given her his robe when she'd stood naked from his bed to get a glass of water. It had all felt too comfortable, too relationshippy, and it had sent her zooming around the room, stuffing her legs into her pants and pulling her sweater over her head so fast she'd yanked out one of her earrings.

He'd insisted on driving her home, though she could have walked. He'd even tried to kiss her goodbye, but she'd lunged from his vehicle before he had the chance.

"The file is redacted," Iris told Marv, dropping a blue folder on his desk.

"Thanks, Walsh," Marv said, lowering his newspaper.

Iris turned away, then whipped back around. "Wait!" She snatched the newspaper from Marv's hand.

Iris studied the small photograph of a girl with light hair parted in the center and a thin-lipped smile. She was skinny, her nose small and upturned, her eyes tired. Iris had seen this girl, but not in the world of flesh and blood. Her spirit had been hovering near Jack Skelling at the bar.

She read the headline.

Still Missing

Norlene Joyce Weaver has been missing since Thursday, August 13th. The twenty-six-year-old worked her regular shift at the Gas Stop.

Her last known whereabouts were at her apartment at 5pm, though it is believed she had plans to meet someone that night.

Police do not currently suspect foul play, but they said her missing person's case is open and ongoing.

Norlene Weaver is approximately five feet two inches tall and weighs 105 lbs. At the time of her disappearance, she wore blue jeans, a green pullover and black tennis shoes. If you have any information on the whereabouts of Norlene, please call the Sault Ste Marie Sheriff's Department.

"What?" Marv asked, peering at the snippet Iris read. "Norlene?" He shrugged. "Probably took off with some guy. She'd turned state's evidence on a drug case, one that I was defending, mind you, and then poof, she's gone. I'd say she got the heebie-jeebies and split."

Iris frowned. "She was a witness for the prosecution in a drug case? Against which client?"

"Sammy Bishop. You've never met him and believe me, you don't want to. Rough around the edges is putting it lightly. He's not big-time. The cops were using Norlene to set up a case against Sammy so he would turn on his supplier."

"And then Norlene vanished?"

Marv eyed her warily. "Then Norlene probably got spooked by the whole deal and took off."

"Who was prosecuting the case?"

"The golden boy, of course."

Iris studied her picture for several more moments and then folded the paper in half. "Can I keep this?"

"It's yours, but give me the want ads. I need somebody to plow my driveway. The last guy moved south. Can't say I blame him."

Back at her desk, Iris opened her laptop and typed in 'Norlene Weaver.'

The information online about the disappearance of Norlene was piti-ful. Not a single front-page story. The best there'd been was a page two story a week after she disappeared with a quote from her sister stating that Norlene wouldn't have left and not told her.

Iris learned that Norlene was twenty-six, lived alone in downtown Sault Ste Marie, and worked at a gas station and did part-time cleaning for a few businesses in town, including Skelling Hall.

"Skelling Hall," Iris murmured.

Two disappearances in Sault Ste Marie, less than six months apart and both with a connection to Skelling Hall, which might be little more than a coincidence. It was a small town, after all. Still…

She typed in 'Brett Stephens' and found a single news piece from the day after he vanished—which also included the footage from Skelling Hall.

She hovered the cursor over the video, but didn't click it.

A number for the sheriff's office was listed at the bottom. There were no family members' quotes in Brett's article.

"Hey," Marv barked from the doorway.

Iris started. "Have you ever heard of a soft approach, Marv?"

He grinned. "Oh, you bet I have. They call me Old Velvet Hands."

"I don't know what that means, and I'd prefer not to."

He strode in and dropped a stack of papers wrapped in a rubber band on her desk. "I've got a DUI case next week. This guy's doing everything in his power to keep his license. See what you can find on issues with sobriety tests. Anything that shows a margin of error."

"I'm on it," she said. Iris closed her laptop and pulled the documents closer.

At one pm, Iris's stomach rumbled and her legs felt stiff beneath her desk. "I'll do the lunch run," she told Nina, standing and bending her knees several times. "Want anything from the deli across the street?"

Nina grabbed her purse from the floor. "Yeah, ham and cheese sub, please." She handed Iris a ten-dollar bill.

Iris poked her head into Marv's office.

"No, Clark, you cannot use your wife's prize-winning donkey for bail. If you want to sell the donkey and get the cash—"

"Lunch?" Iris whispered. "Tony's." She pointed at his window.

He gave her a thumbs up, grabbed cash from his drawer, wadded it into a ball, and tossed it at her. He covered the mouthpiece. "Steak sub, bag of Doritos."

Iris shook her head and grabbed the balled-up money from the floor.

She trudged across the street to the deli and ordered three sandwiches. The bell on the door chimed, and she turned to see the trooper, Andy, walking in with another man in uniform.

"Hi," he said, smiling as if pleasantly surprised.

"Hey." She turned back to the counter as the woman handed her the white paper bag of sandwiches. Iris gave her cash along with a tip and started toward the door.

Andy caught her on the sidewalk outside. "Hey, hold up," he said.

She turned, shivering, as a gust of wind whipped her hair around her face.

"Do you want to get dinner tonight?"

She frowned. She had stacks of work to get done for Marv, but suddenly a night hunched over a desk while Lola plied her with food sounded suffocating. Plus, he was a trooper, maybe he knew something about the missing person's cases. "Okay, sure."

"Great. I could pick you up, say six o'clock."

"No, let's meet somewhere."

"The Burger Boss? They have the best fries you've ever tasted."

"Sure, the Burger Boss it is. I'll see you tonight."

9

The Burger Boss was a typical American diner with red vinyl booths and checked tile floors. The lights were bright and the music louder than Iris liked. Framed posters of Elvis covered the white walls and an old-fashioned jukebox stood in the corner belting out Dolly Parton's *Jolene*.

"I can't stand this song," Iris grumbled, shooting a glance at the music box.

Andy grinned. "Oh, come on, who doesn't love Dolly?"

"Dolly isn't the problem, it's the lyrics in this nightmare of a song. It's like the insecure women's anthem. *Please don't take my man*. I just want to grab the woman singing and shake her. Kick the man to the curb and get a therapist."

Andy laughed, cocking his head as he listened. "I see what you're saying. Now that I'm paying attention this song is a smidge depressing."

"More like oppressing."

"Welcome to the Burger Boss," their waitress announced. She didn't look a day over sixteen and wore her hair in pigtails, a hairstyle that Iris had found, even in childhood, nauseatingly girlish.

Andy ordered a bacon jalapeño burger, fries and a lemonade. Iris opted for a chicken pita and tea.

"Come here often?" Iris asked, taking a sip of her tea, which had clearly come from a fountain machine.

He grinned. "Twice a week, three if it's been a tough one and I need to drown my sorrows in grease and salt."

"I usually opt for booze when drowning my sorrows."

"Yeah, I have those nights too, but inebriated cops aren't exactly smiled upon so I tend to keep my wits about me."

"You should have become an attorney. It's perfectly acceptable to have vodka for lunch."

He laughed. "I prefer something a bit heartier for my lunch."

Iris watched the waitress carrying a tray filled with whipped cream-topped strawberry and chocolate shakes across the room. The girl's pigtails were dangerously close to knocking a cherry off one of the shakes. She slid them onto a table of middle-aged women who flipped through bridal magazines. One of their daughters must have been planning a wedding, or perhaps it was one of them getting hitched.

Iris thought of her own mother, who would never plan her wedding. It didn't matter. Her mother had not been a sentimental woman. Had Iris announced an engagement, her mother probably would have advised her to just go to the courthouse. Weddings were frivolous and a waste of money.

"You're from here? Sault Ste Marie?" Iris asked Andy, averting her eyes from the women.

"Yep, I'm a lifer."

"A lifer? It's akin to a prison sentence then?"

"Nah. I left for a while and no place ever felt like home. This is home." He studied her, tilting his head. "I see the expression you're making right now, but I don't buy it. I think you like it here, Iris Walsh."

She wrinkled her nose. "I like my grandma Lola; I like the Fraser Firm. Beyond that…" She shrugged. "It's just another town. I'd like it a lot more if it was seventy degrees in December and those pine trees were palm trees."

"It'll grow on you. And in the summer those places with the palm trees are sweltering hot, and here in Sault Ste Marie it's our little corner of paradise."

Iris looked at the large window that revealed the snowy street beyond. "Are you the quintessential boy next door who grew up to become a cop?"

"I wasn't the boy next door. Not unless you lived next to a juvenile detention center. I was a terrible kid—fancied myself a James Dean or a Jack Kerouac. I had an insatiable urge to do stupid shit. There was never a reprieve, a breath between high, higher, highest. Fortunately for me, I crashed. Except unlike most, I survived the landing. It's not the fall that kills you—that's just another rush of adrenaline—it's the impact."

"And now you're what? You're Captain America?"

He chuckled, swiped a hand through his tousled blond hair, slightly matted from the knit cap he'd been wearing when he arrived. "I'm Mr. Trying Not to Fuck It Up. That's what I am. I've had a few close calls." He paused and looked at her as if he were contemplating some revelation.

"What?" she asked.

"Nothing." He spooned an ice cube from his water glass and popped it in his mouth. "I've just seen some shit. Some of my best friends who landed on the rocks instead of the sand. I don't know why I was spared. Why I didn't go that way too. But I didn't and somehow I also got the clarity to see it, acknowledge it and realize how lucky I was, how lucky I am." He fished his wallet from his back pocket, flipped it open and pulled a faded photograph from an interior slot. "Harvey and Tom, those were my two best friends."

Iris looked at the picture. Three guys. Andy on the far left. The middle guy had a mop of dark curls. The one beside him wore a Detroit Tigers ball cap. They stood grinning, arms loosely draped across each other's shoulders, not a care in the world.

"They're both dead," Andy said. "We were twenty-five and had a weekend of off-roading planned over by the Porcupine Mountains. I was supposed to meet them, but I'd been seeing this girl who talked me into staying late at her place and driving separately from Harvey and Tom. I got a flat tire on my way there. I was such a careless shit back then. I was already riding on my spare.

"My cell was dead. I had to hoof it four miles before some trucker took pity and picked me up. Harvey and Tom had already gotten to camp, gone into a local bar and started shooting their mouths off, showing off the cash they'd gotten paid for working construction that week. Couple of guys followed them back to camp, robbed them and shot them both in the back of the head."

Iris lifted her eyes from the picture. Andy wasn't looking at her. He'd fixed his gaze on the window, on some far-off place.

"I found them." Andy's jaw had gone rigid as if he were clamping his teeth together between words. "I can still see them. The blood..." He rubbed his hands hard against his face, shook his head. "Sorry. You don't need to hear all that. The point is that I should have been there, would have been there if not for... well, my own stupidity, my own laziness, not buying a new tire. What does that mean? Fuck if I know, but it set me right."

"Just like that, you turned over a new leaf?"

"Well... it was a process. I went on a two-year downward spiral first, made more stupid mistakes, had a couple more close calls. Finally pulled it together, gave up drinking for a few years. I enrolled in the police academy. I sat in the courtroom during the trial of those two dirtbags who'd killed my best friends. They'd shot Harvey and Tom and then blown the money on drugs and beer. One of them bought a spiked collar for his pit mix. I was just... dumbstruck. How could you take two lives for a case of beer and a dog collar?"

"Did they get convicted?"

"Yep. Second-degree murder. Their slippery lawyer almost got them off on a claim of self-defense. Fuckin' defense attorneys." He clamped his mouth shut. "Sorry... Jeez, that was a shitty thing to say. I don't mean you. It's just..."

Iris took another drink of her mediocre tea. "It's fine. In law school I read about a lot of cases with corrupt cops, with sketchy prosecutors. Every level of the justice system is fallible and has questionable characters. It doesn't change the fact that we need an even playing field. Defense attorneys help keep things equal."

"One of the guys who killed Tom and Harvey almost got paroled last year. I went to the hearing and fought to keep them in. I've gone every time they've been up for parole. If it's up to me they'll die in prison."

"And that's what made you want to be a cop?"

"I met the detective working on Tom and Harvey's case and something in me clicked. I grabbed onto the guy's coat tails and prayed he could pull me out of the mud. I ate a few mouthfuls of dirt on the journey out, but eventually I struggled to my knees and then my feet. I didn't do it on my own, not by a long shot. I learned then about asking for help, begging for it if I had to—and sometimes I had to. I'd burned some bridges, had to make a lot of apologies. I don't regret a one of them. Like I said, after they died, I spiraled for a bit. That detective helped me turn it all around."

"Have you ever considered becoming a detective? Climbing the ranks?"

He nodded. "Yeah, still do sometimes. It's been offered, but I have a lot of things I love to do. I don't want to give that up for the job and that's the price most of those guys pay. It takes over your life. Even if you try not to let it. A lot of my detective friends are divorced, don't see their kids… they give up everything for that life. It's not worth it."

"You're not what I thought," Iris told him. "I pegged you for a frat boy who'd been on the honor roll and captain of the football team."

He laughed. "There's no frat that would have had me back then, or university for that matter. I could have gone to community college, but I was too busy getting into trouble."

For a few minutes they ate in silence and then Andy looked at her thoughtfully.

"So, Lola is your dad's mom?"

"Yeah."

"And what does he do, for work, I mean?"

"He's an electrical engineer."

"Lola's son is an electrical engineer?" He grinned as if she'd let him in on a funny secret.

"What?" she snapped, instantly irritated by his goofy smile.

His smile disappeared. "Nothing, just… well, Lola's a character. Shoot, her house is a character. You know the high-school drama class once performed the opening scene of *Legally Blonde* at her house and filmed it."

"Yes, I'm aware." Iris sighed. Her grandmother had a framed article from the newspaper with a picture of the teen girls dangling from her windows and singing. The pink house looked like it belonged on the set of *Guys and Dolls*.

"It's funny you're her granddaughter," Andy mused. "You're so different. She's—"

"Are you like your grandparents?" Iris interrupted.

He blushed. "No, I guess not."

"Frankly I don't appreciate the town looking at my grandma like she's a joke."

He put his hands up. "No, no way. That's not what I meant. Lola is like… like everyone's grandma. The grandma we all wish we had. She's not a joke, Iris. We love her. We love the quirkiness. She's a breath of fresh air in this jaded world."

Iris pursed her lips, satisfied at his explanation.

"What about your mom? What's she like?" he asked.

"She died when I was thirteen."

Andy's face fell. "Damn, I'm sorry. That must have been—"

"Yeah, it was. My dad threw himself into work and I threw myself into school. Graduated valedictorian, did part of an MBA, then switched to law and here I am."

Iris considered the story Andy had just shared. The intimate details of his own progression out of despair. She could share her own troublesome adolescence. Sneaking out, getting high, stealing her dad's car in middle school.

She understood now that she'd just been trying to get her dad's attention. It hadn't worked. Her antics had only pushed him deeper into himself. The days of silence in their house after she'd acted out had been so oppressive that Iris had stopped rebelling. She'd fallen into line —aced her classes. She'd convinced herself the only approval she needed was from the person looking back at her in the mirror and there was a simple way to get it—be the best. Achieve more, fail less, and never depend on anyone.

"It couldn't have been easy doing all that without your mom," Andy said.

"It was fine and I'm fine. Let's not talk about it."

"Gotcha."

They didn't speak for several minutes, but the silence felt heavy with questions Iris suspected Andy wanted to ask.

"So… What drew you to criminal defense?" Andy said finally, wadding his napkin and dropping it on his empty plate.

Iris frowned and thought of the reasons. There'd been an interest that stemmed from a moral high ground, a desire to help the underdog, but deep in her gut Iris suspected it had more to do with self-sufficiency. She wanted to make enough money to ensure she was taken care of— that she'd never need to rely on anyone else to support her.

"The Fraser Firm had a job available, simple as that."

He grinned. "Well don't get emotional about it."

"Listen," she said, thinking about Brett Stephens. "That guy who went missing out by Skelling Hall. Do you know anything about him? Are there state police working on that case?"

"It's not our jurisdiction. The sheriff's office is working it."

"Have you heard anything about it?"

Andy shook his head. "Nothing beyond what I've seen on the news. What has you thinking about him?"

"I wrecked my car right by Skelling Hall the same night he went missing out there."

Andy frowned. "You're right. I hadn't made the connection. That's bizarre."

"You don't remember seeing the guy that night, do you?"

Andy shook his head. "No. It was pretty dead around there. It usually is at night. I saw you in the road, but that's it. Did you see anything?"

Iris remembered the man running, the thing chasing him. She shook her head. "No."

Andy fiddled with the straw in his drink, frowning. "I'm trying to remember if I noticed anything unusual, heard anything. I'll reach out to the guy who towed your car. Who knows, maybe he picked the guy up and gave him a ride somewhere."

"Don't you think he would have reported that to the police?"

"Not if he doesn't realize the guy is missing. He wouldn't be the first person who doesn't watch or read the news. Can't say I blame him if he doesn't."

"How about Norlene Weaver? State police looking into that?"

Andy blinked at her. "Norlene Weaver?"

"Yeah, the woman who went missing in August."

"No. Sheriff's office again."

"Hmm…"

"What's the interest in Norlene?"

Iris picked the onions from her wrap. "I just keep thinking about them both. Two missing persons in less than six months. It seems like a lot for a small town."

"Not necessarily," Andy said. "People go missing every day. Statistically most of them are found within a few days, but some of them take off and it's months before anyone knows what they were up to."

Iris nodded. She knew the statistics, but she'd also seen the ghost of Norlene Weaver and she'd seen something ominous chasing Brett Stephens. There was nothing ordinary about these two missing persons cases.

After they finished dinner, Andy walked Iris to her car.

"Listen, I'm going to my cabin this weekend. Why don't you join me for a day?" he asked.

Iris wrinkled her nose. "What for?"

He laughed. "To get out of town. It's beautiful out there during the winter. Come on, live a little."

"Marv has a hearing next week on a DUI case. He just gave me a stack of documents to review that should take a month and I need to have it done by next Thursday."

"Give me a day, bring the work with you if it's so important. There's no better place to focus."

She sighed. "Fine. But Andy"—she paused, hand on the car door —"I'm not looking for anything serious or exclusive, none of that. I probably won't be up here for long and I'm not trying to get involved with anybody."

"I can follow those rules." He leaned over and kissed her, sliding his hand into her hair and cupping the back of her head.

10

Iris spent the following day hunting on the internet for Michigan case laws regarding DUIs and sobriety tests. She turned on her voice recorder and read from an article on her screen.

"'The National Highway Traffic Safety Administration proposes that the three primary standardized field sobriety tests can accurately predict intoxication eight out of ten times, which means two out of ten positive results are potentially false.'"

"Hey." Marv hurried into Iris's office, cell phone pressed to one ear. "Can you run down to the courthouse and file these for me?" He dropped a paperclipped stack of documents on her desk.

Iris ended the recording. "Sure. My eyes could use a break."

I ris parked on the street in front of the courthouse and stepped from her car.

She glanced up and spotted Jack Skelling on the high balcony above. He stood alone, hands gripping the rail, looking out at the city. The air shivered beside him. The ghost of the young woman, Norlene Weaver, materialized beside him. Iris watched the pale figure as she drifted past Jack and through the rail, tumbling forward, face contorting into a scream that remained silent.

Iris gasped and jumped back, half-expecting the woman to hit the pavement, but she vanished mid-fall.

"Ma'am?"

Iris whirled to see a slender man in a dark suit behind her.

"Are you okay?"

Iris stared at him, mouth half-open. She closed it and swallowed. "Yes, sorry…"

"Did you see something?" The man looked past her, his eyes gliding up to rest on Jack, who had turned and disappeared back into the building.

"I… no. I thought I forgot my purse, but here it is." She tugged on the purse hanging over her shoulder.

"I see. Watch the steps. They get icy."

The man continued past her, and as she watched him slip into the courthouse, she remembered him from Bitters Bar. He'd been talking with Jack Skelling. He was probably a prosecutor as well.

On her way back to the office, Iris picked up coffees. As she waited for the barista to make Marv's peppermint mocha, she grabbed the free weekly newspaper and perched at one of the high-top tables in the corner.

She flipped through, scanning articles about cross-country ski events that weekend, a local band who'd signed with a major record label, and bowling tournaments. Advertisements and classifieds filled the last three pages of the newspaper.

Norlene Weaver stared out from a quarter-page ad beneath the words: 'Have You Seen Me?'

$5,000 Reward

Last seen August 13, 2014 near her apartment in the Views complex located on Miller Street.

Please call Willow Weaver.

"Peppermint mocha," the girl behind the counter announced.

Iris typed Willow's phone number into her cell and grabbed the cardboard carrier of coffees. She started her car, but didn't pull out from the parking lot. She stared at her cell phone. Iris had only to hit send to call Willow Weaver, but what would be the point? She didn't have any information to offer the woman. She couldn't exactly call her and say Norlene's spirit was hovering around prosecutor Jack Skelling.

Not to mention Iris had piles of work to do for Marv. The last thing she had time for was getting involved in the disappearance of some woman she'd never even met.

She quashed her doubts and hit send on the number and waited.

"Hello."

"Hi, is this Willow Weaver?"

"Yep."

"My name is Iris Walsh. I'm an attorney here in Sault Ste Marie and hoped to ask you some questions about your sister."

"An attorney? What kind of attorney?"

"I'm a new associate at the Fraser Firm."

"What does that have to do with Norlene?"

"Nothing actually. I saw an article recently about her missing person's case and thought I might look into it. I consider it my specialty in the law world—digging for information."

"Huh, and what's in it for you?"

"Nothing. I mean, I'm not looking to get paid or anything. I just thought I'd offer some assistance, pro bono. Like I said, I'm an attorney, not a private detective."

"Have you worked on missing person's cases before?"

"No."

"Hmm… well, all right. I'm home all day if you want to come by."

"I'm heading back to the office now, but I can swing by around six this evening."

Iris arrived at Willow Weaver's house at five minutes after six. The sun had already set, but a porch light and Christmas tree lit within the house illuminated the front porch.

The house was small and boxy, with no second floor. Though it looked old, like most of the homes on the street, it appeared well kept.

Iris climbed from the car, grimaced at the cold, and hurried up the steps to the front door. She'd barely knocked when a woman pulled the door open.

"Hi, are you Willow?" Iris asked, thinking if she was, she'd never met a woman less suited to her name.

Willow, unlike her petite sister, was thick with arms that bulged beneath her t-shirt and wide, sturdy-looking legs. She reminded Iris of the women she'd seen doing strongman competitions, though Willow had a softening layer of fat covering whatever muscle lay beneath. Her face was pocked, her hair bleached, and Iris counted half a dozen piercings in her ears.

She smiled at Iris and extended her hand. "I am. You must be Iris."

Iris was taken aback by her voice. It was soft and quiet, more like a purr than the growl she'd expected. "Is now a good time to talk about Norlene?"

Willow nodded and led her inside. The house was warm, clean, but cluttered and smelled of sauerkraut.

"We can sit at the table here," Willow said. "I got out a few pictures of Norlene."

Iris took a seat, pulling her own notebook from her briefcase and opening it to a blank page. She'd never looked into a missing person's case and hadn't a clue where to start. She glanced at one picture on the table. It depicted a little girl, maybe five years old, wearing a white dress and holding a magic wand topped with a tinfoil star.

Willow followed Iris's gaze. "She was six there," Willow said. "She wanted to be a Cinderella for Halloween, but also demanded a magic wand."

Before Iris could respond, Willow spoke again.

"Norlene is dead," Willow told her, shifting her eyes from the photo and staring hard at Iris.

I know, Iris thought, but she didn't speak the words aloud. "What makes you say that?"

"I might not be college-educated, but I know my sister. It doesn't take a genius to put two and two together. She didn't run off; she didn't get carried away by some Prince Charming. Somebody killed her and hid her body and whoever that somebody is needs to pay. Norlene..." Willow swallowed thickly and her voice cracked. "Never got a break. None of us Weaver kids did, but... Norlene was the baby and I tried to help her, protect her, but... well, we all suffered from the same disease. Being born to our parents."

"Are your parents in the area?"

"My dad died ten years ago, drunk-driving. He swerved across the center line and hit a semi—full-on. My mom went two years later, OD'd on heroin."

"I'm sorry," Iris told her.

Willow shrugged. "Probably best thing for us and them. Norlene was the only one still holdin' on to some pie-in-the-sky idea that someday they'd step up. They were never going to. I'm sure they welcomed being done with this world."

"Can you tell me about your sister? Especially what was happening in her life when she went missing."

Willow nodded. "Yeah, I can. She was doin' all right. She'd gotten mostly clean, still drank, but she was off the hard stuff."

"Had she always had a drug problem?"

Willow's eyes teared up. "For a long time, yes, but it wasn't her fault. She… umm… she got raped eight years ago. Buncha college boys rolled into town. They met Norlene at Sid's Diner. She was waitin' tables and they talked her back to their hotel, ended up forcing themselves on her, more than one of 'em. One of the guys drove her out to the woods and kicked her outta the car. It was dead winter. They probably figured she'd die out there. She about did.

"A guy driving in from Marquette spotted her, picked her up. She was…" Tears spilled down Willow's cheeks. "Barefoot. Toes all frostbit. She had to get the pinkie toe on her left foot removed. Wearing nothing but a flimsy little waitress uniform. I wasn't there, but I can see Norlene walking down that black road and I want to kill every last one of those men, rip their arms off, hold their heads underwater until they think their brains might explode."

Iris's mouth had fallen open at the story and she too experienced a burning rage at the men who'd assaulted Norlene. "Were they charged? Prosecuted?"

Willow scoffed. "It was Norlene's word against theirs. They said it was consensual. The police arrested 'em, threw 'em in jail for a night, and the next day a few big black cars rolled into town. Their daddies bailing 'em out. The case never went to court. The only proof that Norlene had was the front desk guy at the motel who saw one of the guys walkin' her out. She was barefoot and crying. They took a deal or whatever, paid a fine."

"That is sickening," Iris said.

"Ain't it? Kurt and I—that's my man—we had a plan to drive down and get those sons of bitches. He'd gotten a few of his buddies rallied up, but it was Norlene who stopped us. 'You're all I have.' That's what she said to me and it about broke my heart into pieces. 'You're all I have.'" Willow buried her face in her hands.

Iris waited. Grandma Lola would have given Willow a hug, wrapped her up tight and rocked her like a baby. Iris had not come from a touchy-feely home. Even the thought of patting Willow on the back made Iris squirm with discomfort.

Willow wiped her face and continued. "Norlene ended up pregnant from one of those sleazeballs. She wanted to keep the baby. It was a big spectacle because if she kept that baby, then she could nail one of those guys for paternity, child support, the works. But she'd also be putting herself in the scope of one of them bastards. None of those men wanted anything to do with Norlene or any baby. I can tell you that without a doubt. She got a few death threats, but man, she was a stubborn little billy goat.

"The baby died in its fourth month. She miscarried. It devastated her. I've never seen anyone so lost. We put her in the hospital for a few weeks. That's when the drugs started. She was in the mental ward, met another girl in there who was hooked on benzos.

"When Norlene got discharged, she and this girl got a place together and she started using. I didn't know nothin' about it until Kurt dragged her home one day by the collar of her shirt and slapped a baggie full of pills on the table. I stood there lookin' at the bag and the dark circles under her eyes and my guts just twisted into a knot.

"I wasn't mad at Norlene. I was mad all over again at those men." She held up her meaty hands as if she was strangling someone. "I wanted to… to commit murder. That's what I wanted. Instead, we shut Norlene up in our spare room and detoxed her. But I grew up with addicts—my parents, aunts and uncles, cousins. You don't get 'em clean once and call it good. Norlene spent the next six years on and off drugs, in and out of the hospital, in and out of our spare room."

"But she was clean last summer when she disappeared."

"Yep. She'd turned state's evidence on Sammy Bishop. He's the kingpin in his little group of thugs. He runs down to Florida or California, picks up a big stash, brings it up here to dole out to his gophers. Norlene sold for him for a while, then she started workin' real hard to get clean."

"Why did she decide to…" Iris thought of the first word that popped into her mind—'rat,' aka turn state's evidence. It was a risky maneuver and one many people came to regret.

"Snitch?" Willow finished for her. "She got busted drunk-driving. It was a stupid thing to do, but I'm telling you she'd been on the straight and narrow for months. One of her friends had a birthday party and Norlene decided to go at the last minute. She'd worked a long shift, barely had a bite to eat all day. She only weighed a hundred pounds. Norlene drank a few beers. A cop snagged her a block away from the bar.

"Kurt and I figured they'd been waiting for her to screw up. They wanted somebody to help them nail Bishop and none of his guys would turn on him. Norlene was their best bet. Problem was, she'd gotten herself out of trouble, so they couldn't force her hand. Not until that night anyhow."

11

Iris considered the story, but it didn't quite mesh in her mind. "If she'd been clean for two years, why would the police believe she could help them with Bishop? Not to mention the wasted resources of paying a deputy to follow her on the chance she messed up."

"Maybe they weren't following her. Maybe they noticed her car that night. This is a small town, in case you didn't notice. All the deputies knew the sheriff wanted to nail Sammy Bishop. Maybe they were keepin' an eye on a bunch of his former gophers and clients. Norlene drove a 1994 Geo Metro, lime green, the ugliest little car you ever saw, wheel wells all rusted out. You couldn't miss her. I figure one of them noticed her car at the bar and saw it as an opportunity."

"You suspect they entrapped her?"

"I don't know the fancy word, but yeah, I think they set her up. They put that deal on the table the night she was arrested, that very same night! This would have been a second DUI offense for her. She woulda lost her license for a year and probably have had to pay a small fortune in fines.

"And Sammy was no good. Not for this town, not for anybody. But she didn't realize the risk, you know? I don't think they looked her in the eye and said, 'He might kill you for this.' If they had, she might have smarted up, taken her punishment and walked outta there."

"You believe he did it then? Sammy Bishop. That he's responsible for her disappearance."

Willow sighed and leaned back in her chair. "Hold on." She stood and left the room.

From somewhere in the little house, Iris heard the sound of a television playing. A small dog appeared in the doorway and eyed Iris suspiciously before turning and darting back into the shadowy living room.

Something else shifted in the shadows and Iris studied it. It barely had a shape, but as she stared, she made out the silhouette of a person, a man, thin and old. A light flicked on and he vanished.

Iris heard Willow moving around, and then she appeared in the doorway, a pad of paper in her hands. She plunked it on the table. The top page was a scrawl of words that Iris couldn't read.

Willow sat down heavily and held the notebook up. "This is me and Kurt's investigation. We realized early on if we didn't look for Norlene, nobody would. Once she'd come up missin' the cops and that fancy prosecutor who'd been giving her so much attention dried up as sure as a mud puddle in the desert." Willow pointed at a word on the first page.

Iris realized it said 'Sammy,' though she'd have been hard-pressed to decipher any of the other words on the page.

"We started listin' off everything we knew about him. Then we asked people around town where he'd been that day, seeing if he'd been braggin' about getting rid of Norlene."

"And?"

"He sure did, but we never got a firsthand account of that. It was always a guy who knew a guy who overheard him sayin' stuff about silencing that bitch. Kurt finally went up to Sammy himself and said we wanted some answers. Sammy told Kurt he had nothin' to do with Norlene's disappearance. He told Kurt the cops probably got rid of Norlene so they could pin a murder rap on him and put him away for good in case the drug charges didn't stick."

"That's pretty far-fetched."

"Probably, but when you don't have a clue, everything feels plausible. We've done some fundraising. Kurt organized a motorcycle ride back in October, a color tour for Norlene. We raised a few thousand towards the reward, but what good is a reward if everyone assumes she ran off?"

Willow fished a photograph from an album and handed it to Iris.

"This is the last photo taken of her, a few weeks before she disappeared. Kurt had it on his phone and we didn't realize it until a month after she'd disappeared and we'd already had the flyers made with the picture of her with dark hair. That was her natural color, but when she disappeared it was kind of dishwater blonde. See, and her roots was showin'. She dyed it herself."

Iris studied the picture of the young woman with stringy hair draped over her shoulders. She wore a paisley top with buttons up the front, tight dark jeans, and faded white tennis shoes. Her eyes were heavy with dark makeup and her lips had the faded red of lipstick that had rubbed off in the previous hours. Willow stood beside her, holding a hot dog and a cup of soda.

"We were downtown for the summer arts festival. Norlene started the evening off in these teensy little heels, but her feet started bothering her. I told her, 'Norlene, you're gonna have blisters the size of silver dollars,' so she went into the resale store and bought those tennis shoes. She was pretty, wasn't she? Too skinny, always skinnier than a fence post, but still pretty." Willow traced her finger along the edge of the photo.

"Ultimately you suspect Sammy Bishop is behind Norlene's disappearance?" Iris asked.

"Seems like it'd be him, right?" Willow continued staring at Norlene's photo. "These days, who's to say what happens when someone disappears? Sex trafficking, tricking women into prostitution, getting them addicted to drugs. I imagined those things for a time—tried to see 'em as holding onto hope." She dropped the picture bitterly on the table.

"It's been four months. There's no hope in imagining her living day and night being tortured, high, getting violated by some psycho. That's not hope. It's cruel to hold on to such an idea. And even if I wanted to, I don't believe that's what happened to Norlene. I think she's dead. Kurt sat me down one day about three weeks after she came up missing. He said, 'Willow, you've always had an instinct about things. What's your gut telling you?'

"And when I got real quiet, I found nothing but silence. That's when I knew she was dead. But not having proof, not knowing what happened or why it happened, that's the hardest part, because what if I was wrong? What if we found her or she came back or she'd been kept alive for some period of time and I'd given up, stopped looking for her?

"And you know what else? I want her in the cemetery next to Mom and Dad because that mattered to her—to Norlene. Not everyone cares about such things. Lord knows I don't, but Norlene had ideas about the end—ideas that bugged me sometimes when she'd bring them up. 'Stop being so morbid, Norlene,' I'd tell her, when she'd go on about the kind of casket she wanted and how she wanted to be buried in her sparkly gold prom dress because that was the happiest night of her life. She saved her dress and even the flowers her date had given her that night —asters. They look like purple daisies. Eventually the flowers dried and crumbled up, and she had to throw them away, but she never got rid of the dress."

Willow swiped at a tear that slipped over her cheek.

"You know what else I feel? Guilt, terrible, gut-eating guilt because more than a few times I ignored Norlene's calls. I got tired of her relapses, her depressions, her rollercoaster life.

"When she first disappeared…" Willow's face pinched with pain. "I was so angry at her. 'Here she goes again, another damn relapse, and I'll have to bail her out because Mom and Dad are dead and there's no one left but me.'" Willow fixed her eyes, filled with torment, on the scattered pictures. "And then nothing. No call. I expected Star to call. That was her best friend. 'Norlene's fallen off the wagon again. Can you pick her up?' No middle of the night call, Norlene sobbing, saying she'd had a bad day, bought a few pills, spiraled. I waited for two days, then I called Star. She hadn't seen her."

Willow touched her throat. "I didn't report her missing right away. It was day four that I called the sheriff's office. I ruined whatever chance police had of finding her. She might have been locked away, still alive, praying that I was out there looking for her, that I would save her." Willow shook her head. "I was just living my life, pissed that she hadn't returned my calls, that she'd blown off work."

"Nine times out of ten when someone disappears, they turn up. It's not your fault you expected the same with Norlene."

"Yeah, that's what Kurt keeps saying."

"Is there anyone you suspected outside of Sammy Bishop?"

"I don't know. I guess I wondered about that prosecutor."

"Jack Skelling? Why would you suspect him?"

"Well, Norlene was real hung up on the man. Once she turned state's, she became his little pet. It was Jack this and Jack that. She talked like they were fixin' to run away together. The last time I saw her, she said she was meeting Jack. She had stars in her eyes." Willow shook her head. "Strung her along is what he did."

"Did you ever ask him about it?"

"Sure." Willow shrugged. "He looked at me like I was a piece of dog crap he had to step over on the sidewalk." She set Norlene's photo on the table. "He said he hadn't seen her, didn't know where she was, but that if I talked to her, she should call him because of the case or whatever."

"Who else would have an idea of what was happening in Norlene's life when she disappeared? Any close friends?"

"One. Star Morton." Willow grabbed another photo and pushed it across the table to Iris. "That's her with Norlene."

In the photo Norlene sat on a sofa, the same one in the living room at Willow's house, feet propped on the coffee table in front of her. A woman around her age sat beside her. Star had black hair, cut just above her ears, and tattoos on the knuckle of her lifted hand. Both girls were grinning and flipping their middle fingers at the camera.

Willow chuckled. "Brats."

"When was this taken?"

"Last year."

"And did Star suspect anyone?"

"She's the one who said the lawyer did it."

"Jack Skelling?"

"Yeah."

"Okay, and if I were to reach out to her, would she talk to me?"

"I don't see why not. Here, I'll write her phone number and address down for you." Willow grabbed Iris's notebook and wrote Star's contact information.

Iris looked at her blank notebook and wrote two names: Sammy Bishop and Jack Skelling. "Tell me everything you remember about Norlene's last day."

"She worked her regular shift at the Gas Stop from six a.m. to three p.m. Left there a few minutes after three. Two people saw her go into her apartment building around three-fifteen. A guy walking his dog called a tip into the sheriff's office that he'd seen Norlene outside the building around five. Nothing after that."

"Was she getting into her car when the guy saw her at five?"

"No. She was standing at the curb like somebody was picking her up."

"Any ideas at all about where she might have been going that night?"

"Well, she was scheduled to clean Skelling Hall that weekend. There's been some confusion about all of that. Her boss at the cleaning company said she'd asked about changing the dates and doing that Thursday night, but she said she'd get back to him. She never called."

"It's possible she went to Skelling Hall?"

"I don't think so. Her car was at her apartment."

"Did she ever go with other cleaning people? Carpool? That's an enormous place for one person to clean."

"Yeah, they had a heavy crew bi-weekly and one person went three times a week to vacuum, empty the trash. That kind of thing."

"You talked to her boss at the gas station?"

"Yeah. Jerome Randolph."

"Any chance he'd be there today?"

Willow nodded. "He's always there in the evening."

"Do you think he'd be open to talking to me?"

"Oh, sure. Jerome is good people. He put five hundred dollars toward our reward for finding Norlene, not that the paper ever bothered to publicize that. Oh, and one more thing." Willow stood and lumbered to the counter. She opened a drawer and pulled something out, returned to Iris. "This is a key to her apartment, a spare."

"It's still there? They didn't lease it to someone else?"

"It's a shithole, not exactly a top priority for the guy who owns it. He owns a dozen places, most of 'em short-term things, vacation rentals, and doesn't do much with the two buildings. The city's been after him to make some updates for about two years. About a month after Norlene went missing, they condemned it. The owner apparently is workin' on some big deal to tear it down and turn it into condos, but for now, it's there and we still have a key. He promised to call me before he started working in there so I could clear out Norlene's apartment."

"Why haven't you done it yet?"

Willow sighed. "'Cause I hoped the police would realize something bad happened to my sister and go in there to search it."

"They've never searched her apartment?"

"Nope. Told me she's an adult who can leave if she wants and they don't have any right to go in without proof of a crime, warrants, yadda yadda. They're just trying to keep me off their backs, is all. They don't want to waste their precious time on Norlene, simple as that."

Iris took the key. "No one else is living there?"

Willow shrugged. "Not legally anyway. Like I said, the city condemned it, but that won't keep the squatters out. Norlene's apartment is locked, so nobody coulda got in there unless they picked the lock or busted down the door."

"Which apartment is it?"

"The complex is called the Views—hilarious, considering the only view from that place is a back alley with overflowing dumpsters. She lived on the third floor. There's two apartments per floor. Hers was apartment six. No elevator, so if you go, you'll have to take the stairs. Are you going to look at it?"

Iris gazed at the key in her palm. "Sure. I'll try to get over there in the next couple of days." Iris stood, gathering her notebook, and then thought of something else. "Did Norlene know Brett Stephens?"

"The kid on the news?"

"Yeah, the one who disappeared from Skelling Hall."

"I'm not sure. Norlene knew everybody in a way from working at the Gas Stop. She never forgot a face."

"And they both worked for Skelling Hall in some capacity," Iris added.

"Yeah. But they're saying that guy was on drugs." Willow's eyes widened. "Maybe he was connected to Sammy Bishop."

Iris slid her notebook into her briefcase. She hadn't considered a potential drug connection between Norlene and Brett, but that was another possibility. "Maybe it's totally unrelated," Iris told her. "I'll see what I can find out."

I ris left Willow's house with a promise to dig deeper into Norlene's case. Before she pulled from the driveway, she searched online for a phone number for Brett Stephens' mother. She was the one who'd reported him missing and she might know if he had a connection to Norlene.

She found a number for Bonnie Stephens and punched it in. A woman answered sounding annoyed.

"Hi, is this Brett Stephens' mom, Bonnie?" Iris asked.

"Yes. I only have a minute though. Make it quick."

Iris frowned, surprised. Surely the woman was desperately waiting for news on her son. "My name is Iris. I'm looking into Brett's case and hoped to ask you a few questions."

"I've answered questions for the police already."

"I'm not working with the police."

"Then what the hell do you want?"

Iris cringed away from the phone. "I want to help you find him," she said, resisting the urge to meet the woman's hostility with her own.

Bonnie released a harsh laugh. "Then start looking at his tweaker friends' houses. He lifted twenty bucks from my wallet the day he disappeared. I'm sure he got good and high and won't be showing his ugly mug around here again for a couple weeks."

"If you thought he took off, why did you report him missing?"

"So they can arrest his ass. Didn't you hear what I said? He stole twenty dollars from me, the little shit."

Iris fought the urge to end the call and rid her brain of the woman's vicious tone. "Do you know if he knew a woman named Norlene Weaver?" Iris asked.

The woman had begun talking to someone else in the room. She came back on the line. "Huh, is there anything else?"

"Yes, I asked if Brett knew Norlene Weaver."

"Never heard of her."

Iris started to ask another question, but the phone went silent. Brett's mother had hung up on her.

"Wow... just wow..." Iris muttered, tossing her phone on the passenger seat.

She was tired and her stomach grumbled, but she wanted to make one more stop before returning to Lola's.

Iris pushed open the glass door into the Gas Stop. It was a typical gas station with rows of chips and candy, refrigerators with pop and beer, a counter offering coffee, and a hot dog machine, the hot dogs shiny and taut beneath the heat lamp. The guy behind the counter stood and stocked cigarettes.

"Hi," Iris said, pausing at the counter.

He turned around. "What can I get ya?"

"I'm looking for information, actually, on Norlene Weaver."

He raised an eyebrow. "Are you a cop?"

"No, an attorney. I just spoke with Willow Weaver."

The man, nametag Jerome, nodded. "I can't tell you a whole lot I haven't already told the police and Willow. Norlene worked her shift, left at three when I came in. She said it had been a pretty quiet day, considering it was August. Summers get awfully busy around here. She drove off, and I never saw her again. But she was seen after that shift. I wasn't the last person to see her."

"Do you have video cameras here?"

"Yep." He pointed to a corner behind the cash register. "Got one here, one in the back, two in the parking lot."

"Did the police look at the footage?"

"Nope."

"Did you?"

"Nah, I mean, like I said, this wasn't her last known place, so I didn't see any reason to."

"Do you think I could look at it?"

"You could, but I tape over it every thirty days."

"Damn… and no one made a copy?"

"Afraid not."

"Did anyone ever come in to visit Norlene—a boyfriend, friends?"

He knitted his brow. "The trouble is, we didn't work together. She worked in the day and I worked in the evenings."

"She always worked alone?"

"Except for holiday weekends."

"Do you know a young man named Brett Stephens?"

Jerome nodded. "I surely do. He gases up here on the regular. His dad and brother too. I saw something on the news about him taking off. Too bad. He was the only one in that family with any sense."

"Do you know if he and Norlene knew one another?"

"Probably did on account of him coming in here now and then, but I couldn't say for sure."

Iris took out her wallet and handed the man her card. "Thanks, Jerome. If you remember anything else about the day Norlene went missing, give me a call."

~

Before Iris returned to Lola's, she dialed the number for Star Morton. It was disconnected.

The address Willow had given her for Star was on her way back toward Lola's. She drove there and parked on the street. The seedy apartment building was spray-painted with the words 'Jesus Died for Your Sins.'

Iris found Star's apartment and knocked. No one answered, and she heard nothing inside. She jotted a quick message on a legal pad asking Star to call her and slipped it beneath Star's door.

12

Mid-morning the following day, Iris gathered her work from the law firm into her briefcase and waited for Andy to arrive.

Iris walked from the house when Andy's blue Jeep pulled to the curb.

"I would have come to the door," Andy told her as he climbed from the driver's seat.

"I saved you the trouble."

"It's no trouble. I could have said hi to your grandmother."

"She's at her friend Minnie's. They've been working on some giant puzzle over there that's apparently over twenty thousand pieces. My head hurts just thinking about it."

Andy opened the passenger door and Iris slid in. "That would take ages."

"Yeah, they've been at it for a few months. I don't suspect it will be finished anytime soon."

As they drove out of town, they passed the road that led to Skelling Hall.

Iris twisted in her seat as the snowy drive flashed by. She half-expected to see Brett running towards them, waving his arms wildly as a black shadow bore down on him.

Andy noticed her gaze. "Thinking about the accident?" he asked.

"Yeah," she lied. "So, this cabin we're going to, what do you do there?"

"Oh, the usual—hunting, fishing, mushing the dogs."

"Dude stuff."

"Pretty much."

"Wait. Did you just say mushing the dogs?"

He laughed. "Dogsled racing. I'm part of a team. We have eight dogs. Two are technically mine, though they live in a kennel outside of town. Every second weekend and every Thursday, they're mine. I work with the dogs at the cabin. I'll be running them in the Brutus Sled Dog Race this year. You should come."

"You race sled dogs? That's such a Yooper thing to do."

He grinned. "Hardly. It's a dying sport. But my granddad did it. He got me into it when I was young. He was the real deal, living in a rustic cabin. Sled dogs were his transportation in the winter. In the summer he rode a motorcycle he'd built himself or canoed to get around. He taught me a lot."

"Did he live in the cabin we're going to?"

"Yep."

"Hmm… okay. How about your romantic life? Had any serious girlfriends, wives, ex-wives?"

"Ex-girlfriends, no wives. One almost-wife, but that ended a few years ago."

"And why is that?"

"My God, you're nosy like an attorney, aren't you?"

"It's my job to ask questions."

He laughed. "I've used that line a handful of times myself. Our relationship ended because it wasn't meant to be."

She narrowed her eyes at him. "That's the most Hallmark explanation I've ever heard. Now tell me the real-world answer."

He shook his head. "Has anyone ever told you that you have the disposition of a rattlesnake?"

"Oh, please, a few pointed questions and you're ready to drive me back to the city."

"I'm strongly considering it."

She leaned back in her seat. "Perhaps that was my plan all along, make you so uncomfortable you take me home so I can get some work done."

"Nah, I like to be uncomfortable. We broke up because Linda didn't like my job. She thought it was dangerous. We started fighting about it and eventually the fights took a toll. We decided to date other people, and she met a mortgage broker from the Lower Peninsula when he was up here vacationing. She followed him back down."

"That must have hurt."

Andy glanced at her. "For a little while, but… what do you do? In a way, I was relieved. She did the thing I was too chicken to do, end it once and for all. Your turn. Tell me the gory details of your latest break-up."

"Nothing gory to tell," she said. "We were in law school together. I decided to come up here, and he had a clerkship in Detroit. End of story."

He shot her a look. "I get the sense you're leaving out some details, but at the risk of having you sink your fangs into my arm while I'm behind the wheel, I won't push."

"What's that?" Iris asked, turning around in her seat to get a closer look at an open cardboard box that contained an object made of twisted forks and spoons.

"A gift for my mom, a clock she pointed out in a shop last year. I picked it up yesterday for Christmas."

"Do you and your mom get along?"

"Yeah, absolutely. She's my number-one fan, somehow managed to not kill me during my troublesome years. I feel bad about it now. I'm sure most of her gray hair and wrinkles could be attributed to my antics. She basically raised me as a single mom. You said your mom is gone, but were you two close before she passed?" he asked.

Iris looked out the window and watched the snow-heavy trees streak by. "No, not really. We were nothing alike."

Even as she said the words, she knew they weren't true. How many times had people commented on how much Iris was like her mother? Even Grandma Lola had noted the similarities now and then, though she was also quick to say 'in only the good ways.'

Iris's mother had always had a slightly cool, detached personality. Of her two children, she'd favored her son and when he'd died, well… the bit of warmth she'd carried seemed to die along with him.

"How about your dad?" Iris asked. "You said you had a single mom. Where was your dad?"

Andy turned his head and cracked his neck, massaging the opposite side. "He split when I was twelve."

"Just left out of the blue?"

"To me, it was out of the blue. My mom had seen it coming. A lot later, she told me she suspected he was having an affair. Turned out he was."

"What a jerk."

"Pretty much."

~

The drive took a half-hour, much of which included dirt roads so packed with snow the only thing distinguishing road from forest was the tree line.

They pulled into a clearing. A small log cabin sat in the center.

"This is it, huh?"

"Yep. My grandpa's cabin. He built it himself in 1932. He and my grandmother lived here. She gave birth to my father and my aunt here."

Iris stared at the little rough-hewn structure, snow piled to the windows. "I can't imagine," she said. "Why? The hospital was too far away?"

Andy laughed. "It wasn't close, that's for sure, but they just lived differently. It was a choice they made being out here. By the 30s they could have built a house in town or bought one, but they'd grown up in the Great Depression. They took pride in being self-sufficient, not getting sucked into the false opulence of the cities. They loved this place."

Iris stepped from the Jeep and trudged through the snow, following Andy to the front door. He pushed it open.

"Don't you lock it?" she asked.

He looked back at her and grinned. "There's nothing in this cabin that any thief would want. If somebody breaks into this place, it's for shelter and they can have it. I don't want anyone freezing to death because I'm worried my grandmother's quilts might get stolen."

Iris turned a circle in the single room, which contained a sagging full bed strewn with quilts, a worn couch and a pocked kitchen table. A pot-bellied stove occupied one corner. Wood was stacked in a rack beside it. The kitchen included a short counter, a laundry tub that she guessed doubled as a kitchen sink, and a single shelf with a scattering of plates, glasses and silverware. One bookshelf, handmade from the looks of it, held old board games and paperbacks with grooved spines.

Andy loaded firewood and a fire log into the stove. He adjusted the flue and then lit a match and set the log on fire.

"Where's the bathroom?" Iris asked.

Andy gestured out the window.

Iris spied a wooden outhouse at the edge of the property. "That looks cold."

Andy grinned. "It is. You learn to go quick in the winter. Though truth be told, I've got a space heater I pop in there this time of year. Want a hot toddy?" He grabbed a bottle of bourbon from the shelf behind the sink.

"Yes, most definitely." She scanned the cabin. "What about water? How do you take a shower?"

Andy set a kettle on the stove and then walked to a corner of the cabin. "Here, check it out." He pulled back a curtain to reveal a claw-footed tub. "I have a basin outside that collects rainwater. It gets piped in back here. It's great, right?"

Iris grimaced and held up a hand, folding a finger with each flaw. "Isolated, buried in snow, no running water, no internet, an outhouse. I don't have enough fingers to tick off everything that's wrong with this place."

Andy laughed, grabbing the kettle from the stove and making them each a drink in mismatched coffee mugs. He handed one to Iris. She walked to the sunken bed and sat on the edge.

"Ugh," she grumbled, looking at the window. "More snow."

"Tell me, what is it you so dislike about winter?" Andy asked.

Iris took a sip of her drink. "Where do I begin? How about the perpetual cloud that arrives in November and doesn't depart until April? Permanently soaked and salted hems of pants, stepping out of my car and sinking knee deep in snow, black ice, a cold so brutal my heart feels like a slab of frozen steak behind my ribs." She held out her palms. "Chapped hands and lips. Feet so dry and cracking that you have to soak them in a bathtub of olive oil to soften them up. Shoveling snow, walking in snow, driving in snow, looking at snow, waking up to a new layer of—you guessed it—snow."

Andy laughed. "Okay, okay, you've made your point. But let me remind you of the good stuff, because you clearly need a bit of yin to your yang. Or yang to yin. Whatever. There's ugliness and there's beauty." He pulled the curtain back on the window. "Look at the white powder on those pine branches, the crystals on the glass, that blue sky that will never look as blue as it does in winter when everything beneath it is white."

He walked to the fire. "A roaring fire, a hot toddy"—he held up his cup—"a spine-broke paperback. Skiing, snowshoeing, sledding, ice-skating, snowballs, snow forts."

He moved to where she sat on the bed, gently nudged her onto her back. He kissed her, leaned over and set his drink on the table. "Cozy beds and blankets and warm bodies."

An hour later, Iris sat beside the fire reading the legal briefs Marv had asked her to go over. She set the file down and surveyed the cabin. It was completely silent, not a sound. No car engines, honking horns, distant sirens.

Her cell phone rang, the shrill call slicing the quiet, a sound tantamount to someone shrieking in the middle of church. Iris grabbed it and hit silent, glancing at the screen. It was her dad, probably calling for his monthly check-in, which comprised five minutes of small talk. She ignored the call.

"Everything okay?" Andy asked.

"Yeah." Iris switched the phone to vibrate. "My dad. I'll call him later."

She opened the file, but her bladder demanded her attention. She shot a reluctant glance toward the outhouse beyond the window.

"Three… two… one," she murmured and stood up.

"What'd you say?" Andy asked, looking up from his paperback, a shabby copy of *True Grit*.

"I counted backward from three. It's the secret to my success." She pushed her feet into her boots and grabbed her coat from the hook.

"Explain."

Iris zipped her coat. "I read it in a book somewhere, counting backwards to motivate yourself to do something you don't want to do, like walk out in the snow to pee in a wooden box."

Andy returned to his book. "I might have to try that. The cold would be a lot less miserable if you had decent winter gear. Does that coat even have a lining?"

"Yes, see?" She opened the coat to reveal the thin silk lining.

"That doesn't count. No wonder you're freezing. But FYI, I turned the space heater on in there. Your butt won't freeze."

"Lovely." She inwardly rolled her eyes and trudged out into the snow, which had begun to fall harder, heavier. They needed to leave soon, or they'd get trapped in the little cabin overnight.

"We better head back into town," she told him when she returned.

Andy set his book down. "How come?"

"Because it's snowing buckets out there. We're liable to get stuck."

Andy stood and walked to her, unzipped her coat. "Would that be so bad?" He traced his finger down her jaw and leaned down to kiss her.

"Yes, it would. I have work to do."

He kissed lower, moving from her jaw to her neck. He slipped his hands beneath her shirt. She didn't want to stop. She kissed him back hard, grabbed the button on his pants and pulled it loose.

"Fine, this first, but then we're going back into town."

~

They didn't go back into town. They had sex a second time on the creaky bed, with snow obscuring the world beyond the windows. Afterwards, Andy heated soup on the single burner and they sipped it from camping mugs.

When it grew dark, there was only firelight in the cabin and Iris watched it leap and shiver behind the wood burner's grate.

It all felt so good, so easy, which made something squirm in her belly. She didn't need this distraction, this getting sucked into some relationship void where weekends were spent in isolated cabins. She was just beginning her career and didn't have time for the slow life of Andy Bale.

Andy slept, but Iris lay on her side and watched the fire. She thought of Norlene Weaver and Brett Stephens. People who'd gone missing with little fanfare. How easy it was for someone to disappear. Or, worse, for a person to make someone else disappear. Except it wasn't a person who floated in her mind.

It was the shadow man.

~

Iris woke in the dark of the cabin.

Something was moving around outside.

She lay facing the wood burner, its orange glow the only light that remained in the room. She listened, but no sound other than Andy's breath broke the quiet.

The instant she closed her eyes, she heard movement again—feet crunching through dense snow. The sound jerked her back to alertness, and she sat up, staring at the cabin door, stomach clenched as she waited to see the metal knob turn.

It didn't.

She could wake Andy, demand he investigate, but Iris had spent too long doing it on her own. In the years after her mother's death, she'd often been plagued by nightmares, but learned early that her father would not be peeking in closets and under beds. In part, the issue was that her father just slept too hard. It was almost impossible to wake him. On the rare time she roused him from sleep, he'd be grumpy and disoriented and bark at her to go back to bed. Iris sensed he was furious that she'd robbed him of the only reprieve he found in a life where he no longer had a wife or son. In sleep, he could sink into oblivion. Iris herself felt that way, but nightmares and occasional insomnia often stole that bit of peace.

Iris stood and crept toward the door. She paused and listened. There were no curtains on the windows. Whatever lurked out there could see her, but she could not see it. The glass reflected her face, her skin less pale in the fire's glow, her long hair twisted and snarled from Andy pushing his fingers through it. She glared back at her face, wanting the thing beyond the window to know she was not afraid. A lie she almost believed.

Lola had said on many occasions that spirits were harmless, but Iris sensed the shadow thing hovering in the dark woods beyond the cabin.

There was nothing harmless about him. He wasn't merely curious about human beings, he wanted them.

He *took* them.

"Nonsense," Iris whispered.

Across the room Andy stirred, but didn't wake.

The shadow man wasn't real, not in the flesh-and-blood sense, and yet… whatever he was, he was dangerous.

13

———

Andy parked at the curb in front of Lola's house, and Iris reached for the door handle.

"Hold up," he said, pulling her towards him and kissing her. "Thanks for coming with me."

"It was fun. I didn't get enough work done, but"—she shrugged —"that's what Sundays are for." Iris opened the door and let out a breath as the cold air hit her.

"I thought Sundays were for rest and prayer."

She scoffed. "Not in my world." She started to close the door and paused. "Shit," she muttered. "I forgot my folder at your cabin. Damn it!" She kicked the snowbank behind her and winced. It was mostly ice.

"I'll run back out there this afternoon and get it."

"You sure?"

"Yeah, not a problem. I'll drop it off later."

"Thanks, I'll be losing my mind without it." She turned and hurried up to the house, nearly slipping on the icy sidewalk.

The interior of the house smelled like roasting garlic and coffee.

"I've got a pot roast in," Lola called down the hallway. "Did you have coffee yet?"

"Yeah, Andy made a French press at his cabin."

Lola appeared in the hallway. "Andy?"

"Yeah. Andy Bale. We stayed at his cabin last night."

Lola's eyes lit up. "He's a very nice young man."

"Yeah, he's all right."

Lola gave her a knowing look. "I'm happy you've made a friend."

"Thanks, Grandma."

Iris walked upstairs, showered and changed into clean clothes. She considered her basket of dirty laundry, the short list of items she needed to pick up from the store, including shampoo, a few pairs of heavy socks and the other winter clothes she'd continued to avoid buying. She couldn't work without her file, but she could do her chores.

Instead, she thought of Norlene Weaver and the things Willow had told her. She fished the key to Norlene's apartment out of her purse and stared at it. What would it hurt to just poke around?

The Views apartment building was much as Willow had described, a wretched-looking structure in a slummy part of town that included mostly industrial-type places, many of which appeared as if they'd been empty for years. An alley ran behind the complex with a rusted fire escape clinging to the crumbling brick. A single dumpster stood there, overflowing with trash—odd considering the building had no residents.

The door into the building stood half-open. Iris walked in. A dark hallway, carpeted and smelling of mildew, stretched before her. To her right was a heavy door marked 'stairs.' She pushed inside. No lights in the stairwell and it was pitch-black and reeked of urine.

Iris stood in the open doorway and pulled out her phone, slid on the flashlight. She pulled her sweater up over her nose and started up the stairs, her footsteps loud and echoey.

She passed the second-floor doorway and ascended another level. The third-floor door hung half off its hinges. She stepped into the hall, this one dimly lit by grimy windows at opposite ends. It stank less than the first floor, but had a strong odor of something floral, as if someone had sprayed the hall with air freshener.

Norlene's door was closed and looked undisturbed. Iris still wore her fleece winter gloves, and she intended to keep them on. The key slid into the lock and turned with a click. The door was lightweight, flimsy, an easy door to force open.

Iris stepped into the apartment, again lit only by the gray light filtering through the windows. The living room and kitchen occupied a single room, kitchen lining the wall to the right with an old-looking pea-green refrigerator, a sink surrounded by a brown counter with the laminate peeling at the edges, and a stove. A piece of wood screwed to the wall appeared to be a makeshift fold-down kitchen table. A timeworn blue sofa with two mismatched chairs occupied the living room. A television sat on a coffee table that was also scattered with books, magazines, and two coffee mugs. A single framed photo of a field of purple asters hung on one wall. Above it the plaster was discolored as if the ceiling had leaked.

Iris touched nothing as she moved through the apartment. She paused at the counter where a stack of mail sat as if Norlene had collected it the day she disappeared and never opened it. The top letter was an overdue notice from the library. Beneath it, Iris saw a grocery store circular and several credit card offers. The sink was empty, but there was a single plate and spoon stacked in a plastic drying rack.

On the wall next to a window hung a calendar. The date was opened to August, the last month Norlene had been seen alive. Iris studied the little white boxes, noticing cryptic notes someone, likely Norlene, had written. A few were clear enough—'dentist 9 am,' 'Jerome's birthday.' Others had only initials, or not even that. On August ninth, Norlene had written a plus sign next to a little smiley face. That had been four days before she vanished. Iris took a picture of the calendar.

She left the main room and stepped into the short hallway that opened into a bedroom on the right and a small bathroom with a stand-up shower on the left. Iris peered into the bathroom. Makeup littered the counter around the sink. A towel hung from a hook beside the shower. Clothes lay crumpled on the floor.

Iris backed up and moved into the bedroom. It was cluttered. A full bed took up nearly the entire room, but Norlene had crammed a long dresser against one wall. Piles of folded laundry lay on the surface. In the center stood a snow globe with a miniature replica of Skelling Hall inside. Tiny dark pines surrounded the hall, which in the snow globe version was painted with glitter. A handkerchief lay on the corner of the dresser. Two lion's head cufflinks rested in the center.

A purple curtain served as a door to the narrow closet. Iris pulled it aside. Clothes hung from hangers next to a canvas organizer, typically used for shoes. Norlene had filled the cubbies with a range of items from folded magazines to hats and scarves. Iris pulled clothes aside to reveal a long gold dress. The beloved prom dress Norlene had told Willow she wanted to be buried in.

Iris turned away from the closet. A stool sat next to the head of the bed, apparently doubling as a nightstand. Two framed photos sat on the stool. In one photo, Iris thought she recognized the child versions of Norlene and Willow standing between a man and a woman who were likely their parents. The other photo was Norlene alone, wearing the gold dress from the closet and standing in front of the Soo Locks. It was likely the fondly remembered prom night. Norlene looked young and hopeful.

Iris studied the picture of the dead woman. She was dead. There was no doubt about that.

"Norlene?" Iris asked the quiet room.

Nothing stirred.

Why had Norlene's spirit attached to Jack Skelling? Why didn't she appear here in her own apartment?

On the opposite side of the bed stood an actual nightstand. Iris opened the single drawer. A Bible lay in the corner along with several tubes of chapstick and a tabloid magazine. Iris grabbed the Bible and flipped through it. A slip of paper drifted out. Iris picked it up. Norlene had doodled the name 'Jack Skelling' a dozen or more times and surrounded his name with little hearts, the type of thing a schoolgirl did over her crush. Iris slid the paper back into the Bible and returned it to the drawer.

Rather than framed photos, Norlene had decorated the walls with pages cut from glossy magazines. Iris studied the images of country houses and long tables set for formal dinners. The dreams of a country life coated the uneven drywall—simple dreams with white picket fences and tables adorned in flowers. There were also pictures of male models, all with dark hair and blue eyes. They wore suits and drove sports cars and they all vaguely resembled Jack Skelling.

Iris heard a sound from the living room and froze. She'd closed the apartment door behind her, but wondered if someone had followed her in. The sound came again—a scratching.

Quietly, she slipped from the room and back down the hall, looking for the source of the noise.

She found it at a window behind one of the living room chairs. A black and white cat, his fluffy fur matted, stared in at her, pawing at the wood frame. He meowed and pushed his face against the glass.

On the kitchen floor, tucked into the corner, Iris spotted a bag of dry cat food next to two plastic bowls.

"Fine," she muttered when the cat meowed again. "I'll feed you, but that's it."

Iris unlatched and opened the window. The cat leapt into the apartment, rubbed against her legs and limped to the food bowl. Iris filled the bowl and watched the animal scarf it down in big gulps. He barely chewed.

The cat favored his right front leg as he ate, keeping the paw lifted. After he ate, the cat cleaned his paws and face. Iris reached for his neck, searching for a collar, but found none. He rubbed against her hand and then flopped sideways and stretched out long.

Reluctantly, Iris petted the cat. She'd never had pets, dogs or cats, and the interest in the creatures had mostly eluded her. She vaguely remembered being jealous of a girlfriend's new kitten in childhood, but the feeling had been short-lived when the girl came to school grief-stricken because the kitten had been run over by a car.

"Got a name?" she asked the mangy-looking cat, who merely continued with his bath.

Iris stood, monitoring the cat to make sure he didn't do his business on the floor. She took a second walk through the apartment, looking for anything unusual that jumped out. This time, she took photos of every-thing that might be important.

She saw nothing extraordinary as she snapped pictures, but one thing did bother her. Nothing appeared to have been removed from the apartment. Norlene's makeup, toothbrush, and clothing all seemed to be in place. If Norlene had run off, surely she'd have taken things with her, but there was no empty space in the closet where clothes had been pulled from hangers and tossed in a bag.

Iris studied the closet, considering again that gold prom dress. Willow had said Norlene had loved the dress. More evidence the woman hadn't left. She didn't have much and she surely would not have left such a prized possession behind.

She returned to the kitchen and opened the refrigerator. A half-gallon of milk, likely curdled, stood on the top shelf next to a stack of yogurts. Condiments filled the door. On the bottom shelf sat an unopened turtle cheesecake, mold growing on the surface of the dessert. Iris read the price tag—fourteen dollars ninety-nine cents. A lot of money to spend on a dessert only to not take a single bite. In the back of the refrigerator, Iris spotted an unopened bottle of Brut champagne.

The champagne and cheesecake looked out of place in the refrigerator, the types of things someone bought to prepare for a celebration. Even if she'd left of her own free will, Iris thought Norlene, having lived on so little most of her life, would have taken those items in particular with her.

The cat joined Iris by the fridge, poking his head inside.

"No, go on," Iris told him.

The cat went back to the food bowl and watched her.

"No more," Iris said. "You ate that whole bowl. I'm not cleaning up your puke."

After a few more minutes of scanning the apartment, Iris decided there was nothing to be seen. She opened the window and put the cat back outside, not looking him in the eyes as he continued to stare at her through the glass.

14

That evening, Iris opened Lola's front door to Andy, who stood with her folder in his hands.

"Thanks," she told him, taking it and pressing it to her chest.

"If it isn't Andrew Malone," Lola said, coming up behind Iris in the hallway. "Come on in here. Get out of the cold."

Iris stepped aside. Andy knocked his boots against the doorframe before stepping in.

"Hi, Mrs. Walsh. How are you?"

"Oh, I'm just splendid. Been enjoying having my little Iris up here. I see you two are getting acquainted."

Iris saw the mischievous gleam in her grandmother's eye. "He's just dropping off my folder," Iris grumbled, waving it in explanation.

"Come have a cup of cocoa, Andrew. Or the pot roast is nearly done. Stay for dinner."

"I'm sure he's busy," Iris said.

"It sounds delicious, but I'm on the clock tonight. I didn't want Iris to be without her work. Good to see you both."

He winked at Iris, gave Lola a wave, and walked back out the door and down the steps.

After Andy left, Iris joined Lola in the living room. "Why did you call him Andrew Malone? His last name is Bale."

"Malone is the name he had as a boy. Don't you remember him? He used to chum around with Frankie."

Iris considered the name Andrew Malone. The name did ring familiar, but why wouldn't he have mentioned that he'd been friends with her brother?

"Come sit on this stool and let me rub your shoulders," Lola told her. "You've got 'em arched right up to your ears."

Iris held up the folder. "I've got to get work on these briefs."

"Iris Lee Walsh, sit your bottom down. You can spare five minutes to talk about Andrew Malone. Plus, you'll work better if your shoulders aren't knottier than a hawthorn tree."

Iris sat on the stool, and Lola rested her hands on Iris's shoulders as if telling them to settle down.

"Andrew Malone," Iris murmured. "Okay, yeah, I kind of do remember that name."

"He took his mother's last name, Bale, after his parents' divorce. It wasn't just a divorce, though. His father abandoned the family. He started having an affair and then one day he drained their bank accounts and left town. It was terrible for Katherine, his mother. My goodness, I remember seeing her around town with these red crying eyes, all hunched up like somebody had ripped her heart right out of her chest."

Iris frowned. Andy had told her about his parents' divorce, but he'd left out the magnitude.

"They moved away when Andrew was a teenager." Lola dropped her voice, though there was no one in the house to overhear her. "I reckon it was because Andrew had started getting into some trouble. But then maybe five years later, they came back. Katherine is remarried now to Lincoln Mastoff, and he's a good man. I was happy to see it all work out in the end."

"I'm surprised he hasn't mentioned knowing Frankie," Iris said.

"Well, poppet, you're not exactly keen on talking about the stuff that hurts. Feel this tension here?" Lola pressed on a tight muscle in Iris's neck.

Iris winced.

"That tension is called armor," Lola explained. "The useless kind, might as well be tinfoil. And those grumpy looks you're always passing out and that tone you used earlier with Andrew—more tinfoil armor. And that won't protect you. We didn't come into this world to play it safe."

"What tone? That's the way I talk."

"Hmph." Lola continued massaging Iris's neck. "All I'm sayin' is the world delivers what you need, not what you want or think you want. When I was twenty-two, I fell head over heels in love with a man named Morris Humphrey. My Lord, he was a handsome devil with black hair and a black mustache and the brightest blue eyes you ever saw. He got drafted, went off to war. It wasn't meant to be."

"Did he die?"

"No, he didn't die, but he came back a changed man. Two years after he got home, he went to prison for beating his own brother to death with a shovel over some petty squabble. Maybe it was the war that turned him. Maybe something dark had already taken root in his heart. I'll likely never know, but had the world left it up to me, I'd have married that man and never met your grandad. But you know what, poppet? I don't believe anything could'a changed what was in the cards for me, or for him. We've all got our destiny. You feel like your world is falling apart, but Iris, all of life looks that way depending where you focus. It comes together, it falls apart—life is just one big game of Jenga."

Iris moaned when Lola hit a sore spot and her grandma rubbed gently there.

"You need a nice long bath," Lola told her. "Jan bought me a big glass bottle filled with bath salts and lavender. Why don't I go upstairs and start you a bath?"

Iris patted her grandmother's hand. "I appreciate it, but no. I've got to get to work on this brief. Marv's expecting it tomorrow morning." Iris stood, grabbed the folder from the table, and retreated to her desk to work.

~

"D amn it!" Iris snapped, slapping the back of the printer as if that might spur it into action.

The black box merely continued grumbling and releasing a stream of beeps while flashing an error screen.

"What is it, poppet?" Lola asked from her game table as she carefully removed a wooden block in Jenga.

"This imbecilic printer is not doing its one and only job," Iris fumed, pulling out the paper tray, adjusting the stack of pages and shoving it back in. She'd already unplugged it once, opened the top and searched for a jam. Nothing had worked. "I'm going to have to walk downtown to the copy shop and get this stuff printed," she grumbled.

"You could drive. It looks chilly out there and it's getting dark."

"No, it's only a few blocks."

Iris shrugged on her jacket, shoved her feet into her boots and stomped into the snow. She had no reason to feel as angry as she did, but the emotion was there, boiling like a kettle reaching its screaming point. She'd wanted to march the printer down the driveway and toss it into Lola's big plastic trash bin.

Iris walked the five blocks into the icy wind rolling off the bay. The print shop was warm and overly bright, with one bored-looking guy manning the desk.

"I need to print this," Iris told him, holding up her USB drive.

"That kiosk is self-serve." He pointed at a desktop. "Do you know how to pull up your documents?"

"Yep." Iris veered toward the computer, inserted the drive, and opened her files. She clicked print and relaxed when the industrial-sized printer purred to life and spit out the ten pages in half as many seconds.

She paid the guy at the desk, tucked the papers into her folder, and started back for Lola's.

When she stepped from the store, her cell phone rang. Willow Weaver's name appeared on the screen.

"This is Iris," she answered.

"Hi, Iris, this is Willow Weaver."

"Is everything okay, Willow?"

"Oh, yeah, sure. I mean…" The woman let out a mirthless laugh. "Just another day, but I thought of something and wanted to mention it to you."

"Go ahead."

"Well… Norlene had some money over the last few months. A couple of times, she took me out for dinners. I tried to pay and she wouldn't let me. She also had a pair of new sandals the last time I saw her. Leather ones. I asked her if she bought them used, but no, she hadn't. I asked where she'd gotten the money and she got kind of mad at me, said I was being nosy."

"Do you have any idea where the money was coming from?"

"No."

"Okay, thanks for calling, Willow."

"One of those dinners was the last time I saw her. She took me out to

Prior's Steakhouse. I'd never been. We shared a bottle of wine and both ordered the fettuccine. I didn't know then that it would be the last time I ever saw her. I was lying in bed thinking about that dinner last night. I kept thinking that eventually I will have a last day with every single person I know. Kurt, my friends. Every one of us will have a last day together and we won't know it. We'll never know it's the last day until after one of us is gone."

Iris swallowed the lump gathering in her throat. Visions of Frankie and her mother were instant figures in her mind. The last days she'd spent with them that she'd not known were last days. It was a hugely troubling thought and as she imagined Lola, her father, the people in her life, she grew colder.

"It's hard to comprehend," Iris said, starting down the street, holding her papers carefully so they didn't blow away.

"Anyway, that's all. I wanted to tell you about the money," Willow said. "Thank you, Iris."

"You're welcome, Willow. I'll call if I find out anything at all about Norlene."

She ended the call and tucked the phone in her pocket. The wind stirred up the snow as she crossed the street.

Irisss… it breathed.

She stopped and scanned the street, but it had been merely a whisper on the wind. Her mind playing tricks on her.

The sky had been growing dark on her way into town and now, though only minutes had passed, full night had descended as she headed back to Lola's.

Winters in Michigan's Upper Peninsula were not so very different from those in the Lower Peninsula, but they were different enough. Her black tweed coat suited her downstate, but in Sault Ste Marie, where the wind-chill often pushed the temperatures below zero, it didn't suffice. The cold didn't merely chap her lips and cheeks, it seemed to gnaw on her very bones. It was cruel weather, killing weather, as she'd recently read in the newspaper after a homeless man had been found frozen to death in an alleyway.

Even as winter had descended that year, Iris had avoided buying the appropriate winter attire. Everyone else lived in their heavy down jackets, waterproof boots, thick wool sweaters. Iris, insisting in her mind that she'd soon be applying for jobs elsewhere—Florida, for instance—had refused to give in and buy the necessities. Instead, she got by wearing Lola's old winter gear, boots half a size too big, fine if she wore two pairs of socks, pilled sweaters, and misshapen knit hats.

Before her, the sidewalk was murky. Clouds obscured any moon or starlight that might have offered illumination in the absence of streetlights. A block down the road, purple and silver lights twinkled from the front yard of a house, but the houses between where Iris walked and that glimmer of faint light were dark. Snow piled in their driveways, a sure sign they were summer people who rarely visited in the winter.

Iris heard a strained whimpering like a trapped puppy, followed by soft scratching. She wanted desperately to burst through her grandmother's front door, but she couldn't simply ignore the sound. To her left, a house loomed. A black silhouette. The sound came again. It seemed to emerge from behind the house, and Iris could make out the shape of a shed back there.

She stared at the structure, at the high snow between her and it.

"Damn it," she muttered, stepping off the icy sidewalk. She sank into the snow and it passed her knees, instantly saturating her jeans with icy coldness.

The whimper came again, and she plodded forward. When Iris reached the shed, she listened, tilting her head, suddenly unsure what had compelled her off the safe path into this desolate backyard.

Another whine emerged from the shed. A dog was trapped inside.

Despite her gloves, her fingers were numb as she fumbled with the metal latch on the door. She prised it open and yanked on the door. It didn't budge. Snow more than a foot high held it closed.

Iris kicked at the snowbank and then bent over and shoveled it out of the way with her hands. Her lips grew dry and cracked and her hair fell in her face. Her body trembled with the cold, but she refused to give up, cupping her hands and scooping snow to the side.

Finally, she wriggled the door open. She expected the trapped dog to leap out, but nothing stirred when she cracked the door. Iris tugged it further, peering into the dark shed.

"Come on," she called, false cheeriness barely covering the sudden brittleness that coursed through not only her voice, but her entire body.

Something lurked in the shed. But it wasn't a puppy, and though Iris couldn't exactly see it, she felt it. The shadow man crouched in the corner watching her. No eyes glowed in the darkness because it had no eyes, no face.

Iris stood frozen with her hand clutching the shed door, her brain spitting at her to shut the goddamn door and run, but a sudden para-lyzing fear had taken hold. If she turned, the thing would leap and drag her back into the shed.

Something shot forward, a black vaporous wind that smelled of scorched, rotted meat. It pushed through Iris, blowing her back. She staggered and fell on her back as the dark shadow pressed down on top of her.

15

For several seconds, she couldn't breathe, felt as if the thing had invaded her mouth and nose. Her throat was thick with it like someone had stuffed cotton down her trachea. She gaped at the night sky, which blurred as she struggled for air.

It was crushing her. She'd die there, suffocate in a snow drift behind a stranger's house.

The weight suddenly lifted. Iris sucked in a painful breath and turned on her side, clawing away from the shed. She stood, snatched her folder from the ground, and ran for Lola's house.

Iris burst through the door and slammed and locked it behind her.

"Got your stuff printed?" Lola called from the living room.

Iris gazed at her disheveled reflection in the hall mirror. She took a shuddering breath and patted her hair down.

"Yeah…" Iris murmured. The folder beneath her arm was wet, but the pages had stayed mostly dry.

Lola glanced up at Iris as she passed the doorway into the living room. She frowned. "Are you okay, poppet?"

Iris forced a smile. "Yeah. I'm fine. I'm going to head upstairs and work for a bit and then call it a night."

Lola blew her a kiss. "Sweet dreams."

Monday passed in a blur with Iris having little time to contemplate her disturbing encounter from the night before.

Marv had Iris running all over town. She went to the courthouse three times in addition to working on a brief for an upcoming case.

At the end of the day, just when she'd begun to fantasize about an evening on Lola's couch, Marv asked her to drive documents to a client who lived ten miles outside of town. Marv would have done it himself, he told her, but he had a date. Iris had been tempted to argue with him, but he'd left her office before she had a chance.

Grudgingly she drove to the client's house, which was closer to fifteen miles outside of town than ten. Iris delivered the papers and got stuck in a twenty-minute conversation with the client about his recent bunion surgery.

"You owe me, Marv," she grumbled, cranking the heat in her car and heading back to town.

As she drove, Iris tried to concentrate on the audiobook emitting from her speakers, Gary Spence's *How to Argue and Win Every Time*, but found herself perpetually drawn back to thoughts of the thing in the shed.

Was it a ghost? Or had something else followed her from Skelling Hall the night of the accident? Had it somehow taken Brett Stephens or had it merely spooked him and he'd run off and... what? Fallen in the icy lake? Gotten lost in the woods and succumbed to the elements? Or maybe he'd made it out alive, been picked up by a friend, or gone on a bender, as the rumors seemed to suggest.

As Iris rounded a curve in the road, a loud pop emitted from beneath her car. She gasped and clutched the wheel. The left side of the car sagged slightly and in her side-view mirror she watched a hunk of her back left tire fling away and tumble toward the opposite ditch.

"Nooo..." She moaned, letting off the gas and coasting to the side of the road.

Her hands trembled when she pulled them from the wheel. The memory of her accident from days earlier had her heart pummeling against her breastbone. "I hate cars," she muttered, unbuckling and wrenching off her seat belt.

After grabbing her cell phone, she stepped from the car and surveyed the damage. The entire back driver's side tire had exploded. Only tatters clung to the rim.

She could call Lola, but a fat lot of good that would do, considering she had her grandmother's car. Iris dialed Nina, but got her voicemail.

Iris ended the call. Marv had said he was going on a date. She hated to call and interrupt him even if he completely deserved it.

She scrolled to Andy's name, but didn't hit send.

The quiet crept in, and Iris thought again of the shadow man.

The forest, benevolent when she'd been speeding down the road, appeared suddenly menacing. A shiver twisted down her spine and as she studied the endless trees stretching before her, something moved. Iris took a faltering step back, fumbling one hand behind her for the door handle without taking her eyes off the snow-laden trees.

The sound of a car engine split the quiet, and Iris swung her gaze away from the trees as a black Mercedes rolled to a stop on the opposite side of the road. Jack Skelling climbed from the car.

He walked toward her. "Got a flat?"

"Sure do."

"Need some help with it?"

"I was just going to call someone."

"I'll save you the call. Here, pop the trunk. You have a spare, I presume?"

"I hope so." She realized she'd never checked Lola's trunk for a spare. She reached through her driver's door and pulled the lever to release the trunk.

At the back of the car, Jack dug beneath her floor mat. The spare was in place. He hauled it out along with the tools to fix it. She'd never changed a flat tire and watched him with interest.

"You don't strike me as mechanically inclined," she said.

He grinned. "I sense that's not a compliment." He got down on one knee and she grimaced. His trousers would be covered in snow and salt.

"Well, it's not a compliment. I took you for a typical attorney who only gets his hands dirty if it's other people's dirt."

He loosened the lug nuts and set them in a neat pile on the road. "My grandfather had strong opinions about what men should be capable of. Changing a tire was one of them."

"I hope loading a dishwasher made the list."

He smirked. "He was a wash-the-dishes-by-hand kind of guy. It was a bit of quality time for him and my grandmother. They'd turn on a Johnny Cash and June Carter album and stand side by side washing dishes and bumping along to the music."

"Sounds like a scene out of *Little House on the Prairie*."

"I'm pretty sure the Ingalls family didn't have a record player."

"Fine, it sounds like something from some all-American family sitcom."

"It was. They were. I'm grateful to have known them." He slid the jack beneath the car and cranked it up.

"They're gone now?"

"Yes, my grandmother passed when I was fifteen, my grandfather eight years later."

"I'm sorry."

He said nothing, just continued on with the tire, rolling the new one into place.

"Is there anything you can't do?" she asked, mildly irritated by this handsome man who was not only a successful chief assistant prosecuting attorney, but also stopped for stranded motorists on the side of backcountry roads.

"All kinds of things. I can't ice-skate for the life of me. Chopsticks at a Japanese restaurant? Forget it. I'd be better off trying to levitate the food into my mouth," he told her, screwing on the last of the lug nuts and standing, wiping the dirty snow from the knees of his slacks.

"Now I owe you a pair of pants."

"Hardly. I'm happy to help and make sure you're not stranded on a dark road somewhere."

"Can I say thank you and buy you a drink?" she asked.

Iris thought of her conversation with Norlene's sister, Willow, how she'd referred to Norlene as Jack's little pet. She could ask him about the case, get his sense of what had happened to Norlene.

He glanced at his car as if he had somewhere to be, then seemed to change his mind. "Do you want to go grab a drink at the Wicked Sister?"

"Instead of Bitters?"

"If we go there, I'll be working."

"Sure. I'll follow you."

~

Iris had never been to the Wicked Sister. It was on the opposite side of town, tucked into a brick building on Ashmun Street. A few people sat at the bar. A family of four occupied a table near the back. It was definitely a different crowd than the one at Bitters.

"This is the bar you go to when you don't want to be seen, huh?" Iris asked, sliding into a chair opposite Jack.

"Pretty much. I come here sometimes for lunch because then I can just think. I rarely get interrupted."

The server arrived. She smiled at Jack as if she recognized him.

"I'll have a glass of red, please," he told her.

"The house red?"

"Sure."

Iris started to order her usual martini, then changed her mind. Those drinks went down too easy and tonight she wasn't within walking distance to Grandma Lola's house.

"I'll have the same," she said. Iris liked red wine well enough, but more than one glass and she'd wake up with a raging headache. "I hear you're the youngest assistant prosecutor they've ever had in Chippewa County?"

He unfolded his napkin and placed it in his lap. "Yes, that's true."

"Do you like it?"

"The work or the title?"

"All of it."

He smiled, but little creases appeared between his dark brows. "Yes. I love the work. I've been called obsessed a time or two. The title isn't important. Well…" He tilted his head to the side. "It's important to my parents, my father in particular. It's not important to me."

"Then why go for it? Why not just stay a prosecutor?"

"Because they offered it to me."

The waitress delivered their wine.

"Thank you," Jack told her. "Could we get the Brussels sprouts as well?"

"I'll get those in right away, Prosecutor Skelling," the woman told him.

Iris widened her eyes. "Prosecutor Skelling. My goodness, your reputation precedes you."

"Hardly. She's a part-time legal secretary. She's probably the only person who calls me that outside of the courtroom."

"Why the D.A.'s office? What propelled you towards that?" Iris asked, noticing how the server's eyes lingered on Jack when she walked away.

"When I started law school, I suspected that my calling was in criminal law," he explained. "It was confirmed in my very first criminal class. I'd gone through a civil procedure class and a few other courses. None of them sparked much interest in me. The moment I began the criminal law classes, I knew I'd found my place."

"Did you ever consider working as a defense attorney?"

Jack smiled. "My grandfather was a judge, a good one. He died years ago, but he left a lasting impression. There was an expectation in my family that we boys pursue certain careers—law, medical, or business. It was my grandfather who made me fall in love with the pursuit of justice.

"I don't believe the state is always right or that we're quote good guys. Both sides, the prosecution and defense, have shades of light and dark. There's honor in defending the innocent who are being unjustly prosecuted. There's honor in protecting people's rights. For me, the greatest honor is giving a voice to the victim, giving the families of victims a modicum of peace after a harrowing tragedy. It's not always that dramatic, as you well know, but when it is, it makes every sleepless night, every eighteen-hour day completely worth it."

Iris shifted in her chair, wishing she'd felt that fiery pull towards her law career. The drive for her had been less about making a difference than making a good paycheck.

"And how about life outside the courtroom?" she asked. "Do you have one of those?"

He leaned back and stretched, angling his arms across his chest and shifting his head from side to side. "Sure. You've seen me at Bitters, right?"

"If I remember correctly, you called that working."

"Touché. I don't mind work being my life. I'll slow down at some point, make room for other things, but..." He shrugged. "There are few things I'd rather be doing than standing in a courtroom. The paperwork, the meetings, the investigations. I love every minute of it."

"You're not much for dating, then?"

"I've dated my fair share. I need to be a well-rounded person after all. Dating is like lettering in a varsity sport." He laughed. "I'm joking. Yes, I've dated."

"Recently?"

"My last girlfriend and I broke up in August."

"Not too long ago then."

"Long enough."

"And why did you break up?"

He studied her, balanced both elbows on the table and interlaced his fingers. "Shouldn't we work up to this conversation? Don't you want to talk about something more relaxed? Like the weather?"

"I hate small talk and I'm not good at it."

The server arrived with their glasses. She served Jack first, offered him a playful smile, which dropped away when she slid Iris's glass across the table.

"My ex wanted a job in big law. We don't exactly have those firms in these parts."

"And that's it? She left, and you stayed. No drama?"

"I do my best to avoid drama." He took a drink and set his glass down. "Your turn in the hot seat. You're fresh out of law school. What brought you all the way up here to the edge of the world?"

Iris thought of the moment she now pinpointed as the beginning of her downward spiral-the great implosion.

It had started with a voice in the night, a voice so long forgotten that Iris hadn't recognized it when it drifted to her in the darkness of the bedroom she and Cody had shared.

"Iris, wake up," the voice had said, clear as day, but it had been sometime after midnight, and Cody had been out of town. At first, she'd thought one of their friends had shown up and let himself in, but when she groped for the bedside lamp, she discovered her room empty.

Once she'd come full awake, the memory of the voice crawled up, the silhouette of a memory. It was Frankie's voice, the voice of her dead brother.

And as if Frankie speaking her name had cast a spell, Iris's ordinary reality had flipped. Two days later, as she sat in the law library cramming for another exam, she'd watched a man walk by and directly into a shelf of books. The shelf didn't topple over. He simply drifted through it and vanished.

Too much coffee, too many late nights, not enough sleep. She'd had a list half a mile long to explain away the hallucination. A week after that, as she'd ridden the bus to class, a group of students climbed on. One hurried toward a seat occupied by a woman wearing an oddly old-fashioned dress. The student had sat directly on the woman because suddenly the woman was not there.

Iris had skipped class that day and gone straight to the university health clinic. Headaches, she lied, blurred vision. She needed a CAT scan, an MRI, whatever they had for neurological problems. They'd done the tests and after a week they had given her a clean bill of health. No tumor, nothing strange in her blood work, nothing at all.

Which had only concerned Iris more. She'd gone from applying for internships in sunny Florida to not wanting to leave her apartment. She'd cheated on Cody, nearly slipped into academic probation, and started drinking nightly.

And then, out of nowhere, as if she sensed her granddaughter's unraveling, Lola had called and invited her up north, said she had an attorney friend whose office was looking to hire a new associate.

Iris lifted her glass and sipped her wine. It was dry, bitter. She wished she'd ordered a martini. "The Fraser Firm had an opening, and I needed a job. Lola offered me a place, so I took it."

"You graduated Cooley Law School with top grades, passed the bar with flying colors. You must have had your pick of firms downstate, but you packed up and moved to Sault Ste Marie? Something's not adding up."

"It sounds like you've been checking up on me."

"In small towns, information comes easy. I didn't exactly have to use Google to get the scoop on the new girl in town."

She laughed. "Yeah, well, that's precisely why I don't intend to stay up here. Too much of everybody in everybody's business. To say nothing of the endless snow."

"Ahh, that's right, you're migrating south."

"I am."

"Going to set up shop in Florida, defend the wealthy elite with ocean-front houses? Or are you looking out for the poor man? The underdog?"

"Whichever one pays their bill."

"And yet here you are, a hop, skip and a jump away from Canada, living in a city that is arguably one of the coldest places in the entire country, save Alaska. Is the Fraser Firm so fantastic you willingly brave negative twenty-degree days to work there?"

"It's fine, it's a job. Plus, my grandma is here and..." Iris shrugged. "I haven't seen her much these last few years. I'm grateful to have the time with her."

"She seems nice," he said.

"She is. But I don't want to talk about her. I want to hear more about you. Tell me some of your dirty secrets, Jack. Where are the cracks in the façade of the all-American guy? Ever been arrested? Gotten expelled from school?"

"No. My father would not have looked kindly on a son who got into trouble. Have you?"

"Never been arrested or expelled, though I got suspended a few times in middle school. After my mother died, I… got angry for a while. My dad seemed to forget he still had a child. I think I was trying to get attention. My brother died too, a few years before my mom. You might have heard of him. Frankie Walsh."

16

———————

Jack gazed at her, unblinking. "I remember Frankie," he told her. "I met him the summer he and Duncan drowned. He was a cool kid."

"You knew him?" Iris asked, stunned.

"Yeah. We'd only been friends a few weeks when the accident happened. I'm sorry, Iris."

"It's okay." She finished her wine and caught the eye of the waitress, pointing at her glass. "Water under the bridge, as they say. It screwed my family up, screwed me up. Somehow, I got my head back in the game, but I acted out for a while first."

"That's pretty typical. I've met with a lot of families who've experienced major traumas. Everyone copes differently."

Iris gazed at Jack, his expertly pressed suit, his clean-shaven face, the way he paused and inhaled the scent of his wine before each sip. He made her uncomfortable, his seeming perfection.

She imagined how she looked with her wind-blown hair and chapped face, her too-big blazer. She'd lost weight in the previous months and never bought new clothes. She was attracted to him, but also insecure in his presence. He was the embodiment of what she herself wanted to be, and her discomfort made her want to fill every ounce of silence.

"I'm fine, my childhood was fine, the death of my brother was fine, the death of my mother was fine. I've reared myself on a diet of fine. Except none of it was ever fine and internally I knew that, but I learned from my mother to put on a brave face, to bury my grief. Of course, that's probably what caused my mother to drive herself into a tree."

Iris released a hoarse laugh. The server had barely finished refilling her glass when Iris picked it up and took a long drink. Jack watched her now, and she imagined in his head he searched for a way out, any excuse to cut the evening short.

On the opposite side of the room, the hostess turned on the lights on the Christmas tree. They blinked in reds and greens.

"After my mother died, we never had another Christmas tree," she continued, suddenly incapable of closing her mouth.

Shut up, shut up, shut up, a tiny enraged voice called in the back of her mind. She ignored it and barreled on. "My dad never felt strongly about celebrating Christmas. We weren't religious after all. After the death of Frankie and then my mom, he gave up the charade. No Santa Claus or Tooth Fairy or Easter Bunny. Fanciful things did not exist and their benefit to children, as far as my dad was concerned, did not outweigh the humongous lie they represented."

Iris gazed at the tree across the room, the sparkling star perched on the top of the branches. "But once every few years I'd be up here, in the magical land of Grandma Lola, with her decorations and her house adorned in Christmas lights, her reindeer on the lawn. And I'd join in on the lie for a bit because it felt good to leave the real world behind, the angry, jaded, everyone-dies world."

Iris finished her wine and avoided looking Jack in the eyes.

"We have a lot in common, I think."

She looked at him, surprised. She'd expected him to clear his throat, insist he'd forgotten about a meeting and run for the door, or offer some bullshit sympathy response.

"Your dad hijacked Christmas?" she asked.

He chuckled. "Not quite. We celebrated Christmas, but it was not… real. If you looked in the window, it was. We had the biggest tree, perfectly decorated with whatever color scheme my mother decided was in that year, strategically placed decorations. The presents were professionally wrapped. My parents hired a Santa Claus every year and did a fundraiser at our house. It was a big deal. One year, I walked downstairs the next day and saw my mother tossing these beautifully wrapped gifts into the fire and I started crying. I was so upset. I'd thought Santa had brought them for us. My mother opened one. It was filled with air. They'd put empty gift-wrapped boxes under the tree just for show."

"Did you still get gifts for Christmas?"

"Oh, yeah, of course. The Skelling kids would never be the have-nots. She'd just paid someone to wrap a bunch of empty boxes so it looked like…" He frowned. "I still can't decipher why exactly she did it, but yes, we always received gifts on Christmas day. I think my mother literally printed a list of the season's hottest toys and ordered them. Sometimes I got things I actually wanted, but when I was a teenager, I realized why. Hilde—our maid—would pick them out. She'd get the stuff on my mom's list, but she'd add a few of the things my brothers and I actually wanted.

"I don't want to sound ungrateful," he said, rotating his wine glass. "I'm grateful for my parents and I love them. They're flawed people—we all are, I've come to realize—but… it colors things, doesn't it? The first Christmas that I had my own place, I went out and bought this huge real tree and then I went to the department store and bought the ugliest, most homemade-looking decorations I could find.

"I got home and my girlfriend had had the same idea, except she'd put up a little fake tree. Our apartment was small, after all. It was in the center of our kitchen table, which we never ate at because it always held both our school books. She'd strung popcorn on it and little homemade ornaments from when she was a kid.

"She looked at what I'd brought home and asked if I'd lost my mind. It was such a crazy thing to have done, not to mention we were barely scraping by financially, both full-time students working side jobs and barely making rent each month. And I'd spent a month's grocery and gas allowance on a Christmas tree I couldn't even fit in the apartment." He laughed and shook his head.

"Your parents didn't pay for your education?"

"No. They tried, but… I'm indebted enough to them. I wanted to do it on my own. I took out loans and worked and got it done."

"I've never had a tree on my own," Iris said. "I thought about it a few times, but… whenever I'd go look at them, I felt like such a phony and then I'd get really cynical and find myself judging all these families taking sleigh rides out into a field so they could cut down a bona-fide tree and play make-believe."

He smiled. "I get that. I don't put up a tree anymore. As I've gotten older, I've stripped away the excess. I keep things simple now. Work is my focus and I give so much of myself to that, there's no time for Christmas trees. But I'm okay with it. I prefer it that way."

The revelation made Iris feel sad, and she wanted another glass of wine or to sit in a quiet room and cry. The impulse was odd, as if she were full suddenly, full of tears, of grief, of regrets. Immediately following it was anger because it felt like a weak feeling, an out-of-control feeling.

"We could go back to your place," Iris suggested, zipping her coat higher on her chin as they walked into the parking lot.

She wasn't doing the tease thing, dancing around the issue like a lot of women did. Usually that was enough, the mere mention of something more intimate had the opposite sex salivating, but she saw Jack's eyes dart away, and she second-guessed the suggestion.

"I have to be in court early, otherwise… I would." He said the last two words so quietly she barely caught them.

She shrugged. "No big deal either way. I'll see you around, Jack."

Iris headed for her car and didn't look back. A voice in her head tried to chastise her for putting it out there, damaging their future working relationship, but the voice she'd been cultivating for far longer silenced it. No man, Jack Skelling or otherwise, was going to reduce her to a woman who played games. She stated what she wanted, end of story. If he wasn't interested, then so be it.

Still, as she pulled into Grandma Lola's driveway, Jack's expression niggled at her. Had he not wanted to sleep with her? Had she been off about the chemistry between them?

"Oh, who cares?" she grumbled, climbing out and planting her foot in a huge snowdrift.

Icy flakes poured into her boot. She gritted her teeth, slammed the car door, and stomped toward the house.

Iris was not a woman who slept her way to the top. Her interest in Jack Skelling was in part due to his position, but it wasn't a desire to further her own career. Instead, she felt an almost magnetic pull toward his focus. Though she'd only encountered him a handful of times, she sensed his togetherness. He was organized, detached, driven. He was all the things she wanted to be and the things she was on her best days, when she could blot out the trauma of losing her brother and mother and avoid the issue of seeing dead people. When she could stay sober, sleep in her own bed, and face the day with tenacity. She wanted to be like Jack Skelling.

Iris walked through Lola's door. The warmth enveloped her and the frustration and shame gripping her throat loosened.

"Is that you, poppet?" Lola called.

"Yep, it's me." Iris found Lola in the living room at her game table.

"Come on, get over here. Turn off that overworked brain and play some Scrabble with me." Lola tapped her finger on the Scrabble board.

Iris groaned. She'd intended to go back to Lola's and get lost in work, sifting through legal briefs and attempting to forget how she'd unloaded a couple decades' worth of childhood trauma on the handsome prosecutor who'd made the mistake of helping her with a flat tire. "Grandma, I'm swamped—"

"Iris Walsh, don't argue with me. Grandma knows what's good for you and you need a game of Scrabble." Lola perked up. "And some of Hannah Truvy's caramel popcorn." She stood and headed for the kitchen.

Iris followed her. "Hannah who?"

"Oh, the little girl down the block. Her Christmas fundraiser this year was caramel popcorn. Much better than last year, which was poinsettias. They're pretty enough, but you can't eat them." Lola filled two bowls with caramel popcorn and nudged Iris back to the game table. "Did you work late, honey? Or go out to dinner with Andy?"

"I had a drink with Jack Skelling, actually. I got a flat in your car and he stopped and changed my tire."

Lola looked at her, nodding slowly. "The prosecutor Jack Skelling?"

"Yep. Do you know him?"

"I know of him," Lola said, arranging the word 'wily' on the board.

Iris considered her grandmother's tone. "You don't like him?" Iris gathered the letters for 'yarn' and added them beneath Lola's word.

"It's not that. I'm sure he's a nice enough young man."

"But...?"

"Well... all those years ago when Frankie and Duncan disappeared, the Skellings were not very helpful. They didn't want anyone out by Skelling Hall. They didn't want Jack to be interviewed by the police. The Skellings were very tight-lipped."

"But why would there have been a search on that peninsula at all? They went into the water near Shallows Bay."

"That was the eventual conclusion, but originally Andrew Malone said the boys had been talking about meeting on the Skelling Peninsula because of some cave Jack had told them about. Police intended to go out there and search and found a big chain blocking the road. Before they got access, a local man found the row boat washed up on Shallows Bay with the boys' backpacks. Duncan's father, Harry, got in Winston Skelling's face that next week. Right in the middle of the street, Harry started screaming at Winston that he'd hindered the search for the boys and he'd see him in court. Of course, nothing ever came of it."

"But I thought the Skellings didn't own Skelling Hall, that it belonged to a foundation."

Lola frowned at her letters. "Who do you think heads the foundation? Winston Skelling, although I saw something a few years back about Jack taking that position."

"I just don't understand why the Skellings wouldn't let police search it." Iris was surprised, but then again, Jack Skelling's grandfather had been a judge. Perhaps they were wary of getting tangled up in any type of investigation. "It's hardly Jack's fault if his father complicated the investigation."

"I didn't say it was," Lola agreed, adding 'un' beneath Iris's 'r' to form the word 'run.'

17

"He changed your tire?" Nina asked from across their office. "That man is a saint. I wish I could get him to pump one of my flats."

Iris laughed. "You're as bad as Marv."

"Hardly. Marv's love life makes me look like a nun."

"Marv does get around. Has he always been that way?"

"Pretty much. I heard him mention a fiancée once, but that was ages ago. I've never seen him date anyone longer than a couple of months. But who cares about Marv? Tell me more about Jack. How was the date?"

"It wasn't a date."

"You drank wine. That's a date."

"It was nice. We talked about family stuff, mostly."

"Really? Any skeletons in his closet?"

"Not that he mentioned," Iris admitted, wishing she could forget all the skeletons she'd marched out of her own closet and put on display for Jack Skelling.

"Hey." Marv stuck his head in the office. "I need you in court this afternoon, Nina. The Turners have a hearing and I've got a meeting I can't miss. Iris, I need these documents redacted ASAP." He dropped a stack of papers on her desk. "Scan 'em and email them to me when you're done."

"Your wish is my command," Iris told him, pulling the paperclip loose.

Beyond the windows, the sun had set. Iris's eyes and back ached. Nina had left for court that afternoon, and Iris sat alone in the office.

A stack of documents that needed to be scanned sat on her desk. On top, she saw Sammy Bishop's name, the same man Norlene had supposedly turned state's evidence on. His name, address and phone number were listed on the paper.

The clock on the wall stated five forty-five. She'd already put in a nearly ten-hour day.

What would it hurt to stop by the guy's apartment, ask him a few questions about Norlene? She didn't have to mention she worked at the Fraser Firm. Marv would never know.

Iris scrawled his address on a sheet of paper and slipped it into her pocket. She grabbed her briefcase, turned off the light, and headed out of the office.

Sammy Bishop lived on the second floor of a set of squalid apartments in downtown Sault Ste Marie. The hallway in the building was claustrophobically hot, but when she pushed into the stairwell the temperature plummeted. A wood block sat on the floor and she nudged it with her foot in the jamb to hold the metal door open.

On the second floor, Iris knocked on the door to Sammy's apartment. The lower right corner of the door was splintered as if someone had kicked it. From within the apartment, she heard loud music. She knocked a second time.

The door opened a crack and the thin face of a woman peered out.

"What?" she growled.

"Is Sammy Bishop here?" Iris asked.

"Who wants to know?" The woman narrowed her eyes.

"My name's Iris Walsh."

"Get outta the goddamn way," a voice snarled behind the woman.

A man jerked her away from the door. He pulled it fully open.

Iris could see the shabby apartment. A threadbare couch faced a dirty coffee table scattered with ashtrays. A boom box sat on top of an old television. Someone had smashed the screen of the television in. The music continued to blare, heavy metal that made Iris's head ache. Her eyes watered as the man blew a puff of cigarette smoke into her face.

"What do you want?" he asked. His expression changed when he got a good look at Iris. He lowered his cigarette and crooked his arm in the doorway, leering at her.

"You're Sammy Bishop?" Iris asked.

"I sure am."

"I'd like to talk to you about Norlene Weaver."

His face wrinkled in disgust and he started to push the door closed. Iris shoved her foot into the apartment before he could shut it, knowing he might decide to slam it anyway.

Sammy looked down at her boot and then back at her face, grinning. He was missing one of his front teeth. "Brave girl. I've broken a few toes in that doorway. I ain't afraid to add you to the list."

"I just want to ask you a few questions. Here." She held up the twenty-dollar bill she'd brought, crumpled it into a ball and tossed it onto the dirty carpet in his apartment. "There's twenty, and I'll give you another twenty once you answer my questions."

"Maybe I'll just pull you in here and take the twenty plus whatever else you got." He smirked.

"By all means, though my friend in the car downstairs will probably have the cops crawling all over this place if I'm not back in ten minutes. Got anything in that apartment you don't want 'em to see?"

He sneered. "They ain't got a warrant."

"No, but if I don't come back down, they've got probable cause. That's even better."

"Fine, it's your money. I don't know shit about Norlene. I already told the police that and her sister too. I didn't know she was fixin' to narc on me until after she went missin'."

"How did you find out?"

"The cops told me. Dragged me into one of them rooms with the bright lights and said they knew I'd killed her. I said, 'Killed who?' I thought they was talking about Gert, my old lady." He hooked a thumb toward the woman who'd opened the door. She sat on the couch smoking a cigarette and glaring at Iris. "Finally, they said, 'Norlene Weaver. We know you killed her because she was testifying against you.' I said, 'Huh? I ain't seen Norlene in months.' And I hadn't."

"Were you doing any business with Norlene around the time she disappeared?"

"Business?" He chuckled. "The only business I ever did with that little bitch was sell her a few ounces, which she chopped and sold as dime bags for a little extra cash. I ain't stupid enough to use her as a soldier. Jesus, I ain't dumb."

Iris cringed at the word 'bitch.' The man in front of her made her deliriously angry and she wanted to shove him or slap him or both. He was everything that was wrong with the world, and Iris wondered why people like Norlene disappeared instead of guys like this maggot. She found herself siding again with her parents, who believed the world began and ended in chaos. How could there be any divine creator if monsters like this walked among them?

"Do you have theories on what happened to Norlene? Any people talking?"

"I ain't a snitch."

"Listen," Iris said through gritted teeth. She wanted to unleash her fury on this man, scream until spit flew into his beady little eyes, but she tempered her emotion. "I am not a cop. I don't give a shit what illegal stuff you or your friends are doing. I'm trying to do the family a favor and see if I can't track down someone they happen to love. Try, if you can, to imagine in that teeny little brain of yours how you would feel if this was your sister, your mother. You'd want answers, right? If you had nothing to do with it, what do you care about offering some information? If anything, it'll get the police off your back."

He stared at her, reaching into his pocket. Iris recoiled, half-expecting him to pull out a knife. It was only a toothpick, which he inserted between his teeth, digging around and then licking the end of the toothpick. Iris tried not to gag as a puff of his sour breath blew into her face. "Word is she took off. Maybe scammed that hotshot lawyer out of some cash, hopped on a bus, and went south."

"Is that on good authority? Somebody saw her get on a bus? Heard of her getting money from someone?"

"Nah, nobody saw her. And if you want it from me, I'd say she's dead."

Iris frowned. "Murdered?"

"Doubt it. She's peanuts. Ain't nobody taking a murder rap to get rid of the likes of Norlene Weaver. I'd bet she couldn't take bein' clean. Life is a whole lot uglier when you're straight. Probably in the spring some hunter'll find her in the woods. Suicide. Maybe she went into the water. They say women do it different from men. If it were me, I'd put a gun in my mouth."

"The hotshot lawyer? Who was that?"

"That Skelling prick. Who else?"

"Why would he give her money?"

Sammy's eyes sparkled, and he unleashed a lascivious grin. "Because he was screwin' her and he didn't want it gettin' out."

Iris started away, but Sammy's hand snaked out and caught the sleeve of her coat. She ripped it out of his grasp.

"Where's my other twenty?" he demanded.

She grabbed the crumpled money from her pocket and tossed it at him, hurried down the hall toward the stairs.

~

I ris was halfway across the street, jogging toward Lola's car, when something stopped her. Not a sound, more like a sense that she needed to walk back into the building. She had the keys in her hand, unlock button ready to push. The cold seeped through her clothing. She wanted to be in the car, heat on, but she shoved the keys into her pocket and strode back to the apartment building. She slipped through the door into the stairwell. A voice drifted from above her, but it was distorted, echoing in the stairwell. Iris walked up a few more steps and listened.

"Some bitch. Norlene. I don't know." Sammy Bishop's voice floated down to her.

She caught only snippets of the conversation, but it clearly centered on Norlene.

Biting her lip, and staying close to the wall, Iris crept further until she was right beneath the voice. Sammy wasn't in the stairwell. He seemed to be walking in the second-floor hallway.

"What should I do? Norlene's apartment? Okay, yeah."

Iris waited, but heard nothing else. Had the call ended?

Above her, footsteps stomped toward the stairs. Iris bolted, taking the stairs two at a time. At the bottom, she grabbed the metal handle and pulled. It didn't open. She'd forgotten to put the wood block in front of it.

A door banged open and footsteps pounded down the concrete steps.

It was dim in the stairwell, and there was nowhere to hide.

Iris's blood pumped in her ears. She released the handle and pressed her back against the wall, sliding into the far corner, clearly visible when Sammy reached the first floor.

His footsteps clapped on the concrete and then stopped. The steps started away, growing fainter. He'd turned around. He must have forgotten something.

Iris waited until she heard the door close overhead. She lunged for the metal handle, jerked it up and down so hard something twinged in her wrist. It still didn't open, and a strangled cry erupted from her throat.

Suddenly, the handle turned on its own. The door shoved in and Iris screamed, leaping backward.

A young woman stood there, eyes wide.

Iris streaked past her and rushed from the building, hit the unlock button and jumped into Lola's car. Sinking low in her seat, Iris watched the front door to the apartment building.

After several minutes, Sammy emerged, a lit cigarette in his hand. He marched to a faded black sports car with rusted wheel wells and climbed in, flicking the cigarette to the curb.

He pulled onto the street, and Iris followed him.

18

———————

Sammy Bishop drove across town to the now-defunct apartment building where Norlene Weaver had lived. He sat outside for nearly ten minutes, but didn't go in. Iris thought she saw the blue glow of a cellphone from the interior of the car, but she couldn't be sure. At fifteen minutes, he drove away without climbing from his car.

Iris followed, but when he pulled into the driveway of a grimy duplex, she turned around and drove back to Lola's.

~

The following morning, she found Marv in her office, shuffling through the papers on her desk.

"Where's the transcription for that DUI case? I need it."

Iris opened her desk, grabbed a file, and handed it to him. "It's all in here."

"Good, thanks." He tucked it under his arm. "Don Fraser is meeting with the Skelling Foundation today about a lawsuit by Brett Stephens' mother. I need you to sit in and take notes. Fraser's assistant is out with mono."

"Brett Stephens' mother is suing?" The woman Iris had spoken to had seemed uninterested in her son's disappearance.

"Yep, premises liability. She's alleging negligent security. It's a cash grab."

"How can she even afford an attorney? I thought the family was—"

"Destitute? Pretty much, but there are always a few bottom-feeders who get a gleam in their eye when anybody with money is involved. She's being represented by some schmuck from Marquette. Just be in the meeting. Starts at nine in conference room A."

I ris sat in a corner chair at the opposite end of the long table in conference room A. Don Fraser occupied the other end along with two men Iris didn't recognize, who were apparently part of the Skelling Hall Foundation. She'd expected, perhaps hoped, to see Jack Skelling, but neither he nor anyone in his family attended.

"The suit is simple. Bonnie Stephens is claiming premises liability and general negligence. She's citing lack of video cameras in and around Skelling Hall. Her attorney pointed out that Brett was expected to work at night."

"According to Miles Fincher," one man cut in, "Brett was explicitly told not to plow the property at night."

"Okay." Fraser made a note. "The question is whether that was in writing. Did the hall have a written agreement with the Stephens boy? Anything that stated the expected working hours?"

The two men exchanged a glance. "I'll call Fincher," the shorter man said, standing and walking from the room.

"Shall we wait for Mr. Portsman?" Fraser asked.

"No, go ahead."

"Bonnie's attorney also cites lack of emergency options, an available telephone or any way to summon help if needed."

"Does she have a case?"

Don Fraser took off his slim black spectacles and rested them on the papers before him. "In court, I doubt it. Brett drove a plow truck. He got out of his truck for whatever reason. That's not on his employer unless they can prove something forced him out of the truck or drew him out of the truck that night. Marv Booker says the Stephens family has a history of drug abuse. It's very possible the kid was out there getting stoned, had some kind of episode and ran off into the woods. That being said, if the mother wants to make a stink about this, she could. If she drags Skelling Hall through the papers she might… bring up other instances."

The man shifted in his seat. He turned his head slightly, as if remembering Iris sat at the end of the table.

"Perhaps we should speak in private?" the man murmured.

Don Fraser looked at Iris. "You're all set, young lady."

Iris looked at Fraser and the other man. She hadn't written much down. "Oh, okay. You don't want me to record anything else?"

"No."

Iris fumbled the cap on her pen and stood as the door opened and the shorter man hurried in.

She paused by Fraser on her way out. "Would you like me to type these up?"

"Yes, and email them to me directly. Thank you."

Iris slipped into the hallway and eased the door closed behind her. Fraser had referred to other instances. Was he talking about Norlene Weaver? Was it possible the Skelling Foundation suspected something had happened to her at the hall?

She returned to the office she shared with Nina, troubled by the way the man had looked at her, as if he specifically didn't want to talk in front of her. More than likely, he didn't want to speak of anything that reflected poorly on Skelling Hall in front of anyone except their lawyer. Still…

Marv strode into the office and thrust a paper onto her desk.

"What?" she asked, recognizing the transcription she'd just given him.

"Did you proofread this?"

Iris blinked. "I think so… Is it full of typos?"

Marv studied her, his expression a mingling of concern and irritation.

She read through it quickly, unable to find a single misspelling. Halfway down the page, she stopped.

Norlene is dead. Norlene is dead. Norlene is dead. Norlene is dead. Norlene is dead.

Iris held the paper closer to her face, confirming it did in fact say what she feared it said. "I didn't type that."

"I sure as hell didn't say it in the recording."

"I know… I…" She set the paper down, unable to offer an explanation. Had she typed it? She'd transcribed the recording the night before after following Sammy. She'd been uneasy after the encounter, made worse by getting stuck in the stairwell. Perhaps she'd zoned out.

"I'm sorry. I don't know how that happened," she admitted.

"Fix it," he told her and walked from the room.

After the long day, she agreed to meet Nina at Bitters for a drink. When she arrived, she spotted Jack Skelling.

Jack sat at a table, a half-empty glass Iris suspected was club soda in front of him. His jacket was off, slung over the back of his chair, his cuffs rolled up and his tie loosened. Two other guys sat with him.

Jack glanced up, but didn't catch her eye. He returned to his conversation, and irritation flared in Iris's chest. She was furious that she'd confided so many personal things to Jack Skelling, and she was vaguely humiliated that he seemed content to ignore her now when she stood mere feet away from him on the other side of the room.

Her turbulent emotions stemmed largely from the screw-up in the transcription for Marv, and she was dreading seeing him at Bitters.

"I'll take a dirty martini," she told Dandy.

She drank half the martini, glaring at the mirror beyond the bar where she could see Jack's reflection at his table.

He stood and made his way to the bathrooms. Bolstered by her drink, Iris jumped up and followed him.

Before he could push into the men's room, Iris cornered him. "What's the story on Norlene Weaver?"

Jack gave a little start, as if he hadn't seen her.

"Iris, hi." He frowned, glanced toward the table where the two men sat, and then returned his gaze to Iris. "I'm sorry. What did you say?"

"Norlene Weaver, your informant, who disappeared in August."

He scratched at his chin and looked at the ceiling. "Norlene Weaver, twenty-six years old, lifelong Sault Ste Marie resident, two stints in rehab. In January of last year, she became an informant on a case involving a local man suspected of dealing schedule I narcotics. In August she went missing. Investigators suspect she took off to avoid testifying."

"Well, thanks for the Cliff's Notes version of events, but I'm asking for your instinct, Jack. You worked with her pretty closely from what I've gathered. What do you think happened to her?"

"What do you mean 'from what you've gathered'?"

"I've talked to her sister and Sammy Bishop. More than one mentioned her relationship with you."

"Her working relationship," he corrected.

"Sure, whatever. The point is, do you think she took off?"

Jack squinted at the ceiling, rubbed his eyes, and looked back at Iris. Behind him a shape flickered—Norlene. She stepped close to Jack and her lips moved as if she were whispering in his ear. Jack didn't so much as twitch.

He had no idea the girl was haunting him. He was totally oblivious to her. The knowledge of that, that an entity could whisper in someone's ear and they'd be unaware of it, gave Iris a chill. She looked away from Norlene and focused on Jack.

"I don't know, Iris. It's possible she left. She was afraid to testify and word around town was that she'd been running her mouth about the case, about being an informant. It's possible that someone threatened her."

"It's also possible that someone killed her."

Behind Jack, the spirit grew agitated. She materialized and vanished, flickered into the corners like a caged animal.

"What are you looking at?" Jack asked, frowning and looking over his shoulder.

"Nothing."

"I don't know if someone killed her. I consider it unlikely. The dealer she was testifying against has never committed a violent crime that we're aware of."

"Did anyone question him?"

"I imagine the police did."

"Fine. Thanks." She turned and stalked away, mad for reasons she knew and others she didn't.

In front of her, the door opened and Marv and Nina walked in, bringing with them a blast of icy air.

"It's colder than a gold-digger's heart out there," Marv bellowed. His eyes locked with Iris' for an instant and then slid away. "Dandy, get us three shots of whiskey, pronto."

"Happily, Marv, if you'd close the damn door before we all freeze," Dandy told him.

Marv grinned and pulled the door closed, following Nina to the bar. Both Nina and Marv's eyes skittered past Iris and landed on Jack Skelling.

"And what do we have here?" Marv murmured when Iris slid onto a barstool next to him. "A quickie in the bathroom at Bitters Bar? I can't say I haven't had a few myself, but Iris Walsh, I expected more propriety from a young woman such as yourself."

Iris relaxed, grateful that Marv seemed happy to forget the strangeness from earlier that day.

"Hilarious, Marv." Nina laughed, elbowing him. "Iris has significantly higher standards than you."

Iris slid the shot Dandy placed in front of her to Marv. "Here, double down, Marv. I'm on a one-drink maximum tonight."

He wrinkled his nose. "What? My God, tell me those religious converts didn't get to you. Are they here now?" He made a show of spinning on his bar stool, sweeping the room with a suspicious gaze.

Nina rolled her eyes. "Marv, do you have a serious thought in your head?"

He lifted his eyes and pursed his lips. "Nope."

"I'm only staying for a bit. I've got a meeting," Iris told them.

"A meeting? It's five o'clock. Haven't you heard of business hours?"

"Says the guy who's been known to leave the office at ten p.m.," Nina countered.

"It's not for work," Iris said.

"Ooh, tell us more." Marv waggled his eyebrows, then flicked his gaze to Jack Skelling. "Is it a secret rendezvous?"

"No," she snapped. "Now drink your whiskey."

19

Iris drove to Skelling Hall and parked in the lot behind the enormous mansion. Miles Fincher greeted her at the door.

"Hi, Mr. Fincher. I'm Iris Walsh."

When she'd called Fincher about the meeting, she hadn't mentioned that she worked for the Fraser Firm. She wondered if Don Fraser would get wind of her visit and, if he did, how he would react.

"Ah, yes." The man smiled. "The young lady interested in the history of Skelling Hall. Few come with questions, I'll tell you." He paused, took a long look at her. "You were here with Marv Booker the other day."

A blush crept into her neck. "Yes, and I caught a snippet of the tour, but had hoped to learn more."

"Most folks are satisfied with the thirty-minute presentation. Attention spans getting shorter and shorter. Half the visitors are on their phones during the entire tour. It's a shame."

"Yeah, the pace of the world seems to get faster."

"It sure does. Though we still keep things slower up here than they do south of the bridge. The further south you go, the busier it gets. I visited my sister last year in Detroit. Gridlocked highways, four or five lanes each. I missed my exit twice because I couldn't change lanes. Never have I so understood the term 'rat race.'"

"I don't miss the traffic downstate," she admitted.

"That traffic sends more folks to these parts than just about anything else. Sitting in those traffic jams gives you time to consider what matters in life and rarely do they conclude it's whatever office is at the end of that daily commute. But I'll end my rant there. Never do I more show my age than when talking about the traffic." He chuckled and led Iris into the grand hall.

"I appreciate your taking some time to give me a bit more history on this place. The guide the other day alluded to some tragedies that happened here at Skelling Hall. It piqued my curiosity."

Fincher paused beside a row of oil paintings. "Here are Felix and Angelique in the early years. She was quite lovely. Many considered Felix a foreboding figure."

Iris studied the man and woman perched stiffly on an ornate sofa. Angelique had delicate features, wide green eyes, and black hair pulled tightly back from her face. Her hands were folded in the skirt of her dress. Felix sat beside her, face grim, pointed mustache extending from his Roman nose.

"These are the children." Fincher stepped to the next portrait.

Iris looked at the image. Two young boys, dark-haired like their parents, stood on either side of a little girl with light hair and eyes. Skelling Hall towered behind them.

"Andre is this one, the tallest, oldest boy. Phillippe was the youngest child. The one with all the freckles and light hair is Beatrice, the only surviving child."

"The guide the other day said the boys vanished. Was it ever confirmed that they had died?"

"It's assumed they died, but unfortunately, no, it was never confirmed. The disappearance of the boys destroyed Angelique and Felix. It happened in the summer. People assume the boys went swimming and drowned. It's hard to say since they did not find their bodies. The disappearance of the boys triggered a gradual end to Skelling Hall, what this place had been in its prime. Angelique died of consumption a few years later. Some mothers simply can't survive the death of their children."

Iris shuddered and crossed her arms over her chest. It was not Angelique Skelling, but her own mother who appeared in her mind. Her mother, who too had died of a form of consumption, consumed by the loss of her son.

"How did you end up as the... caretaker here?" Iris asked, remembering the story Marv had shared about Miles Fincher meeting Felix Skelling in an insane asylum.

"That was a long time ago indeed. Suffice it to say that Felix and I became dear friends. He was much older than me. Perhaps he thought of me like a son in some way…" Fincher looked wistfully at the painting of Felix and Angelique. "I consider myself a steward of Skelling Hall. This house needs to be preserved, remembered. I do my best to pass on the lineage of this noble house and family."

"But Felix sold the house, right? Put it into a foundation rather than pass it on to his child to live in."

"After Angelique died, Felix was not well. He started to see things that weren't there. Eventually they institutionalized him. It was during that time he created the Skelling Foundation. The house was put into the hands of the trustees. His fortune went to Beatrice, but most of his worldly possessions, as well as the house and property, went into the control of the foundation. Of course, several Skelling family members are on the board, so this is all still family-controlled in many ways."

"What types of things was Felix seeing? It must have been extreme to warrant admitting him to a mental hospital," Iris said.

Fincher continued down the hall, pausing next to a portrait of the house itself. "He claimed to see many things, including his dead children and wife. He insisted the forest was not safe, that the very ground beneath the house was evil. He wrote often of a being he called the 'dark man.' When Felix established the foundation, the dark man was his reason. He was sure if Beatrice stayed here, she too would die at the hands of this fictitious being."

"The dark man…" Iris murmured, looking at the painting of Skelling Hall. It was a summer painting. The trees and foliage around the house were so thick they might have been walls.

"Yes, clearly Felix was hallucinating."

"You've never experienced anything unusual here, then?"

"Oh, I didn't say that." He continued briskly down the hall.

Iris hurried behind him. "Can you tell me about that? What you saw or felt?"

Mr. Fincher pulled a handkerchief from his blazer pocket and wiped at a tall vase on the floor. "Little smudge there. Kids. You tell them a hundred times during a tour, 'Don't touch anything.' But when they leave, their sticky fingerprints smear everything in sight."

"Have you seen things here, Mr. Fincher? Unexplainable things?"

Fincher pursed his lips and looked at the window. The view beyond was the snowy woods, tinted orange as the sun began its descent. Mr. Fincher looked scared when he turned back to face her. "Best if we end our talk now. Less than an hour until full dark and I like to be locked up and well on my way."

Iris followed him as he hurried back toward the front door. "Mr. Fincher, one more thing, please."

He turned. The look of agitation, of wanting her out of the house, remained on his face.

"Do you have any idea what happened to Brett Stephens or Norlene Weaver? Brett was last seen here at Skelling Hall. Norlene was possibly cleaning here the night she—"

His eyes narrowed on her as if she'd just revealed her true form—a wasp rather than a butterfly.

"I'm not sure where you are getting your information, Miss Walsh, but I find it highly unlikely our attorney, your superior, Don Fraser would be comfortable to know one of his associates was asking such questions."

"I apologize," Iris stammered. "I didn't mean to pry. Thanks again for your time."

Iris pushed open the heavy door to the frigid day beyond. As she climbed into her car, Miles Fincher watched her from the open doorway.

20

In the days that followed her meeting with Fincher, Iris waited for a confrontation at work. Surely Don Fraser would call her into his office and demand to know why she'd been asking questions at Skelling Hall about Brett and Norlene.

No summons came from Fraser. Marv too seemed intent on forgetting her minor mishap with the transcription, though he must have been curious about why Iris had typed such an odd message into a document she'd prepared for him.

Grateful that she still had a job, Iris focused on work and tried to force Norlene and Brett from her mind. She worked ten-plus-hour days and fell into bed at Lola's each night, exhausted and questioning what compelled her to practice law.

That Friday, Iris arrived at Lola's house after another long day at the office. Lola's Christmas lights twinkled from the eaves and fresh snow fell in big flakes. Lola's friend Minnie's white SUV was parked in the driveway.

Iris walked in the front door, instantly soothed by the laughter of her grandmother and the smell of something sweet and cinnamony.

Iris paused in the living room archway. Lola sat in her chair, slippered feet propped on her stool. Minnie and Jan sat on the couch.

"Hi, Grandma," Iris said. "Hi, Minnie, hi, Jan."

"Welcome home, poppet," Lola told her, raising something to her mouth.

Iris started away and then paused, turning back to stare at Lola. Her grandmother was holding a joint to her lips.

"Grandma, are you smoking pot?" Iris asked, gaze moving to Lola's friends to see if they were as shocked as she was.

They weren't. Minnie leaned forward and took the joint from Lola's fingers.

"Sure we are," Lola said after she'd released a puff of smoke. "Me and the girls like to smoke a bit of grass now and then. Come on in here, have a toke and try one of Jan's cinnamon brownies. They're better than marmalade." Which was apparently an inside joke, because all three women burst into peals of laughter.

Iris tried to wipe the startled look from her face. "I've got work to do, but you enjoy yourselves." She started away and then paused.

"I can hear you thinking from in here," Lola called. "Come on, honey. Come get the giggles with us."

Iris turned and strode back into the room, took the joint from Minnie's outstretched hand and drew in a big inhale before her better judgment took over.

The women started laughing at once. Iris released the smoke and coughed. She handed the joint to her grandma and sat down in an oversized chair, leaning her head back and closing her eyes. She wasn't stoned from one hit, but the mere act of drawing in a breath of cannabis brought a calm over her she hadn't experienced in months.

"About time they legalized it," Minnie said. "Look at Iris. I just saw ten years drop off her face."

"Do you feel a decade younger, poppet?" Lola asked.

Iris sat up and gazed at the three women. "I don't know. Let me take another drag and then I'll tell you."

I ris's cell rang. She lay sprawled on the sofa, her legs draped over the side. Minnie and Jan had left a half-hour earlier and Lola snoozed in her chair. The television played a romantic comedy that Iris had only been half-paying attention to.

She saw Andy's name on the screen.

"Hello," she answered.

"Hey there. How are you?"

Iris released a relaxed sigh and watched the red and green lights flickering on the tree. "I'm grand."

Andy laughed. "You sound grand. Good week at the office?"

"Let's just say I survived." She paused. "Oh, maybe that's in bad taste, considering your job actually puts you in mortal peril."

"In that case, I survived as well. Listen, I'm on patrol tonight, but I have the dogsled race tomorrow. I'm running the dogs from Paradise to Sault Ste Marie. The race ends downtown around eight p.m. Do you want to come down and check it out? See dog mushing in real life?"

Iris closed her eyes. The couch seemed to swallow her. She'd become one with the couch.

"Okay," she said.

"Really?"

"Mmm…hmmm."

"Great. I'll see you tomorrow. There's a big banner where the race ends. Not to mention half the town will be there. You won't be able to miss it."

~

Iris stood in the crowded street, shivering and wishing she'd taken Lola up on the offer of her knee-length winter jacket. On a side street, she recognized Jack Skelling's Mercedes pulling to the curb.

Iris watched Jack step from his car. He gazed down the city block. Garlands and Christmas lights wound up the street lamps, ending at droopy red ribbons. Snow fell in soft lazy flakes and clung to his hair and eyelashes. He closed his eyes and tilted his head up, caught a snowflake on the tip of his tongue.

The act was so innocent, so vulnerable. She stepped closer to the building. She didn't want him to see her watching.

He hadn't moved, stood there with his face toward the sky. He slid a hand up to his chest and she thought she saw a flicker of pain on his face, but the distance made it impossible to say for sure.

A moment later he was gone, slipping into the throng of people gathered beneath the banner that read '10th Annual Brutus Sled Dog Race.'

Iris stepped away from the building and continued to the folding table where a woman was passing out Styrofoam cups of hot chocolate.

"Thank you," Iris told her, wishing she had something stronger to add to the cocoa. The cold had her longing to duck into a building and stand by a heat vent.

She spotted Marv making his way toward her in the crowd. "You're quite the lady about town," Marv mused, smoking a cigar and blowing it sideways.

"What's that supposed to mean?" she grumbled, sipping the cocoa and cringing when it scalded her chapped lips.

"Oh, nothing really. Last week you're dining with Jack Skelling and tonight you're watching the handsome trooper mushing his dogs. You have your pick of the litter in this town, don't you?"

Iris shook her head. "I cannot believe you of all people feel the need to point that out."

"Listen, it takes one to know one, Walsh. I just like to call it out."

"Who are you here with tonight? Some woman you met in a coffee shop this morning?"

"Bakery actually." He nodded toward a woman in white fur boots and a red ski jacket. "Jessica. She's up here with girlfriends for a bachelorette weekend." He winked at Iris.

"Lucky girl." Iris smirked. "And for your information, I'm not involved with Jack Skelling. We had a drink once because he fixed my flat tire."

"Do you think I was born yesterday, Iris Walsh? I see the way you look at Skelling. Not that I'm surprised. If I were a lady, I'd have my sights set on him too."

"Marv! Marv!" Jessica waved her hands and pointed up the road. "They're coming!"

Marv grinned and held up his cigar. "You have fun tonight, Walsh. Don't do anything I wouldn't." He cut back to Jessica, grabbed her around the waist and kissed her flushed cheek.

Iris focused on the road.

The first pack of dogs appeared on the hill, the driver standing on his sled, his face impossible to distinguish beneath his green balaclava.

Then Andy came into view, six smiling dogs in front of him. He wore a fur-lined coat, goggles. The number thirty-three was pinned to his chest.

When Andy passed through, he waved at her as he passed beneath the finish line.

Nearly a half hour passed before Iris saw Andy again. He'd removed his heavy coat and hat as if hot from the ride. He wore a gray thermal shirt beneath cold-weather overalls.

"So, what'd you think?" he asked, brushing a hand through his matted hair. His smile lit his face and his cheeks were rosy. He'd clearly loved it.

"It was neat," she said. Iris had never seen a dog race before and wasn't sure she'd endure the cold to witness another one.

He grinned. "All right, I'll take it. I sense you're not one to be jumping up and down at the finish line."

Iris lifted her hands and attempted to curl her fingers. "I lost sensation in my fingers and toes about ten minutes ago. I'll be lucky to limp, let alone jump."

Andy laughed. "That's because you're still dressing like a lower peninsula girl. Here, put this on." He draped his heavy coat around her.

It smelled like him, piney aftershave and sweat. It also still held the heat from his body. She swam in the coat and pulled it tight around her, tucking her hands into the long sleeves.

"Better?" he asked.

"Much."

"I've got to get the dogs fed and bedded down at the kennel and then we can go to the cabin if you'd like?"

"I don't remember agreeing to anything other than watching a dog race," she told him.

He grabbed the front of her coat and pulled her closer, studying her. "Do you want to come to my place, Iris?"

She stared back at him, unnerved by the extended eye contact, by the tremor of attraction gripping her.

"Fine," she said. "But the cabin will be freezing cold."

"Not once I build a fire."

"I'd prefer a hot shower and a furnace blasting waves of hot air into my face."

He smiled. "Okay, you humored me by coming out, I'll get you warmed up."

~

After they arrived at Andy's house, Iris took a hot shower to thaw her frozen limbs. She dried off and slipped on one of Andy's sweaters, which hung nearly to her knees.

Iris found Andy at his kitchen table, eating a plate of eggs.

"There's more in the pan," he told her.

"Eggs at midnight? I'm good."

She walked to the cupboard and grabbed a mug, adding an herbal tea bag from the box on the window ledge and pouring water from the still-hot tea kettle. When she turned, he was watching her.

"I like you in my clothes."

She took a sip and broke the gaze. Snow fell beyond the window. "Oh, look, more snow," she muttered.

He stood and walked to her, pulled the mug from her hands and set it on the counter. He kissed her and slipped his hands beneath the sweater. His hands were warm as they slid up her back. He picked her up and carried her to the stairs.

Andy lay naked beside her, an arm draped across her belly. She wriggled from beneath his touch and stood, casting an indignant glance at the billowing snow outside his bedroom window. His sweater lay over the back of the chair and she didn't put it back on. Instead, she slid into her own clothes, still cold from hours standing outside.

"Stay the night," he told her.

"No. I have a million things to do tomorrow." She dressed, feeling his eyes on her.

"I'll walk you out," Andy said, jumping out of bed and pulling on black sweatpants.

When he opened the front door, snow blew into the foyer. Beyond the stoop, Iris could barely make out Lola's car in the driveway. The wind howled, and the trees writhed in the front yard as if in worship of some treacherous ice god.

"Damn, that wind has really picked up," Andy said.

Iris stepped back and shoved the door closed. "Okay, I'll stay, but I'm leaving first thing in the morning."

Andy grinned and unzipped her coat, kissing her.

21

Iris woke to find Andy's side of the bed empty. It was just after seven a.m. She'd slept later than she intended.

The kitchen was empty when she walked downstairs, but a full pot of coffee sat on the counter. She took a mug from the cupboard and filled it, walking to the window.

Andy stood in the driveway scraping snow off her car. As she sipped her coffee, she softened against the window frame, but when he looked in her direction, she stiffened and turned back to the kitchen.

A binder lay open on the kitchen table, and Iris gazed at a photograph, startled when she recognized Frankie's face looking back at her.

The photo depicted four boys, her brother among them. He was thirteen in the picture, the age of his death. She studied his baby face and his freckled nose. His hair, the same coppery color as hers, was shaggy and poking at weird angles from beneath a ball cap. Someone must have taken it the summer Frankie drowned.

Andy stood at one end, barely recognizable. He was thin and gangly, slightly taller than Frankie. His hair had been longer and paler then, a flop falling over his right eye.

Andy walked in and she looked up. He brushed snow from the shoulders of his jacket. "Good morning," he said, smiling.

"Why didn't you tell me you were friends with Frankie?" Iris demanded.

Andy walked to where she sat and stared down at the picture, small wrinkles forming around his frown. "Honestly, I didn't make the connection until I dropped you off at Lola's and then…" He shrugged. "I thought you might not want to talk about it. You seemed reluctant to talk about your mom and I assumed you might feel similarly about Frankie."

"Why get this out then?" she asked, gesturing at the album.

"I was thinking about it this morning and figured now was as good a time as any. We were going to have to talk about it eventually."

"When was this taken?" she asked.

He sat in the chair beside her. "A few weeks before the accident. This is Duncan, the boy who—"

"Drowned with him," she finished.

"Yeah."

"Who's this?" Iris pointed at the fourth boy, vaguely familiar.

"It's Jack Skelling."

Iris studied young Jack. Same dimples, but little else resembled the man he'd become. In the photo Jack looked dreamy-eyed. "The four of you were friends?"

"Yeah. Duncan, Jack and I had been friends since pre-school. We'd met Frankie that summer when Lola brought him to the beach. He wasn't shy." Andy laughed. "He walked right up to us and cracked some joke. We were struck dumb and then fell over laughing. After that, we spent every day together until… well, the day they went fishing."

"You and Jack didn't go that day?"

"I was grounded. I'd lifted one of my dad's nudie mags to show the guys, and my mom found it in my backpack. I think she was more pissed at my dad than me, but… in retrospect, they were fighting all the time by then. Anyway, I couldn't go. I don't know what happened to Jack. He was supposed to meet us, but when I talked to him later, something had come up for him too."

"The place they went, Shallows Bay. Had you been fishing there before?"

"Yeah, every summer my whole life."

"And there'd been no accidents? Was the water rough that day?"

Andy scratched at the stubble on his chin. "Yeah. There was some wind that had come up out of the west. I figure… Frankie must have fallen over—he was the inexperienced one—and Duncan must have gone in after him. If the tide is just right, it can pull swimmers downriver."

Iris frowned, trying to remember that summer. It was the summer she'd gotten sick. Meningitis that had put her in the hospital. She'd been in a coma for four days. She'd never made it to Lola's, but Frankie had spent a month with their grandmother as Iris's parents took shifts at their daughter's bedside.

Iris remembered the last time she'd seen Frankie. She hadn't been admitted to the hospital yet, but was going on day two of a fever. He'd come into her dim room, the shades drawn, the humidifier pumping eucalyptus-scented air, and given her his favorite Batman Pez dispenser to keep her company.

Iris had been so jealous of Frankie's extended stay with Lola, but he'd reassured her, as soon as the fever broke, her parents would drive her to Sault Ste Marie as well. But the fever hadn't broken. It had ratcheted up to one hundred and five degrees and her parents had rushed her to the emergency room. She'd spent two weeks in the hospital and when she returned home, her parents had taken the trip to Lola's off the table. She needed to rest—end of discussion.

Iris had spoken with Frankie on the phone a few times, secretly seethed as he told stories of fishing and swimming and Lola's butter pecan cookies, but she'd still been out of it too and couldn't remember those conversations in any great detail.

And then one afternoon, Iris had woken from a nap and found her parents downstairs. Her mother stood at a window crying, her father paced the kitchen.

Frankie went fishing with a friend and now he and the other boy are missing, they told her.

One of her mother's friends came over to watch Iris and her parents sped north. They stayed for a week, but no trace of Frankie was ever found.

Iris flipped the page, expecting to see more family photos of Andy, maybe more photos from his childhood, but the following page held a newspaper article.

Local Boys Missing since Sunday. Suspected Drowned,

Side-by-side photos of Frankie and Duncan stared out from beneath the headline. They'd chosen Frankie's seventh-grade school photo for the article. His hair had been wild as usual, his cowlick especially prominent. He'd widened his eyes for the photo and done a goofy grin, which their mother had scolded him for later.

Iris skimmed the article.

Local boy Duncan Stewart (12) and downstate resident Franklin Walsh (13) disappeared Tuesday while fishing in Shallows Bay. The rowboat it is presumed the boys took that day was found beached by a local man. Both boys' backpacks were discovered in the boat, as well as one fishing pole and a container of worms.

The coast guard and local search-and-rescue team have launched an extensive search of St. Mary's River.

Iris found another article on the next page of the album.

Search Ends for Missing Boys

The search for two missing boys, local Duncan Stewart and out-of-towner Franklin Walsh, ended Tuesday, three weeks to the day since they were last seen.

The sheriff suspects one or both boys fell from the boat and were unable to swim to safety. He believes their bodies will eventually be recovered.

Iris threaded her fingers through her hair, frowning at the article. "Frankie was an excellent swimmer."

"Duncan too. But the water is… unpredictable. They didn't have life-jackets. We never did back then. What kid bothered with stuff like that?"

"What had you guys been doing in the days before? Anything unusual?"

Andy studied her as if trying to gauge where she was headed. "Nothing that stands out. We were always into stuff back then, trying to catch chipmunks, searching for old hunting cabins to break into. Duncan had been pestering Jack about all of us going out to Skelling Hall. Jack had let something slip about a cave out there and Duncan was obsessed. His dad had taken him cave hiking in Tennessee earlier that summer."

"Skelling Hall…" she murmured. A shudder rippled down Iris's spine. "Would they have gone there instead of fishing?"

"A guy found the rowboat with their backpacks inside. They'd left their bikes at the trailhead to Shallows Bay. It's pretty obvious they went fishing."

"But they never found their bodies."

"Yeah. It's sad, but it's not uncommon."

"Whose boat was it?"

"No one's. A little wood rowboat was always tied to a rock on the shore. I guess somebody must have owned it, but it seemed like they put it there for anyone who wanted to take it out fishing. Sometimes we'd go and some other kids would be out in it, but I don't remember it ever belonging to anyone."

"Did you and Jack ever talk about what happened?"

"Yeah, but… Jack's dad got weird after it happened, kind of put him on lockdown. He snuck out once, and we searched the shoreline. A lot changed after that year. My parents split up. My mom and I moved away for a few years. By the time we moved back, Jack's and my lives had taken very different directions. Even in high school he was the superstar, straight As, homecoming king, destined for greatness. I was still screwing everything up, refusing to learn my lesson."

Iris looked away from the picture, unable to block the memory of the night her parents returned from Sault Ste Marie, the night their lives descended into silence. Her mother had looked as if someone had assaulted her—puffy face, eyes red from crying. Her father seemed to have shrunk, lost weight, lost his very essence.

They'd spoken little other than to say they had not found Frankie. Iris had gone to bed that night with the Batman Pez dispenser clutched to her chest. She'd cried herself to sleep.

Iris rubbed at her face. Andy tugged the album away, gently closed it. "I'll never forget that day, the day they went missing," Andy told her. "Mrs. Stewart, Duncan's mom, showed up at my house. She had this look like… like Duncan was dead. I thought maybe they'd been hit riding their bikes. When she said he hadn't come home, I assumed they'd lost track of time. I called Jack because that had been the original plan, to go out to Skelling Hall. He said he hadn't seen them, but thought they'd probably gone fishing. My mom tried to calm Mrs. Stewart, gave her the 'boys will be boys' spiel, said they probably got lost in the woods, but…" Andy closed his eyes and shook his head. "She was right at the edge of hysterical. I'd never seen that before in an adult. That raw panic. It scared me.

"I talked to her later, years later, when I first started on the force. She told me around noon that day a horrible feeling had come over her, just… the most terrible dread and sadness. At first, she didn't understand why, and then when Duncan didn't come home for dinner, she knew something bad had happened. She called Lola and… she said Lola felt it too. Lola had already gone down to the bay in search of the boat, with no luck. Hours started passing and Mrs. Stewart said she knew Duncan was dead. She believed he'd died that day when she'd had that feeling."

"Noon..." Iris murmured, trying to imagine what she might have been doing at that exact moment. Watching television? Pretending to sleep at her mother's insistence that she needed rest?

Had Frankie dropped his pole in the water? Had a fish tugged it in and he'd jumped in to get it and been overcome by a wave?

"Mrs. Stewart and Lola went to the sheriff's office and demanded a search. The sheriff thought they were half-cocked, but he humored them because he could see they were ready to rip the place apart if he didn't comply. I've talked to a lot of detectives and almost all of them trust the mothers. Mothers have an instinct. Sometimes they squash it because they want to hold on to hope, but... more often than not, their gut is right."

Iris thought of Willow Weaver then, how Willow's own gut told her that Norlene was dead, had probably been dead since the beginning.

"I met with Willow Weaver the other day. Norlene Weaver's sister."

Andy leaned back. "And?"

"And she needs help. Norlene didn't run away. She has the same instinct, the mother instinct. She knows that Norlene is dead."

"Who does she think killed Norlene?"

"She doesn't know, but she's leaning toward Sammy Bishop."

"Because Norlene was testifying in a drug case against him, right?"

"Exactly. And I went to Sammy's apartment. He said he didn't know anything, but I overheard him talking on his phone about Norlene after I left. Then I followed him to Norlene's apartment. He sat outside, but never went in."

Andy gaped at her. "Why would you do something like that? If he'd have seen you-"

"He didn't, but he must have something to do with Norlene's disappearance. Why else would he have driven to her apartment?"

Andy sighed. "Christ, Iris. I don't know. It's suspicious, sure, but you following him is not going to get him in jail, it's going to get you hurt."

"I'm not going to do it again, but... should I tell someone? Call the sheriff's office?"

"And say you overheard a phone call and Bishop drove by her apartment? I don't think the sheriff will find that compelling. Just... sit on it, okay. I'll ask around, see what I can find out."

Andy walked her to her car. "I should have started it for you," he said.

"No big deal. Thanks for clearing it off."

"You're welcome, and thank you."

She slid into the driver's seat, but left the door open a crack. "For what?"

"Braving the blizzard to watch me last night. I know it's not your thing."

She nodded. "Now I can say I've seen dogs mushed."

"No more tailing drug dealers, okay?"

"I'll do my best. See ya later, Andy."

Iris backed down the driveway, watching as Andy returned to the house. She felt a tremor of longing to be back in his warm bed, her legs tangled with his, and then crushed it. She had a long day tomorrow.

22

———————

Lola wasn't downstairs when Iris returned home.

She walked to the second floor and paused in the hallway when she heard voices murmuring in her grandmother's room. Iris cracked the door and peeked in, but it was only her grandmother, alone in her rocking chair by the window, a photo album open in her lap.

"I'm home, Grandma," Iris told her, stepping into the doorway. "What are you up to?"

Lola looked up and smiled. She brushed a hand across the images sealed beneath plastic. "I'm talking to my ancestors."

Iris walked in and glanced at the black-and-white photo of a woman with wide-set dark eyes and hair pulled so tight it made Iris's head hurt to look at it.

"Which one was that again?" Iris asked. Lola had shown her the pictures the summer before when she'd first started seeing and hearing strange things, but she'd been in such a state of distraction she'd paid little attention.

"This is Leona Dherurbin, my grandmother, your great-grandmother. She's been visiting me lately, telling me about things to come."

Iris pulled a steamer trunk from the foot of Lola's bed and sat down. "Is that so? Can she tell me if I'm destined to be Marv Booker's minion for all eternity or if someday I might actually try a case?"

Lola traced her finger along the woman's shape. "I'm afraid the dead don't meddle in such things, poppet."

"They meddle in everything else," Iris grumbled.

Lola looked at her, tilted her head to the side. "It gets better. You'll see."

A gust of snow blew against the window. Iris crossed her arms over her chest, cold at the sight of it. "Can we talk about Frankie?"

Lola closed the album. "Of course we can. I'm surprised you've waited so long to bring him up."

Iris tucked her hands beneath her knees. "Andy told me about that summer. How Frankie and Duncan went off fishing."

"Mm-hmm."

"Have you ever seen Frankie? Spoken to his spirit?"

Lola smiled and nodded. "In the beginning, I did. He came to his funeral and made faces at me from behind his casket. He kept sending me this thought. 'Why did Mom put me in that shirt? I hated that shirt.'"

Iris widened her eyes. "He *did* hate that shirt. I asked Mom that too when I saw her leaving to take it to the funeral home. I don't think she even heard me. It was a button-down with stripes. Frankie wouldn't have been caught dead in that shirt." She considered her words. He *had* been caught dead in it.

"Did you ever tell my parents that you saw him?"

Lola smiled sadly. "I tried once. I too had lost a child, Melody, when she was barely twenty and I'd seen her a few times over the years. She was at peace and that had helped me to accept her passing. I told your mother I'd seen Frankie, and that he'd moved on from this life and he was okay."

"She didn't believe you, did she?"

Lola sighed. "No, she didn't. She got angry at me. Your father called me afterwards. He was very upset and told me to never spread that nonsense in his house."

"I don't get it. He's your son. Why is he so skeptical of it? Against it all?"

"Perhaps for the same reason that the children of doctors become rockstars and the kids of hippies join the military. There's a peculiar balance in the universe. We often see it between parents and children, as if the very thing one is most afraid of the other will become."

Iris thought of her own recent shifts in life. Until she'd started seeing them, she hadn't believed in spirits either. Had thought people who spoke of such things were fantasists reaching for the shiny allure of the supernatural to lessen the dullness of reality. She couldn't imagine sitting her father down and telling him she was investigating a woman who'd gone missing because she kept seeing her ghost.

"Did Frankie ever communicate anything about his death? About what happened that day?"

Lola picked at the edges of the album. "I had a dream the night he didn't come home. A dream that he and Duncan had not gone into the lake. They were in the woods being led by something. They were like moths to the flame, unable to turn away from it. Then everything went dark. I woke up weeping."

Iris frowned. "What did you think it meant?"

Lola shifted her eyes up to Iris. She looked haunted. "I don't know, poppet. I don't think I'll know until I see Frankie again."

"I just… I don't get it. What's the point of the dead coming back if they can't communicate anything that matters? Just to make our lives harder?"

Iris thought of Norlene hovering by Jack Skelling. She imagined Frankie's voice whispering to her in the darkness. She'd lived twenty-eight years without a visit from a ghost and now suddenly they were everywhere. Why her? Why now?

Lola smiled. "Oh, honey, you're so much like your mom and dad. Everything needs to have a rational explanation. What's the rational explanation behind falling in love? Crying over a sunrise? Maybe they come back because they miss us. Maybe they're not ready to move on. Probably we'll never know while we're in these bodies the reasons for so many things in this beautiful and complicated life."

Iris stood and walked to the window. Snow cast the world in white. Tendrils of grey streaked up from chimneys. In the distance, she could see the top of the courthouse. She thought of Jack Skelling, unknowingly haunted by Norlene Weaver.

"Why do some spirits cling to a particular person?" Iris asked.

"Same reason we cling to people in life, I suppose," Lola said. "They like 'em, they're drawn to 'em. Some spirits stick by their still-living spouse or child, struggling to hold on to a life that no longer exists. Some of 'em don't seem to know they've died. Others latch onto somebody. I can't tell you how or why, but it happens. Remember my friend Edna-Sue?"

Iris wrinkled her brow. "Vaguely. She was the one who baked the weird cupcakes with faces on them?"

Lola chuckled. "The one and only, but that was a hobby. She worked as a paramedic for thirty-some odd years. She went to the scene of a suicide one night. A man had taken his life with a shotgun. She got a real weird feeling in his apartment and it stayed with her. That night, she woke up to somebody sitting in her rocking chair across the room. It was that man sitting there and rocking, a shotgun resting on his knees. He followed her for a year until she finally called a Catholic priest and had some kind of cleansing done to get rid of him."

"It worked?"

"Seemed to. Sent him back into the light, helped him to move on. He wasn't hurting her or nothing but he scared her and she could feel his sadness. She told me once that whenever she woke to find him in the room, she felt as if there was no purpose to life, no light at all, that she might as well just die herself. She started thinking he was somehow transferrin' his thoughts and feelings to her. Sometimes, she'd go through a spell of ten days where she wouldn't get out of bed. I took soup over to her. She wasn't sick, just… terribly sad. She didn't speak like herself and then when she came out of it, she knew she had to get rid of that ghost."

"Had she seen ghosts before? The way you and I can now?"

"Nope. She'd had a brush now and then. I doubt a human alive hasn't had one, whether or not they realize it, but this one was undeniable. Scared the daylights right out of her."

Iris thought of Skelling Hall, how Fincher had told her that Felix Skelling was seeing a dark man. Was the dark man a spirit like the suicide who'd haunted Edna-Sue? She wanted to ask Lola about such things, but her grandmother looked tired suddenly, her eyes drooping.

Iris took a blanket from the foot of Lola's bed and covered her up. "Have a nap, Grandma. I'm going to go downstairs and get some work done."

Lola's eyes fluttered up to her. "You work too hard, poppet."

Iris kissed Lola on the top of the head.

Downstairs, Iris eyed her desk stacked with briefs. She had work for days, but she couldn't stand the thought of sitting at the desk and willing her brain to focus on those cases. She grabbed Lola's keys and headed to the car.

Iris drove to the beach where Frankie and Duncan had disappeared nearly eighteen years before. When they'd gone missing, Shallows Bay had been little more than an isolated beach at the end of a dirt trail. It had become more popular in the intervening years. A gravel lot now offered people a place to park. Three picnic tables and as many firepits sat on the snowy beach.

On this sunny but cold December day, the bay stood empty. The water beyond lapped against the icy shoreline.

Iris stepped from the car. Her boots crunched over the frozen ground.

She thought of Willow Weaver, the haunted, confused look in her eyes when she talked about Norlene.

It had to have been Sammy Bishop who murdered Norlene. It was the logical explanation. And yet… when she imagined Norlene, Iris's thoughts pulled her to Skelling Hall and the shadowy figure pursuing Brett Stephens.

The wind picked up on the river. Iris shivered and returned to her car.

She drove, first to Skelling Hall, though she didn't turn onto the peninsula. She merely sat on the side of the road and watched the woods. She didn't know what she expected. The shadowy thing to appear? Brett or Norlene to come strolling out of the forest?

When a car turned off the peninsula road, Iris ducked in her seat, feeling foolish for sitting there, but peeking out just the same. It was Miles Fincher. He glanced toward her car, likely recognized it, but passed by without slowing.

Iris drove back to town and parked in front of Norlene's apartment building. She didn't know if Sammy had come back later and entered the apartment, but she wanted to see if anything had been taken since she'd gone in the last time.

Iris got out, jogged across the street and pushed into the building. She paused, remembering Andy's warning, but she wasn't following anyone, merely checking out an empty apartment. The hallway was dim and smelled more mildewy than her previous visit. The cold dampness of outside followed her in and she hurried up the stairs to the third floor. As she approached the door to apartment six, she paused.

It was slightly ajar.

Iris listened, but heard nothing from within. Sammy must have gone there after all and removed something that linked him to Norlene's disappearance.

"Shit," she muttered.

She should have gone to the apartment sooner, but how could she have known what he intended to take?

As Iris pushed open the door, someone darted at her, shoving her so hard she smacked into the opposite wall and fell to the floor.

The person, clad in black, face covered by a dark balaclava, lurched through the door and was gone.

23

Iris winced and touched the back of her head where it had hit the wall. She'd left a rounded indent in the plaster. She stood and hobbled quickly across the room to the window, hoping to catch a glimpse of the fleeing man.

As she neared the window, something popped up from the fire escape and Iris shrieked and leapt back. It was the black and white cat she'd seen on her first visit to Norlene's.

"Jesus Christ," she snarled, yanking the window open.

The cat leapt in, and Iris leaned out, scanning the alley and the road beyond.

No one. He'd gotten away.

Iris returned to the apartment door, locked it, and shoved a chair beneath the doorknob. She fed the cat, checked in the mirror that her head wasn't bleeding, and then set about the apartment searching for what might have been taken.

She scrolled through the photos she'd snapped of each room and held the images up to see if she could discern a change. Nothing in the kitchen or living room appeared out of place. The bathroom still looked intact.

When she paused in the bedroom, holding the photo of the dresser up, she saw the discrepancy. On one corner of the dresser, there'd been a white handkerchief and in the center a pair of lion's head cufflinks. The cufflinks were gone. Iris searched the carpeted floor, double-checking they had not fallen. They weren't there.

Iris sat on the edge of the bed and zoomed in on the photo. There was nothing extraordinary about the cufflinks except perhaps that Norlene had them. They were a man's accessory and not many modern men wore them at all. Iris wished she'd looked at them closer on her previous visit to the apartment.

Now they were gone.

~

After she'd left Norlene's apartment, Iris had driven home, eaten dinner with Lola and gone to bed. She'd mentioned nothing about Norlene's apartment to Lola. She hadn't called the police to report the break-in. She'd carried on as if nothing unusual had happened.

What was the alternative? She'd realized the moment she'd closed Norlene's apartment door behind her that she had no authority to do anything.

She wasn't a cop. She didn't have evidence. She was trespassing on private property, sifting through the belongings of a woman the police believed had skipped town. Reporting any of it was a quick way to get into legal trouble herself, not to mention jeopardize her job at the Fraser Firm.

As Iris sat at work the following day, attempting more research for Marv on DUI laws, she realized she didn't have a clue what she would do if she figured out who murdered Norlene.

Most of what she'd discovered in her novice investigation wouldn't be admissible in court. It hadn't gone through the chain of custody, hadn't been found using legal avenues such as warrants. Sammy could stand in front of her and confess, and it wouldn't be admissible in court.

The cufflinks niggled at her. Sammy Bishop made the most sense as the perpetrator of Norlene's murder, but why would a drug dealer be concerned about cufflinks? Maybe the break-in had nothing to do with Norlene's death and it had just been a random burglar looting the entire building.

"No…" she murmured.

The man had had nothing on him, no bag, no other valuables that she could see. Virtually the only thing obviously missing from Norlene's apartment were the cufflinks.

"Hey." Nina paused in their office doorway. "Candace ordered takeout from Lou's Pour House and I've got to go down to the jail and talk with my client about the video surveillance that shows him pawning the television he said he didn't steal. Can you pick it up?"

"Anything beats reading DUI case law," Iris said. "Where's Lou's Pour House?"

"It's three blocks down, tucked into an alley of sorts. Don't let the appearance scare you. They have the best pizza in town. Candace put it under Marv's name."

"All right, see you in a bit."

I ris pushed open the door into Lou's Pour House, a windowless dive bar that stank of stale beer. She stepped to the counter where the bartender stood watching a talk show.

"I'm here for a pick-up order," she told him. "Under the name Marv Booker."

The man didn't look at her. "Five minutes on the pizzas," he said.

"All right, thanks." Iris turned and scanned the bar.

Only a few people sat at the tables and as she gazed around the room, her eye caught on a woman who looked familiar.

Iris studied the woman, sunk low in her chair, chin resting on her chest. She looked drunk or high. The guy she was with had six empty glasses on the table in front of him. His eyes were glued to the television in the corner of the room, where someone on the talk show was standing on stage, beating his chest like a gorilla.

Iris continued to watch the woman, trying to place her, and then she noticed the woman's hand hanging limply at her side. She had tattooed knuckles.

This was Star Morton, the close friend of Norlene Weaver she'd been unable to track down. Iris made her way to Star's table. The woman didn't look up, but the man across from her did.

"Hey," he said, leaning back and spreading his already wide stance as if in invitation.

Iris scowled at him and directed her attention to Star.

"Star Morton?" she asked.

The woman's eyes didn't flicker up to Iris. She stared straight ahead, though there was nothing there save the sticky tabletop.

Iris squatted down and got right in Star's line of sight. "Hey!"

Star's eyes drifted over her and then steadied on Iris. "Huh?" she mumbled.

"Leave her alone," the guy muttered. "She's chillin'."

"She doesn't look chill," Iris snapped. "She looks drugged." Iris stood and glared at the man. "What did she take?"

He sneered. "What's it to you?"

Iris grabbed Star's wrist and shook it. "Star. Hey. I need to talk to you."

Star's head lolled to the side and her eyes drifted closed.

The man kicked out one leg as if he intended to buckle Iris's knee.

She sprang to the side and scowled at him. "Do that again and I'm calling the cops."

He held up his hands and made a face. "Oh, no, not the cops. Bitch, you'll be dead in the dumpster out back before they ever get here."

The bartender who'd been rinsing glasses raised his eyes to the scene across the room. "Floyd." The bartender's voice held a warning as he stared down the man.

Floyd shrugged as if he were doing nothing wrong and flipped the bartender his middle finger beneath the table. "Cocksucker," he muttered.

Iris returned to Star. "Star. Hey, wake up. Can you hear me?"

Star blinked at the floor and shook her head slowly. "Tired…" she grumbled.

Something wet splashed the side of Iris's face and hit Star full on. Floyd had dipped his fingers in a glass of beer and flicked it towards them. Iris wiped it away with her sleeve, gritting her teeth and turning on Floyd. "Listen to me, you piece of shit. If you think—"

Before she could finish her statement, Floyd jumped from his chair. He stood a foot taller than her and shoved his face close to hers, grabbing both of her arms so tight she feared they'd snap.

"No, you listen to me, cunt," he hissed, his hot breath spraying into her face.

Iris tried to pull away, but his grip was impossible to break.

"Goddammit, Floyd." The bartender stepped from behind the bar with a baseball bat in his hand.

Floyd's eyes had gone black. He seemed unaware of the bartender or the bat, and Iris realized she'd made a grave error screwing with this guy. He could do a lot of damage before that bat would stop him, if it stopped him at all.

Iris felt a blast of cold air as the door opened and suddenly Floyd was jerked away from her and shoved sideways. He stumbled, lost his balance, and crashed onto a spindly round table that collapsed beneath him.

Andy followed him, grabbed the collar of his shirt and hauled him back to his feet.

Floyd threw up his hands and ducked his head. "Okay, okay. I didn't do nothin'. This is battery or some shit."

"I just watched you grab that woman through the window. It looked to me like you were about to do something," Andy snarled, cuffing Floyd and marching him outside.

Andy loaded Floyd into the back of his cruiser and returned to the bar.

"You okay?" he asked Iris.

She nodded, rubbing her biceps where Floyd had squeezed. She'd likely find bruises there tomorrow. "That guy's nuts."

"Yeah, he's not one to mess with. Sorry about the table, Rich," Andy told the bartender.

The guy shrugged and slid two large pizzas across the bar. "It was ready for the garbage dump anyway. Here's those pizzas, miss."

"Thanks," Iris said, pulling cash from her wallet.

"On the house," he told her.

Iris shook her head. "I appreciate it, but this can go toward your new table."

Rich took the money and popped it in the register.

Andy took her hand and drew her out of earshot of the bartender. "I wanted to give you a heads up. We pulled Sammy Bishop in yesterday evening on an outstanding warrant. The detective grilled him on Norlene, told him a witness had spotted him outside her apartment."

"Yesterday? What time?"

"I picked him up around three pm. He's still in jail waiting on a bail hearing."

Iris had encountered the man at Norlene's apartment closer to five. It couldn't have been Bishop.

"What did he say about Norlene?"

"He said he went by her apartment to see if anyone was hanging around. Sammy's got this half-cocked idea that Norlene is still alive and planning to testify against him. He's convinced Norlene and Jack Skelling cooked up this missing person's story to hide her until his trial."

"That's absurd. Do you believe him?"

Andy shrugged. "As many drugs as he's on, I'm surprised he didn't throw out a bigger conspiracy than that one."

Across the room, Star grumbled and nearly slipped out of her chair.

"I want to get her out of here," Iris told Andy, gesturing at Star. "Could you help me?"

"Sure."

Iris lifted Star's hand and squeezed. "Star, hey. I'm going to give you a ride. Okay?"

Star nodded, but didn't move. Iris and Andy each took an arm and pulled her to her feet. They guided her to Iris's car and into the passenger seat.

Star's eyes focused for a moment, and she caught sight of Andy. She recoiled, jerking her arm from his grasp. "Don't touch me," she hissed.

Iris shot a confused look at Andy, but he put his hands up and backed away. "Call me if you need anything," he told Iris.

She nodded, opened the driver's door and slid inside. "Thanks, Andy."

I ris dropped the pizzas off at the Fraser Firm and told Marv she'd had a family thing come up that had to be dealt with.

As she steered the car toward her grandmother's house, she glanced at Star. The woman had nodded off against the passenger window.

L ola carried a cup of cocoa to Star, who sat on the couch beneath a pink blanket.

"Thank you," Star told Lola, taking the cup and inhaling. She'd spent the first half-hour on the couch dozing, but in the previous few minutes had come back to some level of awareness. "Smells good."

"It's my secret recipe," Lola told her with a wink.

Iris sat in a chair kitty-corner to the couch, watching the woman.

"Why are you being so nice to me?" Star asked, eyeing Iris suspiciously.

"Because I want to ask you questions about Norlene. I've been looking for you. I left a note under your door."

Star frowned. "I was evicted. The super changed the locks. I can't get back in to get my stuff, so I haven't bothered going by there."

"In winter? Did he give you any notice?"

"About a week. I'd missed the December payment for rent."

"Legally, you have rights as a tenant. He can't just kick you out."

Star tucked a strand of black hair behind her ear. "Yeah, well, those so-called rights generally don't apply to my type."

"They apply to everyone."

Star sipped her cocoa, but said nothing.

"Norlene's sister said that you weren't using drugs anymore, or at least that you hadn't been."

Star bit her lip. "I wasn't. I got clean like Norlene. Two years and then... everything went to shit like it always does. My guy left. My manager at work grabbed my ass, and I slapped him. Got fired the next day." She blew on the cocoa. "In the middle of it all, Norlene disappeared. I said fuck it. What's getting clean ever done for me? It just makes it all harder. If I'm high, I don't have to see just how ugly it is, how hopeless."

Iris had heard a hundred self-help gurus take moments like the one she was in and launch into an 'it's never too late' speech. She didn't. She didn't live Star's life and any advice she had for her would be coming from a life so privileged, so foreign, that it would feel like a lie. Plus, she herself had wanted to kick in the sparkling white teeth of a few of those motivational speakers when they launched into a spiel about how everything happens for a reason.

"Do you have any idea what happened to Norlene?"

Star took another drink, snuggled deeper into the blanket. "I think he offed her."

"Sammy Bishop?"

Star snorted. "No. Jack Skelling."

Iris sat back. "Why would Prosecutor Skelling kill Norlene?"

"To shut her up and to get rid of the kid."

"What kid?"

"Norlene was pregnant, and the baby was Skelling's."

24

Iris knew her expression was one of disbelief, and Star glared at her.

"I don't care if you believe me."

"It's not that I don't believe you," Iris lied. "It's just… Norlene was a witness for the prosecution. I'm pretty sure Jack Skelling understands the repercussions of getting romantically involved with a—"

"He's got a dick, doesn't he?" Star snapped.

Iris closed her mouth. Arguing with the woman would get her nowhere. "Okay. You think Norlene and Jack had an affair, and he killed her to keep her quiet?"

Star traced her finger along the snowman painted on the mug. "A guy like Skelling isn't payin' child support to the likes of Norlene Weaver. I told her to back off, that maybe if she flew under the radar, she'd be taken care of, but she wasn't having it. She wanted him to marry her. She wanted everyone in town to know she was Jack Skelling's girl."

"Do you have any proof of what you're saying? Or is this all second-hand from Norlene?"

"Well, I didn't see a pregnancy test, if that's what you mean."

"Did you ever see them together? Being intimate?"

Star scoffed. "He ain't stupid. You think he was going to screw her where anybody could see them? Hell, no. They snuck off, did these long drives out to the woods, and she'd come back skippin' like a schoolgirl. Why would she be that way if it weren't true?"

"Maybe because she wanted it to be true."

"Norlene wasn't a liar. She said she was in love with Jack Skelling and she was pregnant with his baby and I believe her."

"I'm surprised her sister didn't mention any of this to me."

"Her sister didn't know."

"Norlene never told her sister?"

"Nope. Willow was always judgin' Norlene. Norlene had this idea in her mind. She'd wait until it was all squared away with Jack. Maybe she'd even have a diamond ring to go over there and show off, some proof like you said. But she never got it."

"I find it hard to believe that a man like Jack Skelling would be involved in the disappearance of a young woman."

"Of course you do. You're just like him. You think you're better than us. Shit, I think you're better than us, but Jack Skelling went slumming with Norlene and when that mistake grew too big to cover up, he took care of it."

Iris scratched at her hairline, mildly irritated by Star's accusations. First of all, Star Morton was scarcely credible. Add to that the pristine record of Jack Skelling. Clearly it had all come on the word of Norlene Weaver, who Willow had implied had an unhealthy fixation on Jack Skelling.

"You don't have to believe me. I don't care whether you believe me or not."

"Did you ever tell the authorities?"

"I called 'em once. Some guy took my statement and said if a detective had more questions, they'd call me. They never did. Shocker."

"When someone disappears, police get a lot of leads. They have to follow the most plausible ones."

Star's eyes flashed. "I'm her best friend. I *was* her best friend. If a lead coming from me isn't worth checking, then I don't know why the police bother looking into it at all. Course they hardly did. To them, Norlene either ran off, or she got killed by a drug dealer she'd turned narc on. Either doesn't mean much to the cops."

"How about a cufflinks? Did Norlene ever mention any cufflinks?"

Star shook her head. "Nope."

"She never mentioned someone leaving a pair at her apartment? They were shaped like lion's heads."

"If someone did, it was Jack Skelling."

~

Iris learned little more from Star Morton than what she'd already known. When they left Lola's, Star sat in the passenger seat staring out the window, quietly fuming.

"Where can I drop you off?"

"Just take me back to Lou's. I have a friend who lives nearby."

As Iris drove back into town, she gestured at her purse. "I have a card in the side pocket. Take one and leave me a number or some way to get in touch. I'll contact your landlord and see about you getting back into your place."

Star plucked a card from the side of Iris's purse and shoved it into her pocket.

Iris pulled to the curb near the bar. "I appreciate your talking to me."

As Star gazed through the windshield, her expression hardened.

Iris followed her gaze to where Andy stood talking to the bartender from Lou's Pour House.

"Why don't you like him?" Iris asked.

"Because he's a piece of shit."

"Have you had trouble with him? Been arrested or something?"

Star narrowed her eyes at him. "No. He knows to stay away from me."

"Why is that?"

"Did Willow tell you what happened to Norlene? That she got gang-raped?"

"Yes."

"Well, that dirtbag was there."

"He was the cop on the scene?"

Star snorted. "He was one of the frat boys."

Before Iris could ask more, Star jumped from the car and started across the street in the opposite direction from where Andy stood. She didn't look back.

Iris watched Andy. His eyes flicked up to Star and then shifted toward her. He waved, but continued his conversation.

Could Star have been telling the truth? Andy had been part of the group who'd assaulted Norlene Weaver? It didn't seem possible. How could he have become a police officer with something like that on his record?

Then again, Iris wasn't naïve. She knew how tightly knit groups like the police operated. They were a band of brothers and there was always a loophole if one of them got into trouble. Andy himself had told her he'd been troubled as a young man, made a lot of mistakes.

She waited until the bartender walked away and then she climbed from her car and strode to where he stood.

"Hey. I'm happy to see she didn't claw your eyes out."

"I need to ask you a question," Iris said, trying to keep her voice even.

"Go for it."

"Were you in the hotel room the night Norlene Weaver was raped eight years ago?"

Andy paled, but he didn't break eye contact with Iris. He nodded slowly. "But that's all I was. I was passed out on the couch. I'd downed a fifth of tequila. I had no idea it was happening."

Iris glowered at him. "Why didn't you tell me when I asked you about Norlene?"

"Because of the look on your face right now."

"You lied to me," she spat.

"No, I—"

But she didn't let him finish. Iris spun away and stalked back to her car before Andy could stop her.

25

———

Iris had intended to go back to the Fraser Firm, but the discovery about Andy had her head spinning. She couldn't focus on legal briefs. She wanted to take a long walk. Walks had always been her thinking time and downstate it had been easy. Even in winter, there were paved walking trails that were shoveled and salted.

She considered where she could find a similar path now. The forest trails were buried in snow and she didn't fancy a walk alone in the woods. If she walked downtown, she was liable to run into Marv or Nina. She thought of the cemetery on the eastern side of the city.

As Iris drove past the cemetery, she slowed, spotting Jack Skelling as he climbed from his car.

Jack trudged through the snow up a large hill toward a cluster of tombstones.

Iris pulled to the side of the road, watching. She thought of her last conversation with Jack, how she'd confronted him. Her face grew warm at the memory.

He paused at a tall headstone, face tilted down, perhaps in prayer. She thought she saw his lips moving, but she was too far away to say for sure.

Iris considered Star's claims that Jack had been sleeping with Norlene, that he'd killed her to silence her. The notion was so absurd, it made her sad for Jack. Sad that people could whisper such terrible lies

152

behind his back. Here was a man who'd devoted his life to giving victims a voice, the last person who would take one away.

Slowly she eased off the brake and pulled further down the road, parking behind Jack's car.

She waited until he made his way down the hill and then stepped from her own car and waved.

He continued toward her, checking both ways before he crossed the road.

"Hey," she said.

"Hi." He offered her a cautious smile. "Do you have family here or…?"

"No, I thought I'd come here to take a walk. I wanted to apologize for the other day at Bitters."

Jack pulled up the collar of his jacket as a gust of wind rushed down from the hill. "Thank you. What was that about, anyway?"

She put both hands in her jacket pockets. "That was me donning my shield of tinfoil armor."

"Come again?"

"Nothing. I'd had a long day and… I don't know. I've been looking into Norlene's case. Don't ask me why because I don't have a reason that will make sense to you. I'm sorry I was so rude."

"You're forgiven," he told her. "Shall we bury the hatchet? Have dinner with me?"

They ate dinner at Prior's Steakhouse, an upscale restaurant that looked out on the Soo Locks.

The hostess seated them at a high-top table with a water view. A mammoth freighter drifted through the icy river toward the straits of Mackinac.

"How can people do that for a living?" Iris murmured, imagining the men on board the freighter, the violent wind gnawing through their winter layers.

Jack watched the freighter. "I loved those boats as a kid. My grandfather did too."

"The grandfather who was a judge?"

"Yes."

"Is that who you were visiting today at the cemetery?"

Jack loosened the collar of his shirt, undid the top button. "Yes, among others. 'Still waters run deep.' That's what's carved on his headstone."

"And that described him?"

"Yes. He was a complex man. A man of few words, but many virtues. He instilled in me the importance of living a life of integrity. I've spoken with a lot of attorneys who respected him, admired him on both sides of the courtroom."

"It's good to have people to emulate."

"I agree. Who do you emulate, Iris?"

Jack was gazing at her intently, his blue eyes bright in the glow from the candle on the table. As she had previously, Iris felt a niggling less-ness. It wasn't a sensation she often experienced. She'd practically devoted her life to never suffering by comparison. But here with the young, handsome, apparently flawless prosecutor, she sensed her answer would fall short of his.

"My grandma, I guess," she admitted because it was true. In all her life, she'd never met a more kind, selfless woman than Lola Walsh.

He smiled. "I've only met her briefly, but I can tell she's one of the good ones."

The waitress arrived and Jack ordered a bottle of cabernet and clams, which he said were exceptional. They drank wine, Jack only a few sips and Iris doing her best to stop at two glasses, and spoke mostly of work-related things. The grunt work she was mired in as a new associate, the cases he'd tried and been changed by.

After the server dropped off their bill, Jack studied Iris. "So, tell me why you're looking into Norlene Weaver's case."

Iris grabbed thirty dollars from her purse and Jack waved it away. "My treat," he told her.

Iris returned the money to her wallet. "I feel bad for Willow Weaver."

"Norlene's sister?"

"Yes. I spoke with her and she's living in perpetual limbo. I keep thinking, what would that be like? Losing someone and having no idea what happened to them?" Iris pursed her lips and folded her napkin into a tiny little triangle. "It made me think of Frankie. His death ripped my family apart, but... he died. We had closure. We had a funeral—without his body, of course, but still, it was a formal goodbye. We knew he was dead. We could go on."

Although that wasn't entirely true. They hadn't gone on. They'd stopped. Stopped talking, stopped laughing, stopped vacationing. Her mother had stopped announcing Friday night was pizza night, had stopped making Jell-O with the fruit in it, something Frankie had loved, but Iris had loved it too. She'd stopped lecturing Iris on brushing her teeth and cleaning her room and then one night, after Iris had spent the day pestering her about Frankie, wanting to talk about her dead brother, her mother had stopped the whole charade once and for all by driving her car into a tree.

"It's Willow who has you concerned about Norlene's whereabouts," Jack said. He handed his credit card to the server as she hurried by the table.

"Yes. And your name has come up in connection with Norlene quite a few times."

"As well it should. She was a witness in a case I was prosecuting."

"I know, but…" Iris thought of what Star had told her: 'Norlene was pregnant with Jack Skelling's baby.' It didn't ring true and yet she had to ask. "Norlene's best friend, Star Morton, told me she was pregnant with your baby."

Jack frowned and pinched the bridge of his nose. "Well, that's a new one."

Iris studied him, tried to imagine the man before her carrying on a secret affair with Norlene Weaver. She couldn't see it. "It's not true, then?"

Jack sat back in his chair, folded his arms across his chest. "It's absurd is what it is. Good God, where would she get an idea like that?"

"From Norlene herself, according to Star."

Jack uncrossed his arms, sat forward and placed both palms on the table. "Norlene was a nice girl, but… I think she became infatuated. I had no clue it was at that level."

"Apparently it was. Star thinks you got rid of Norlene to shut her up."

Jack's eyes drifted to the window. "Norlene was a very unhappy person who hated this town. She was terrified about testifying."

"You think she ran away?"

"I do, yes."

"Why didn't she call her sister, her friend? I've visited her apartment. She left things behind that are unusual… things most people, women especially, would take. Her hairbrush, her toothbrush."

Jack rubbed at his neck. "I don't know about that, but... I could see someone leaving those things behind, wanting a fresh start. Is that so crazy?"

"For a woman who makes nine dollars an hour? Yeah. It's crazy. She left a perfectly good car."

"I'd hardly call it perfectly good."

"It ran and when you barely have money to make rent, a running car is a ticket to freedom. Even if she had some other way out of town, why didn't she sell the car, get a few hundred bucks to fund her trip?"

"Maybe she didn't want to tip anyone off."

"Someone who wanted to hurt her, you mean?" Iris asked.

"Sure."

"Someone like Sammy Bishop?"

"Possibly. Like I told you before, he hasn't committed violent crimes that I'm aware of, but he could have threatened her."

"Did the police ask him that?"

"I would imagine they did."

"But why didn't you make sure they did? She was your witness?"

Jack sighed and brushed a hand through his dark hair. "When Norlene left, I was prosecuting a murder case. I was barely treading water. You're right, I didn't look into it. I figured she got spooked and skipped town, that she'd be back."

"But she hasn't been back."

"I know."

"Maybe it's time to push the police, request they do a more thorough investigation."

"I think you're right," he said. "I'll reach out to the sheriff's office."

"One more thing..." Iris knew it was risky telling Jack she'd been in Norlene's apartment, but if he was going to help in Norlene's case, he had to know everything. "I went to Norlene's apartment twice. According to Willow the police haven't searched it."

"Did you find anything of relevance?"

"I took photos the first time. When I went back the second time someone was in the apartment. They shoved me and ran out. The only thing missing was a pair of gold cufflinks."

Jack shifted, scratched at his neck. "Did you get hurt?"

"No, not really. I'm fine."

"That was not a wise thing to do, Iris. Whoever was there could have attacked you, or worse."

"I know. I'm not going back, but I wanted to tell you because I think the cufflinks might have something to do with her disappearance."

Jack frowned. "I'm not sure how I'm going to work that into the conversation with the sheriff… but… I'll think of something."

"Okay." Iris smiled and drank the last of her wine. "Thank you. I'll drop it now."

Jack unbuttoned another button on his shirt and rubbed at his collarbone. She could see a small gold cross hanging from a chain around his neck. The piece of jewelry surprised her. He did not strike her as a churchgoer.

Iris found the delicate cross on the simple gold chain strangely attractive. The same magnetism she'd felt their first night returned. She wanted to lean closer to him, lift the gold cross in her fingers, feel the warmth of his breath on the side of her face.

Marv's words rang in her mind: 'You can't fill the void by filling your bed.' What an obnoxious thing to say. She swept her hair away from her face and forced his comment from her mind.

After the server returned his credit card, Jack walked Iris to her car. This time she didn't suggest anything more, but when she pulled open her driver's door, he moved closer to her, into the little bubble of space that people rarely breached without reason.

He gazed down at her. "I saw you with Andy at the sled dog race. Are you guys…?"

"No. We're not anything." She pulled his head down to hers.

The kiss was long and Jack's hands roamed down her back, slipped beneath her coat, pressed against the small of her back. When he pulled away, Iris wobbled on her feet, momentarily off-kilter.

"Whoa," she murmured, putting a hand on the hood of her car.

"I've wanted to kiss you since I first saw you in the bar," he told her.

"Me too," she admitted, ready to drag him into the backseat of Lola's car if he was up for it.

"The Christmas party at Skelling Hall is Saturday night, La Fête de Noël. Will you accompany me?"

Iris blinked at him. She'd been expecting an invitation to his apartment, not to a Christmas party. "The Christmas party? Marv mentioned it, but I don't know anything about it."

"You'll enjoy it. It's my favorite event of the year. Dancing, an open bar and a gigantic Christmas tree. I know you can appreciate that."

She smiled and rubbed her hands together. "Sure, why not? Marv insisted it was the highlight of the season."

"It is and it's formal. Do you have a dress?"

Iris imagined the clothing she'd brought to Lola's house the previous spring. A formal dress was definitely not among them. "I can get one."

"Good. Now for my second question. Would you like to come back to my place?" He grinned and leaned in to kiss her a second time.

Iris held up Lola's car keys attached to a fuzzy pink bunny keychain. "I'll follow you."

The ghostly apparition of Norlene had not appeared that night, but as Jack climbed into his car and drove past her, Iris saw the woman materialize in the passenger seat. Her head slowly swiveled, and she gazed at Iris with glittering, hate-filled eyes.

26

The sight of Norlene's ghost bothered Iris. It had bothered her each time she'd encountered it, but this time the young woman held an expression of fury. Had it been directed at her?

Iris thought of Jack's claim that Norlene had been infatuated with him. Was she as obsessed with him in death as she had been in life?

Iris followed Jack to a new brick condominium complex on the shores of the St. Mary's River. He took her hand and led her to the front door, using a key card to gain entrance. He leaned toward her as if he might kiss her in the elevator, but then another woman hurried on and he backed away, winking.

"Good afternoon, Prosecutor Skelling. Did you have court today?" the woman asked, shooting an appraising look at Iris.

"Yes. It went well."

"I'm happy to hear it." The woman stepped off on the third floor.

Iris and Jack continued to the fifth floor at the top of the building.

"Does that bother you? Everyone knowing who you are?" Iris asked.

"I'm accustomed to it. It's a good reminder. People are always watching. Helps to keep me on my best behavior."

Jack unlocked his door and held it open for Iris to enter.

She took in the austere space. No television sat in the living room. The space contained a black couch and matching club chair, a coffee table empty of magazines. The kitchen was equally bare, not a dish in the sink or an errant dishtowel draped over the oven handle.

The walls were white and empty save a single black-and-white image above the couch depicting the scales of justice. A gas fireplace took up one wall, and a picture window overlooking the river filled another.

"Who's your decorator?" Iris asked.

Jack glanced up from where he hung his coat in the closet, sliding off his shoes and adding those to a shoe rack inside. "You don't like it?"

"It's not that I don't like it. It's very…"

"Practical?"

"Bare," she countered.

"I can't concentrate if things are a mess. I realized the more stuff I got rid of, the clearer I became."

"You must be practically transparent at this point."

He laughed. "Yeah, it's unusual, I know, but it works for me."

Iris thought of her grandmother's house packed with figurines, half-finished board games and craft projects. Iris loved the idea of clean, minimal living, but she'd never been able to master it. She tended more toward Lola's side of the equation. Her room at Lola's was littered with stacks of books, clothes draped over chairs, cocktail glasses and coffee mugs scattered on windowsills and side tables.

Iris's cell phone vibrated. She looked at it and saw Andy calling. She ignored the call and tried not to see him on the other end, perhaps wearing the same wounded look on his face she'd seen the day before when she confronted him about Norlene Weaver.

"Do you need to let Lola know you're here?" Jack asked.

"I texted her on the drive over."

"What's that like for you? Living with your grandmother?"

He took a seat in a dark chair, legs bent and wide, large hands palm-down on his knees. She wanted to undo the rest of the buttons on his shirt, see his bare chest, the ripple of muscles beneath. She wanted to get lost in physical touch and forget about Andy, Norlene Weaver, Brett, Frankie, her mother. She wanted to forget every single thing that existed outside of the moment.

"I don't want to talk about that right now," Iris answered.

She stood and pulled her shirt over her head, reached behind her and unclasped her bra. Jack watched her as she unbuttoned her pants and let them slide to the floor. She walked across the room and pulled him to his feet.

"Let's go to your bedroom," she murmured.

In the morning, Iris woke to Jack moving quietly around his room. He pulled on gray sweatpants, white socks and a long-sleeved black t-shirt.

She picked up her cell phone. It wasn't even five a.m. The world beyond Jack's windows was still dark.

"Where are you going?" she asked.

He leaned down and kissed her. "For my run."

"Do you run every day?"

"Yes. Would you like to join me?"

She yawned and pulled the covers up to her chin. "No, I still have two hours before I have to go to the office, which means I can stay tucked under these covers for another hour. I would, however, love to swing by the Superior Cafe and get a latte and bagel when you get back."

Jack frowned. "I eat two eggs and have a cup of black coffee here every morning, but I'll be happy to accompany you."

She'd allowed her eyes to drift closed, but she opened one to look at him. "Two eggs and black coffee? That's the most depressing breakfast I've ever heard of."

"I try to eat light in the morning, fewer energy fluctuations."

Iris closed her open eye and rolled away from him. "Suit yourself, but the Asiago bagel with garlic herb cream cheese is insanely good."

"I'm sure I'll enjoy watching you eat it," he told her.

She heard the door close behind him.

Iris stayed beneath the covers for another five minutes, but found herself thinking about Norlene Weaver and Brett Stephens. She'd found no immediate connection between them, there was a seven-year age difference, they didn't appear to have known each other, but they'd both disappeared from the same smallish town and they both had a connection to Skelling Hall.

Giving up on any additional sleep, Iris showered and slipped into the clothes she'd worn the previous day. She walked around Jack's apartment.

His bookshelf contained many of the books she'd read in law school, as well as a hefty stack that was currently on her TBR pile: *The New Lawyer's Handbook*, *The Art of Prosecution*, *Crime and Justice*. She leaned closer to inspect a book tucked in with the all the rest: *The Manitous: Supernatural World of the Ojibway* by Basil Johnston.

Iris wiggled the book free and looked at the cover. Black stick figures moved along a snowy hill, shining symbols etched into the ground beneath them.

On the opposite side of the room, Jack's laptop computer, the screen black a moment before, switched on.

Iris slid the book back onto the shelf as a file opened on the screen, as if an invisible hand had clicked it on.

"What the hell?" she murmured.

A recording of Jack's voice filled the room.

December 18

Morning Mind Dump

My father called me yesterday. I didn't answer, nor have I called him back. I know what he wants. This weekend is the anniversary of Dylan's death. He wants to mark the occasion as he does annually with a dinner at the yacht club, a place that Dylan despised in life and would surely abhor as a meeting place to honor the day of his passing. If 'honor' is the word. It's my father reciting a laundry list of Dylan's accomplishments and leaving out the ending, acting as if Dylan was a soldier who died in battle.

In the Monroe case, it appears that George will take the plea deal, which is good. I'm overloaded with work and Miles Fincher has called me twice about final approvals on the Skelling Christmas Party.

Which reminds me, I need to have my tuxedo dry-cleaned.

The recording ended. Iris frowned and walked around the apartment. What had caused it to turn on? Some glitch in the laptop?

That was the rational explanation, the one that made sense, but a different idea materialized in Iris's mind. She thought of Norlene's furious gaze from the night before.

"Norlene?" she asked. She didn't expect an answer and none came.

Iris gazed at the computer screen where she saw a list of audio files. Their labels were brief, dates, times and often a single word that made little sense to Iris. It appeared that Jack kept a sort of audio journal.

She saw one labeled 'Brett' and stepped to the computer, hand hovering above the mouse. She shouldn't listen to any more of his recordings, had no right to breach his privacy, especially as he was an attorney who could have privileged information saved on his laptop, but Brett wasn't his client. He was a kid who'd gone missing at Skelling Hall.

Iris clicked play.

Morning Mind Dump

Ask Miles Fincher for a complete work-up of Brett's employment history with Skelling hall, emphasis on any absences or no-shows.

Contact parole officer Ginger Paulson about Brett's record.

Meet with the foundation regarding Brett's disappearance and how best to handle media coverage.

She scanned the list, saw one from weeks before with her name attached. She clicked it.

Morning Mind Dump

Last night I met a woman who intrigues me. Iris Walsh, with long red-brown hair rolling in waves down her back. She is beautiful, but... not soft. She looked hard, strong. Something about her fascinated me and simultaneously repelled me as if she was dangerous, a beautiful flower with poisonous petals.

I haven't dated anyone since Whitney. I've not even had the urge—not to date, not to sleep with a woman. I've understood lately why my brother Neal no longer dates. He told me when I last saw him that he's celibate. Apparently, this notion came from some Buddhist monk he met during his travels. Few things he does make sense to me, but this... this refraining from goings-on with the opposite sex, that makes sense.

But now there's Iris...

The recording ended.

She scrolled down the page of recordings, glanced over the ambiguous titles—'Bitters,' 'Saturday,' 'Lunch.' She saw Norlene's name and navigated to the file.

It was dated three weeks after the young woman had gone missing.

A sound came from the hallway, footsteps, a key sliding into the lock.

Iris exited out of the file and jammed her finger against the shut-down button on the laptop. She lurched across the room, barreling into the kitchen just as the door swung in.

Jack walked into the apartment, a sheen of sweat glistening on his forehead, his dark hair wet.

"Hey." He smiled and held up a white paper bag and a to-go cup. "I ran by the cafe. Figured you could enjoy your latte and bagel here."

27

Iris arrived at the Fraser Firm, aware she should have gone back to Lola's and changed her clothes. It was unlikely that Marv wouldn't notice she was wearing the same thing as the day before. She hurried down the hall to her office.

"—Dylan Skelling," Marv said as Iris passed his open door.

She turned back and poked her head in the doorway. Candace stood next to his desk, holding a plastic container of donut holes.

"Donut hole?" Candace asked Iris cheerfully. "They're cake. I hate how sticky the others make your fingers."

"No, thanks. Marv, did I just hear you say Dylan Skelling?"

Marv popped a donut hole in his mouth, chewed, and nodded. "Yep."

"Who is he?"

"Who was he, you mean?" Marv cocked an eyebrow. "Jack hasn't mentioned him? Can't say I'm surprised. He's screwed on pretty tight, that one. Dylan was Jack's older brother."

"Jack had an older brother?"

"Yeah, he died fourteen years ago Sunday. The coroner ruled it accidental thanks to some strings pulled by Winston Skelling, but Dylan committed suicide."

Iris gaped at him. "Oh, my God."

"Yeah, it wasn't pretty, and your boyfriend found him. Dylan hanged himself on the Skelling Peninsula out in the woods."

"But... why? I mean, does anyone have any idea why he did it?"

Marv shrugged. "I don't think we ever know why anyone does anything, ourselves included. He was in his third year of law school, had a girlfriend who'd won Miss Michigan. He had that picture-perfect thing all the Skellings have, but later word trickled out that he'd been failing a couple classes in law school.

"Before he came home for that winter break, he'd been acting erratically. Went to class one day in his socks, no shoes, even though it was snowing outside. A teacher later said he'd showed up at his apartment in the middle of the night pounding on his door and demanding an explanation for a grade he'd gotten on an exam. Obviously, he was having a breakdown of some sort, but... he masked it. That whole family does. I've never met a more painted-on family than the Skellings. Everything has to appear perfect all the time at whatever cost."

Candace stood eating donut holes, her eyes glued to Marv. "How terrible," she said, though she hung on every word as if she were listening to a soap opera rather than hearing about a real-life tragedy.

"I feel so bad for Jack," Iris murmured, thinking of Jack's voice recording about the anniversary dinner. She'd told Jack about her own unraveling after Frankie's death. He hadn't so much as mentioned the passing of an older brother.

"You should. I doubt he received much in the way of support after his brother's death. Even worse, he had to fill his brother's shoes. He was the next oldest."

"Which he's done admirably," Candace piped in.

"What about his younger brother?"

"He suffers from the same affliction. Everything's perfect all the time. Though I think Neal's busting out of that. I ran into him at a conference last year."

"He's a lawyer too?"

"Yep. But he'd just booked a trip to Thailand. He was taking three months off to travel and see the world. Trying to break the cycle, I think."

"He's an eyeful," Candace said, smiling dreamily. "Jack's a looker too, but Neal could be a fashion model, he's so handsome."

"Yep, a whole family of Don Juans," Marv quipped. "Candace, can you go print those documents I sent? I need them for court in an hour."

"I sure can. One more donut hole?" She extended the container to Marv. He grabbed three and dropped them on a napkin on his desk.

Iris started to follow Candace from the room.

"Hold up, Walsh," Marv told her.

She turned back. He eyed her curiously for a moment and then offered her a sly smile, but didn't mention her lack of fresh clothes. He held up a large white envelope. "I need you to drive this over to Bonnie Stephens' house. The Skelling Foundation is making an offer so she'll drop the suit."

Iris gaped at him. "Why are they paying the woman off if they're convinced Brett got high and took off?"

Marv ate a donut hole, watching her. "Because that's what people like the Skellings do. It's not about right and wrong. If the media gets hold of this, it will damage the reputation of Skelling Hall and by extension the Skelling family. Two or three years down the road, Jack Skelling will run for district attorney. His father is ensuring a clear path to victory, which means no negative press."

"But they don't even own the hall. It's managed by a foundation."

"Which the Skellings are a huge part of. Not to mention it bears their name."

"Still, paying her off makes them look guilty."

"Walsh, I don't have time for this today. Go present the offer to Bonnie the bloodsucker and stop asking questions."

Iris planted her hands on her hips. "Seriously? That's your response?"

"Aren't you dating Jack Skelling? Can't you pose these questions to him? Please just do your job. I don't have the energy or the interest to talk about this right now."

"Fine." She turned on her heel and stalked from the office.

Bonnie Stephens lived in a derelict little house crammed between equally rundown houses on the east side of town. The faded gray siding had largely fallen off the front of the structure and stuck like crooked teeth from the piles of dirty snow beneath the windows.

Iris knocked on the door.

A woman jerked open the threadbare curtain on the window. She regarded Iris suspiciously and then cracked the door.

"What do you want?"

"I'm an attorney at the Fraser Firm. Are you Bonnie Stephens?"

"Yeah." The woman yanked the door open the rest of the way. Her dark hair was oily and unbrushed. She wore a faded purple velour sweatsuit. Something had once been written in rhinestones on the chest, but most of the stones had fallen away, leaving only the letters 'S' and 'C.'

"May I come in?" Iris asked, ready to get out of the cold, though not enthused about stepping into the woman's house, where she could see piles of animal feces on the kitchen floor.

"Fine, but this better be good." The woman stomped back into the kitchen, sidestepping the poop.

Iris followed her in, grimacing at the rank smell of the house. Three dogs lay on the sofa in the living room—the likely culprits behind the poop. In addition to the smell of dog crap, the house stank of garbage. A trash can overflowed in the kitchen's corner and two additional bags of trash had been heaped beside it.

"I'm sorry about your son," Iris told Bonnie as the woman crossed to a kitchen chair and slumped down.

"I'm sure you are," she sneered.

Iris wanted to ask Bonnie questions, find out what might have happened to Brett, but she sensed the woman had no interest in discussing her missing child.

"The Skelling Estate is offering you five thousand dollars," Iris explained, pulling a document from the envelope. "In exchange, you would drop your accusation against Skelling Hall and you would agree not to speak to any reporters."

Brett's mother regarded Iris through bleary eyes. Crying might have been the cause, but Iris doubted it. More than likely, it was thanks to the nearly empty bottle of tequila sitting on the table.

"Five thousand? That's it?" Bonnie released a harsh laugh, picking up a glass and taking a drink.

"That's what they're offering, yes."

The woman appraised Iris, scanning her and pausing at her boots. "Those look new. You probably spend five thousand dollars on a purse, don't ya? On a pair of new boots or a dinner out. Isn't that how you people do it? 'Guess we can skip dinner tonight and pay off this loud-mouthed bitch.'"

"My boots cost thirty-two dollars. Dinner runs around fifty on a pricey night. If you're unhappy with the offer, say the word and I'll let them know. But understand they might not extend another one."

"Cash? Right here and now?"

"It's a cashier's check. But yes, you'd need to sign the necessary paperwork, and I'd leave the money here and now."

The woman drained her glass and slammed it on the table. She lifted the glass a second time and banged it down, watching Iris as if hoping for a reaction. "Don't ya love that sound? A glass smacking on wood. My dad used to do that. Every time I hear it, I think of him. Whiskey. That's what he liked. Tequila for me, but it was whiskey for him, vodka for my mom. Every night was a party at our house." She stared at the glass for another moment.

Bonnie stood unsteadily and made her way to a line of kitchen drawers. "Let me find a pen."

Iris slid the papers toward her. "There are little stickers where you need to sign," Iris explained.

Bonnie hunched over the kitchen counter, angrily flipping papers and scrawling her signature on the bottom.

The air in the room grew heavier, the stench overpowering. The temperature dropped. Iris's skin crawled. She wanted out of the woman's house.

A young man materialized in the corner. He was little more than a trick of the light, watching his mother through empty black eyes. Brett Stephens had slipped into their midst, confirming what Iris had already suspected: Brett was dead.

Black oozed from his hairline down his pale face as if someone were pouring oil over his head. The boy shuddered, and in his place stood the shadow man. He had no distinguishable face, and yet Iris sensed he watched her.

Iris stumbled back, bumping into the refrigerator.

The shadow thing drifted closer, hovered inches from Iris's face. The kitchen was bathed in a cloud of black. A new smell joined the feces and garbage: putrid, scorched meat. Iris cupped her hands over her nose and mouth, tried not to gag.

"What?" Bonnie snarled, glaring at Iris. "Little bit of dog shit making you queasy?"

The shadow dissolved, and Iris blinked at Bonnie and shook her head. She put a steadying hand on the refrigerator. "I had a dizzy spell," Iris lied.

A single photograph hung slightly askew on the wall where the shadow had appeared. Behind the cracked glass, Iris saw a family portrait, an image of better days.

The woman before her was a decade or so younger with curly dark hair in the photo. Her two boys were only boys. The father in the photo was already showing some wear—a wrinkled shirt, stubble on his chin, a foreshadowing of things to come—but in the photo, in that moment, the mother and sons had no inkling of what the future held.

"Did Brett live here with you?" Iris asked.

Bonnie finished signing and shoved the papers back into the envelope and dropped them into a puddle of coffee on the counter. "Yeah, he did. That's why I've got those damn mutts. Those were his dogs. Frickin' things shit and piss everywhere."

Iris looked at the dogs. They seemed to watch Bonnie with cautious, even frightened eyes.

"Have you considered calling the animal shelter? I'm sure they'd come take them."

Bonnie glared at her. "'Oh, no, not Brett's dogs,'" she mocked. "That's what his dad and brother say. Then *they* need to take care of the damn things. Flea-bitten mongrels."

"You've had no contact at all with Brett since the last night he was seen at Skelling Hall?" Iris took the cashier's check from her purse and handed it to Bonnie.

The woman ripped it out of her fingers. "No. I haven't. And if he turns up, they can't make me give this back, right?" She shook the check.

"Do you think he's going to turn up?"

Bonnie wobbled to the table, picked up her glass and drained it. "No, I don't."

She thumped the glass down and disappeared into the living room. Further in the house, Iris heard a door slam and understood she'd been dismissed.

28

Iris backed out of the driveway. As she drove away, she watched Bonnie Stephens' house shrink in the rearview mirror. Only when it was out of sight did the tension in her shoulders ease.

It wasn't merely the shadow man. It was Bonnie herself—a woman who couldn't care less that her son had vanished. By taking the five grand, she'd ensured her child would get no news coverage at all. And then there were the dogs…

Iris wanted to call Andy. He'd know what to do about the dogs, who to contact, but she couldn't will herself to dial his number. Instead, when she pulled back into the office parking lot, she opened the web browser on her cell phone and searched for Sault Ste Marie Animal Control.

A woman answered.

"Hi, I'd like to report a dog neglect situation."

"Go ahead."

"There's a woman in town whose son has gone missing. He left his dogs at her house and it's clear they're not being cared for."

"What's the address, please?"

Iris gave her Bonnie's address.

"We'll send someone out," the woman told her.

"Thank you."

Iris did not feel guilty about making the call. Having the dogs removed would be a relief for the canines and the woman whose house they occupied. She thought of Brett's three dogs, likely his beloved pets, and a hollow feeling spread in her chest. Willow Weaver had been moving heaven and earth to find out what had happened to Norlene. Brett's mother couldn't be bothered to even look after his dogs.

The rest of the day at the office was long and tedious. Marv asked Iris to search for case law on hiding assets for a divorce he was handling. By the time six o'clock rolled around, Iris had been sitting for so long her butt had grown numb.

Marv paused in the doorway to her office. "I'm out of here, Walsh. Have your dress for the ball yet? Nina said Skelling asked you. You'll be the talk of the town." He grinned.

Iris yawned and stretched her legs beneath her desk. "Don't remind me. I have to go from here to a damn bridal shop. Apparently, that's the only place in this city to get a formal dress."

"Paulette's? She's the best. Better hurry though, she closes early in the winter."

"I'll follow you out," Iris told him, standing with a groan.

They walked through the office together, turning off lights and closing doors. In the parking lot, Iris waved goodbye and climbed into her car. She drove back to the house to pick up Lola, who'd been over-joyed at the prospect of helping Iris pick out a dress for the holiday party.

Iris called her grandmother on the drive. "Hey, Grandma, I'm two minutes away."

"I'll just come to the car," Lola told her. "No need to get out."

Lola walked slowly down the porch steps, holding the rail in her gloved hand. She wore her signature pink down coat over a pair of corduroy pants she'd sewn herself in the sixties and still wore at least once a week. A fuzzy pink hat covered her white hair.

She climbed into the passenger seat and leaned over to kiss Iris on the cheek.

"Isn't this exciting?" she exclaimed. "Here, poppet. I brought you an egg salad sandwich."

"Thanks." Iris took the plastic-wrapped sandwich and opened it.

She'd loved egg salad as a child, hadn't eaten it in years until moving in with Lola. Iris took a bite as she backed out of the driveway.

~

"If it isn't Miss Lola Walsh!" the woman at the counter exclaimed when Iris and Lola walked into the dress shop. "My goodness, woman, you are pretty in pink, aren't you?" She hurried to Lola and hugged her.

"Oh, Paulette, I love your window display," Lola told her, gesturing at the window behind them where a mannequin wore an enormous medieval-looking wedding gown tinted red at the bottom.

The floor had been laid with tufts of fluffy cotton to look like snow. Behind the headless bride stood a dazzling Christmas tree adorned in only red and white bulbs.

"Isn't it to die for?" Paulette agreed. "That dress is dip-dyed, which is all the rage right now with the young brides." She turned her attention to Iris. "Good heavens, with that hair and those eyes"—she put her hands on Iris's shoulders—"you would be a sight to behold in that dress." She spun Iris to face Lola. "Wouldn't she be magnificent?"

Lola smiled and took Iris's hand. "She is magnificent, even in her work suit, but I'm afraid we're not here for a wedding dress. This beauty needs a dress for La Fête de Noël."

Paulette released Iris and swept across the room to a wall of dresses in reds and golds. "These are the season's hottest dresses. The ladies have been swooning over this one in particular." She pulled a princess-style dress with an enormous skirt from the rack and swished it about. It was red, silk or satin, and covered in silver rhinestones.

"I'd like something black," Iris told her.

Lola squeezed her hand and tugged her toward the back of the store where a much smaller rack held black dresses.

"Black?" Paulette asked, following behind them. "But darling, this is a winter ball. Black is hardly going to make you shine."

"Oh, she shines all on her own," Lola said, pushing dresses aside so Iris could get a closer look.

Iris selected a long black dress, simple, with a slit up the side. She pulled it out. "I like this one. A size six, please."

Paulette eyed the dress, brow furrowed. She looked from the dress to Iris and back to the dress. "One-shoulder crepe formal. You won't be able to wear a normal bra with that one-shoulder strap."

"I have a strapless bra."

"Okay then, a woman who knows what she wants. Size six coming right up."

Iris closed herself into a fitting room and tried on the dress. It fit perfectly. She stepped into the larger mirrored room where Lola sat on a velvet-upholstered sofa.

"Oh, poppet! You are breathtaking. Will you humor me and stand on that little platform?"

Iris smiled and pushed her hair over her shoulders. She stepped up onto the platform. Six mirrors reflected her image back to her.

"It's perfect," Lola murmured.

As Iris gazed at her reflection, considering what shoes she could pair with the dress, the black shadow suddenly loomed behind her, darting so quickly from one frame to the next, she nearly fell off the podium trying to get a glimpse of it. She spun in a complete circle, but only her reflection looked back at her.

"Grandma…" She started to ask if Lola had seen it, but when she turned, she saw Lola had gone ashen and she held a hand to her chest as if short of breath.

Iris jumped from the platform and knelt in front of her. "Grandma, are you okay?"

Lola swallowed and lifted a shaky hand to her pink hat. She pulled it off and clutched it in her bony fingers as if it brought some kind of comfort.

"Poppet…" She shifted her pale eyes to Iris.

"You saw it, Grandma?"

Lola nodded, reached a hand up to calm the wispy white hairs sticking from her head. "Yes."

"Do you know what it was? Have you ever seen anything like it before?"

Lola frowned and her face went hard, as if she were searching for the memory of something. "I think I may have, but—"

"And how is the dress?" Paulette asked, striding into the mirrored room.

Iris stood up and Paulette gaped at her. "Mamma mia! Black is definitely your color. I don't think I've ever said that before." She laughed. "Shall we get it wrapped up?"

"Yeah. I'll take it. Thank you."

"I'm paying for it," Lola chirped, returning to her usual cheery disposition, though her face remained pale as she stood.

"Grandma, you don't need to do that."

Lola brushed a finger over Iris's cheek. "Let me spoil you, poppet. I didn't get to nearly enough."

Lola followed Paulette from the fitting rooms. Iris shrugged out of the dress and pulled her work clothes back on. As she slipped back through the mirrored room, she paused, focusing on each pane of glass, searching for the shadow man.

He was gone.

29

Iris and her grandmother had not spoken of the dark shadow in the mirror the night before. Lola had attempted to bring it up, but Iris had wanted to disappear into work when they'd arrived home from the bridal store.

The following day, Lola had not broached the subject and Iris simply didn't want to think about it.

"What time is Andy picking you up tonight?" Lola asked Iris.

They stood side by side in the kitchen kneading bread dough for sweet rolls that Lola was making for a Christmas gathering with her girlfriends.

Iris wiped her floury hands on a dish towel. "I'm going to the party with Jack Skelling."

Lola paused and looked at her sidelong. "You're not going out with Andy anymore?"

"I never was—not exclusively, anyway. We went out a few times and…" Iris shrugged. "Then we stopped."

"And now you're seeing Jack Skelling?"

"Sort of."

Lola was silent for several minutes and then she spoke again. "Why Jack rather than Andy?"

No one before Lola had questioned why Iris seemed to be choosing Jack Skelling. For everyone else, it was clear. He was the chief assistant prosecutor, attractive, professional, the guy any parent hoped their daughter would bring home.

Iris shook her hands. The dough stuck to her fingers more than to the floury countertop. "Because he's… he's more my type."

"You mean he's more like you? Or he seems that way anyhow, but many people choose partners who are very unlike them. It keeps life interesting. Your grandpa hated socializing. I dragged him out once a month, but goodness, he preferred to be out in a boat with a fishing pole or hiking through the woods looking for mushrooms. The modern world was too fast, too busy, too bright. But there was symmetry in our marriage.

"We brought each other closer to balance. By compromising and doing what the other wanted, we learned more about ourselves. As a young woman, if you'd have told me someday I'd look forward every year to sitting in a deer blind until my tush was numb, I would have laughed you out of town. But you know what? I did love it. It's one of the things I miss the most."

Iris attempted again to form the dough into little balls, but it clumped and stuck to her fingers. "Argh," she muttered, throwing up her hands. "This is useless. I can't make it do what you've gotten written here, Grandma. I told you I'm terrible in the kitchen."

"Nonsense." Lola stepped close to Iris and took her granddaughter's hands. She guided Iris's fingers back to the dough and nudged Iris with her hip. "For starters, you need to relax, poppet. You're kneading dough, not doing brain surgery."

Lola, steering Iris's hands, rolled the dough into the flour and then created a perfect little ball. "Now you try," Lola told her.

Iris repeated what Lola had done, adding more flour to the dough before rolling it between her palms. "Huh, look at that," she murmured, surprised to see the dough form into a non-sticky sphere.

Lola kissed her cheek and returned to the sink, rinsing the flour from her hands. "All I'm saying is that Andy offers more in the way of adventure. With Jack, I think your life will be very predictable."

"I like predictable."

"I know you do, honey. But it's not real. Life won't let it be that way, even if you try to make it so. That path only ends in heartache."

"Is there any path that doesn't end in heartache?"

Lola smiled. "My wise girl. You used to say stuff like that even at eight years old." Lola dried her hands on a dishtowel covered in pink snowmen. "When you feel alive, when each day is new, heartache still comes, but it doesn't come because our plans got mussed up. That's what I'm saying about routine, sameness. Grieving a real tragedy is part of life. Grieving a disruption to your plans is a tragedy in itself."

Iris opened the oven and slid the pastries inside to rise. "Work is what I have time for right now. Not adventure or excitement or drama."

Again, Lola was silent. She loaded bowls into the sink and rinsed them and wiped the flour from the counter, but Iris could see her thinking as she moved around the kitchen. Iris took the rinsed dishes and loaded them in the dishwasher.

"I know why you really prefer Jack," Lola said.

"Why is that?" Iris asked, shoving spatulas and spoons into the silverware rack.

"Because he's emotionally unavailable. At least that's what Dr. Phil calls it.""

Iris smirked. "Is that so?"

"Yes, it is."

"And how do you know he's emotionally unavailable?"

"Because I've seen the man, poppet. Even exchanged a few words with him here and there over the years. He's an island. One of those men who is just lovely to look at and he does everything right, but… well, he's missing that thing, that bit of wiring that makes him whole."

"Is he an island or a robot?" Iris asked, adding detergent to the dishwasher and closing the door.

"Oh, pish-posh. You know what I mean. He's done really good things, Jack Skelling. He's a good man, but he's never going to make a good husband."

Iris snorted. "Fortunately for me, I'm not looking for one of those."

"Maybe not, but we all need somebody to love, to put our cold feet on when the snow flies, to keep an eye on us when we spike a fever, to hold us when something goes wrong—and it always will. You can be certain there will be pain in your future and there will be joy. The pain is cushioned when we're loved and the joy is made bigger."

"Maybe I'm choosing Jack because I want to avoid the pain. A healthy bit of detachment is what most relationships need."

"Who says it's detachment that makes him the way he is?" Lola demanded. "There's no telling what lies in the heart of another. We can't tell by what they say, often not even what they do. Time is perhaps the only true revealer, but that demands the heart to stay a single course, which it rarely does. You can't know, poppet. You can't ever know for sure. You have to close your eyes and jump."

Iris rubbed her eyes. "Grandma, I really have to get some work done and then I have to shower so I don't stink at this damn Fête de Whatever."

"Okay, okay. I'll get down from my soapbox and make us some lunch. I thought I'd reheat last night's lasagna. Warm up some bread?"

"Why don't you relax? I'd be fine eating some crackers and cheese."

"God did not put me on this earth to relax. Anyway, I like to cook for you. I haven't had anyone to cook for in too long." Lola started toward the refrigerator and paused. She put a hand to her head.

"What is it, Grandma? Are you feeling sick?"

"Hmm... no, just a tad dizzy."

Iris walked to Lola. "Come on, let's go to the living room and you can sit down. I'll heat the lasagna and you can watch those lunatics across the street hanging more Christmas lights."

Lola smiled. "I do love all those lights. I hope they put out their nativity scene this year. Last year someone stole their donkey, but it's beautiful just the same."

30

"Can you zip me up, Grandma?" Iris asked Lola, feeling out of sorts in the figure-hugging dress and Lola's sparkly diamond earrings.

She hadn't been this dressed up since senior prom and that night too the gown had felt unnatural on her body, the makeup too thick, her hair like an immovable mass on her head, secured with so many bobby pins and so much hair spray she could have walked through a hurricane and found it intact on the other side.

Tonight, she'd not bothered with a fancy updo, but left her long hair sweeping down her back. She'd also gone light on the makeup and rather than perfume spritzed herself with the lavender rose water Lola kept in glass bottles in the bathrooms.

"My Lord, you look like an actress about to walk down the red carpet. The men will be falling over themselves to open your door," Lola announced.

Iris smiled. "If I don't trip them first, that is."

Lola laughed and pulled the zipper up. "Goodness me, you're a spitfire. They're not so bad, you know? If you let one of 'em get close enough to know you."

"I have. Don't remind me."

Lola sighed and ran her fingers through Iris's hair. "It's better to have loved and lost than to have never loved at all, as the saying goes. I had three great loves in my life. Did pain follow each and every one of them? It surely did. Would I take any of it back? Not for a million dollars."

"You're more forgiving than me."

Lola caught Iris's gaze in the mirror. "That might be true, but poppet, this life is long and also over like that." She snapped her fingers. "Don't waste it being strong. Be soft, let somebody love you. That chip on your shoulder is only going to get heavier. By the time you're my age, you'll be bent right in half from the weight of carrying it."

Iris sighed and turned, kissing her grandmother's cheek. "This looks okay? I don't have a pair of underwear sticking to the back of my dress?"

"You're so beautiful it hurts. And perfect, not a hair out of place. Your mother would have loved to see you tonight."

Iris faced the mirror, pushing her thick hair over her shoulder. "Do you think so?"

"I know so. You and Frankie were everything to her."

Iris adjusted the thick strap on the dress, a memory of her mother's last evening dropping like a dark curtain over her mood.

She'd been pestering her mother that day, wanting to talk about Frankie. Iris had just celebrated her own thirteenth birthday, the same age Frankie had been when he'd passed, and he'd been on her mind.

Her mother had gotten flustered. "Please, Iris! I can*not* do this tonight." Those had been her mother's last words before she'd put on her coat and walked out the door.

It was odd what the memory marked as significant, gave its own little page in the story of someone's life. So much was abridged, there was no going back to retrieve it, but that memory, that one conversation that should never have mattered—that should have disappeared into the pit of forgotten things—remained embedded in Iris's mind as if she'd torn it from the book and hung it on her wall.

She'd wondered a thousand times what might have happened if she'd not insisted on talking about Frankie that day. If she'd not been peppering her mother with questions, would her mother be watching Iris now get dressed up for a fancy party with a handsome man?

No, the simple answer was no. Because every moment between then and now would have been different.

Iris tugged off the silver bracelet that had once belonged to her mother and handed it back to Lola. "This feels too dressy."

Lola pursed her lips and picked a piece of lint off Iris's dress. "It is a formal party."

"I'm formal enough with the dress."

I ris walked from the house before Jack made it to the front steps.

"I intended to knock," he told her.

"I saved you the effort."

From the picture window Lola, her white hair wild and her pink nightgown glowing in the light from the Christmas tree, waved happily.

"Hi," he mouthed, waving back. He turned to Iris. "You're stunning."

She smiled and scanned him slowly, admiring the fit of his tuxedo. "You're not so bad yourself, Prosecutor Skelling. What will people say about the prosecutor taking a defense attorney to the Skelling Christmas Party?"

"Let them talk." He took Iris's arm and steered her toward the car, opened the passenger door so she could settle inside.

I ris was rarely given to sentimental moods, but when she stepped into the ballroom at Skelling Hall, it took her breath away.

White and red twinkle lights ran along shimmering gold curtains that hung from the ceiling. The Christmas tree was lit in red and white with an enormous sparkling star on the top. The tables were draped in gold linen with red velvet runners down each center. Red candles glowed from gold candelabras in the center of the tables. A fire burned in the enormous brick hearth.

A band played on a stage in the back corner of the room. A woman with a haunting, ethereal voice sang the French version of *Silent Night*.

"My God," Iris murmured.

Jack touched her elbow. "It is something, isn't it?"

Tears prickled behind her eyes and she struggled to quash the sudden and unwelcome wave of emotion rising to a crescendo. She was not this kind of woman and she sure as hell would not burst into tears over a few Christmas decorations in a ballroom full of her peers. She took a deep breath and tried to shift her focus to something neutral—push pins, legal briefs, dull pencils.

"If it isn't Cinderella!"

Iris looked up to see Marv, an attractive blonde in a sparkly blue dress on his arm.

Iris smiled. "Hey, Marv." Her voice cracked a bit on his name and he took both her shoulders in his hands, studying her.

"What in heavens is this? Iris, are you having a moment?"

She scowled and pushed his hands away. "No, thank you, I'm not."

Jack looked at her sidelong, then snaked a hand around her waist and squeezed.

"Don't torture her, Marvin," Jack told him. "I think she only agreed to come with me because I took her by surprise."

Marv grinned. "Wanted to stay home in matching bunny slippers with Grandma Lola?"

Iris rolled her eyes and shifted her attention to Marvin's date. "Hi, I'm Iris Walsh. This is Jack Skelling."

The woman smiled, but more at Jack than Iris. "I know who you are," she told him. "I saw your picture in the paper."

"An unfortunate side effect of my profession," he told her.

"I'm Carrie Henderson." She offered Jack her hand.

Iris looked at Marvin, who waggled his eyebrows and shrugged.

"Come on, Carrie," he told her, "it's time to find the booze. Save a dance for me, Cinderella," he called to Iris over his shoulder as he maneuvered Carrie across the room.

"He's a character," Jack said, though Iris heard an edge in his voice.

"Yeah, I like him."

"Shall we find some seats?"

"Sure."

Iris allowed Jack to take her hand and pull across the room. She continued to gaze at the glittering lights, her chest constricted.

They'd barely sat down when a man Iris didn't know swooped in and took hold of Jack.

"Jack, I need you to meet the Grangers. They're considering a donation to the Skelling Foundation and they've seen you in the paper."

Jack stood and offered his hand to Iris. "Care to join us?"

She shook her head. "I think I'll grab a drink."

"I'll be quick." He leaned down and kissed her cheek.

Iris watched Jack disappear into the throng of people. She wove her way to the bar and considered the menu of options, which included beer, champagne, wine and a cocktail called the Skelling Santa Claus.

"What can I get ya?" the woman working the bar asked.

"I'll try the signature cocktail—the Skelling Santa Claus," Iris said.

"It's divine," the bartender told her. "But watch out, these babies pack a punch."

"Just so long as it doesn't knock me out," Iris told her, taking the plastic glass garnished with sugar-coated cranberries and a sprig of rosemary.

As Iris turned from the bar, she spotted Andy on the opposite side of the room. He was sideways to her, standing next to a petite woman with long, silky black hair flowing down her back. He was smiling and laughing, but as if he sensed her watching, he turned and their eyes met.

Iris swallowed the lump in her throat and lifted her cocktail. He smiled, offered a brief nod and held up his own glass before returning to the conversation.

"My grandmother used to sing this to us," Jack said as he and Iris danced.

She tilted her head, listening. "What song is it?"

"*Petit Papa Noël.*"

"Which means?"

He spun her around and pulled her back against him. "It's about a child asking Santa Claus not to forget him at Christmas, or something like that. My French is rather rusty."

"Mine is nonexistent, so I'll take your word for it."

After the song ended, Iris excused herself to use the restroom. Jack was quickly lured away by a group of men debating a murder case that was soon going to trial in California.

As Iris made her way to the bathroom, children's laughter echoed from the second floor. She looked at the curving grand staircase. Two boys ran down the stairs. They wore knickers and little brown vests. The taller of the two, who chased the younger, wore a tweed newsboy-style hat. Their clothes were antique-looking, the fashion of another century.

Iris watched Andre and Phillippe Skelling reach the marble floor, race toward the front door, and disappear long before they reached it. For several seconds, she stood frozen, hands gripping the little black purse Lola had loaned to her.

"Iris…"

The voice startled her, and she took a faltering step away.

She turned to find Andy behind her.

He frowned. "Are you okay?"

Iris loosened her grip on the purse. "Yes. I'm fine." She started away from him, but he caught her elbow.

"I know you're pissed. I was wrong not to tell you about Norlene and I'm sorry. I'm not going to stand here and make excuses, but Iris…" His eyes were troubled, pleading. "There's something between us. I found you stranded on that dark road and…" He blinked, looked at the ceiling as if he were fighting back tears. "It felt like fate and I wanted to play this cool tonight and act like I don't care that we're not together, but I can't. I don't want to pretend I don't miss you, and that I'm not thinking about you."

For the second time that night, Iris felt the rush of emotion, the sudden tears trying to claw their way up. "Andy, I'm here with Jack."

Andy sighed. "Yeah, I noticed. I get it, but he doesn't have anything to do with us."

Her throat grew thick, her eyes full to bursting. She blinked the tears away. "There is no us. We had a fling. It's over." She tinged the words with dismissal, thought back to the discovery that he'd lied about Norlene and held onto that seed of fury because she didn't need and didn't want what Andy Bale was offering up. And yet her chest grew narrow around her heart and lungs, squeezing, as with the tightening of the hangman's noose.

Iris looked beyond him to where his date stepped out of the ball-room, eyes roving until they landed on Iris and Andy.

Iris nodded toward her. "Better go see about your date."

Iris turned and hurried to the bathroom, shutting herself in a stall. She pulled her dress up and sat, knees quaking. She pressed the heels of her hands into her eyes.

"You're fine… you're fine…" she murmured.

Andy's words tried to squirm in, rupture the walls she'd built around her heart.

"No," she muttered, squeezing her knees together.

He had lied about Norlene and she still didn't know what that meant. She was at a party with Jack Skelling. She had everything she wanted in Jack.

Andy was just a guy she'd slept with, and now she had Jack.

185

31

When Iris returned to the ballroom, Marv intercepted her.

"I hope that wasn't a lover's quarrel I just witnessed in the foyer. I never have found the ménage à trois to work out."

Iris took his drink and finished it.

Marv laughed. "Okay, then. Why don't I get us two more?" A man with a tray of cocktails walked by. "Ask and ye shall receive." Marv grabbed two from the tray and handed one to Iris.

She took a sip and watched Jack smiling and laughing in a group of men near the fireplace.

"Looks like your date is imbibing tonight as well."

"Or he might be drinking soda water."

"Oh." Marv nodded. "True enough, but don't let the golden boy fool you. I've seen him get lit a time or two."

"Really?"

"Sure. What young guy living the dream doesn't tie one on now and then? More then than now, in his case."

"Huh..." Iris hadn't once witnessed Jack drink heavily. Even at the restaurant he'd barely finished his glass of red wine. "After winning a big case? Is that when he'd let loose?"

"Nah, and that's his problem. He doesn't raise one high to celebrate. He drank to drown his sorrows when the cards were stacked against him—oldest tell in the book. But nowadays he doesn't drink whether he's winning or losing."

"When was the last time you saw him let loose?"

Marv adjusted his bow tie in the mirror just over Iris's shoulder. He winked at himself. "Look at those pearly whites. My dental hygienist is a miracle worker, Iris. You should go see her."

"The last time you remember Jack drunk, remember what we were talking about?"

He dragged his eyes from the mirror and back to Iris. "Trying to figure out how to get your new prince a little tipsy? Let's see, the last time I saw him metaphorically crying into his beer was the end of last summer. He lost a case against a guy who'd been abusing his disabled mother. The guy had money, hired a big out-of-town lawyer. I sat in on a few days in court. Skelling painted a pretty disturbing picture of this guy and then worked tirelessly to find witnesses to back it up. He did a helluva job and Skelling should have won it."

"What happened?"

"The guy's attorney cast reasonable doubt. He paraded his own line of witnesses who said the guy was a stand-up son, had dedicated his life to care for the mother. He also threw in some witnesses to do character assassination on the mother—paint her as a grouchy old battleax. He did a helluva job too, and he won."

"What a scoundrel," Iris murmured.

Marv grinned. "Watch your tongue, Walsh. In our line of work, those guys are our bread and butter."

"Don't turn me off of my drink, Marv. I wish I could have seen him trying that case."

Across the room a silver-haired man patted Jack on the back and shook his hand as if congratulating him on something.

"Stick around with him long enough and you'll see more," Marv said. "I like to give him a hard time, pretty boy and all, but he's good at what he does. It's hard to fault someone for that, even if they are the competition."

"Who is that?" Iris murmured, watching a tiny bent woman break away from the group near Jack. She wore a glittering red ball gown and her face was so heavy with makeup she looked wilted.

"That's Beatrice Skelling. The daughter of Felix and Angelique. Your date's great-grandmother."

"You're kidding. She's still alive?"

"As alive as you can be at that age."

"How old is she?"

"In her nineties, at least. She's eccentric, but she's a staple of sorts. This is the only night you'll see her all year. She lives out in the woods with one of her daughters-in-law."

Iris shifted her gaze from Beatrice to Jack, who caught her eye and waved her over.

"Duty calls," she told Marv, breaking away and joining Jack at the fireplace.

"Iris, these are my parents. Winston and Elise."

Iris offered her hand to Winston. Jack favored his father, the same dark hair and eyes, tall, broad, the type of man who looked the part of a wealthy, powerful patriarch. Winston's wife was equally put together. She wore a shimmering juniper green dress and her golden-blonde hair was perfectly arranged in a French twist.

"It's a pleasure to meet you, Iris," Winston told her. "I was amused to hear my son was seeing a defense attorney. He's a lover of irony."

Iris smiled. "You know what they say, keep your friends close and your enemies closer."

Winston laughed. "Funny too. Good work, son."

Jack smiled at his father, but the expression appeared forced. There was a stiffness in Jack with his parents nearby.

Iris shook Elise's hand, but the woman barely looked at her.

"I see the Brownings have just walked in. I must say hi. Excuse me, dear." She air-kissed Iris and slipped away.

Winston gazed around the room, a vague look of disapproval on his face. "I'd hoped Neal would attend the gathering, not to mention our dinner tomorrow."

"Last I heard, he was in Thailand," Jack told him.

"Must be nice ignoring his responsibilities and jet-setting around the globe. At least one of my sons understands personal duty."

Jack said nothing. He moved closer to Iris. "May I?" he asked, gesturing at her cocktail.

She handed it to him and he took a long drink.

His father cast a disapproving look at the cup in Jack's hand.

"How did you end up at the Fraser Firm, Iris?" Winston asked.

"My grandmother pulled some strings. She knows Don Fraser."

"I see, and who is your grandmother?"

"Lola Walsh."

Winston's eyes darted to Jack and then back to Iris. "I think I'll join my wife," Winston said. "Iris, Jack." He nodded at them both and then strode across the room.

"Did I say something wrong?" Iris asked, surprised by Winston's abrupt departure.

Jack drained Iris's glass and set it on the table. He adjusted his bow tie as if it had grown tight around his neck. "No. They can be brusque. I think I'll have a drink of my own."

She raised an eyebrow. "You're living on the edge this evening, aren't you?"

Jack grinned and shook his head. "Shall I get two?"

"That'd be great."

I ris spotted Beatrice Skelling alone near a table.

Iris wove through the crowd to where the woman stood looking at her drink as if in confusion. The champagne glass was nearly empty.

"Would you like me to get you another?" Iris asked her, gesturing at the flute.

Beatrice looked up at Iris, blinking behind her huge fake eyelashes, so large on the woman's frail eyelids they looked like tarantulas. A gaudy gold and ruby necklace rested on her bony chest.

"That would be lovely," she said, her voice little more than a whisper. She swayed a bit on her feet.

Iris took her elbow, steadying her. "Why don't you sit down," Iris suggested. "How about water instead?"

The woman frowned as if unsure and then nodded. "Okay."

Iris leaned across the table and grabbed one of the full goblets of water. She put it into the woman's feeble hands.

"I'm Iris Walsh," Iris told her.

The woman nodded and sipped her water, saying nothing.

"I heard you're a Skelling," Iris went on.

Beatrice didn't immediately respond. She stared at Iris for a long moment, as if trying to place her.

"I am a Skelling," Beatrice murmured, her eyes drifting away from Iris. "My father built this place over a century ago. Not with his own two hands, though he did some of the heavy lifting. He told us stories, my brothers and I, about the bricks coming in on freighters. The natives told him not to build the house. Cursed land, they said. He didn't listen." Beatrice reached for her hair and felt around. After a moment, she pulled out a single gold bobby pin adorned with three pink pearls. She held it in her withered palm. "This was my mother's. Angelique. She died from heartbreak."

Beatrice leaned over and pulled up her dress. Iris saw beneath her tulle skirt the woman wore white orthopedic tennis shoes. She sat back up and held out a watch that she'd worn like an anklet.

"This was my father's, Felix. It doesn't work. He went insane." She turned her milky eyes on Iris and then reached for a gold sequined purse on the table. She dug around and came out with two misshapen stones in the shape of arrows. "Arrowheads." She laid them on the white tablecloth. Her hand trembled as she brushed her fingers over them. "These belonged to the boys, Andre and Phillippe. I bring these things out once a year for La Fête de Noël so my family can be here with me."

Iris nodded, considering the items spread out on the table. They looked like a child's haul after they'd spent the day on a beach with a metal detector.

"Did you say the natives told your father this land was cursed?"

Beatrice tried to get hold of the bobby pin, but could not seem to close her arthritic fingers around it.

"Here, let me," Iris said. She picked up the pin and slid it back into Beatrice's stiff hair.

"Cursed…" Beatrice echoed back to her. "The maji-manidoo, they said. An evil spirit lived on the peninsula. They'd stopped hunting here years before. It was too dangerous."

"An evil spirit?"

The woman fumbled the arrowheads back into her purse. She looked at the watch that had been secured to her ankle, likely because it would have fallen off of her slender wrist. Iris wondered how she'd gotten it there. She doubted the woman had done it herself.

"Mother?" An older woman—in her seventies, Iris thought—paused behind Beatrice and put her hand on her shoulder.

Beatrice turned and looked at her and then patted the woman's hand. "My daughter-in-law," she told Iris. "Florence, I am ready to go home."

"I can imagine you are," Florence said, casting an amused glance at Beatrice's empty champagne flute. Florence turned to Iris. "Thank you for keeping her company."

"Happy to," Iris told her.

Florence helped Beatrice to her feet and looped her arm through Beatrice's.

"I wonder…" Iris asked before they'd turned away. "Could I visit Beatrice sometime? I'm very curious about her life here at Skelling Hall."

Florence considered Iris for a moment. "She rarely has visitors. You'd be welcome. You're here with Jack?"

"Yes."

"He knows how to contact us. Enjoy your evening."

They started across the room, but Beatrice pulled away from her daughter-in-law and returned to Iris. She took Iris's hands in her own, much softer, frailer ones.

"Tomorrow, dear. Come see me tomorrow."

Florence approached Beatrice. "She may not be available tomorrow, Mom," Florence said gently.

"I am. Or I can be," Iris said.

"Okay, then it's settled. Let me give our address."

Iris took out her cell phone and plugged the address into her notes.

She watched Florence and Beatrice make their way across the room and into the great hall.

～

"Breath of fresh air?" Jack whispered in Iris's ear. Iris had gotten drawn into a conversation with a group of women who were debating a school millage that was coming up. One woman was so against the tax she was nearly crying.

"Yes, please," she murmured. "Excuse me, ladies," she told the group, broke away with Jack and hurried out of the ballroom. "Good grief, there should be a three-drink minimum for that conversation."

Jack smiled, pushing through the large door. "You looked like you needed a rescue."

It was cold outside the hall, but surprisingly still. No wind blew off the river. The trees didn't twitch. The pines nearest the hall had been decorated in strings of white lights and they cast a shimmering glow on the snowy ground beneath them.

Outside, Jack led Iris to his car. He lifted the hood on the trunk and pulled out a flannel blanket. "Here, try these." He held up a pair of rubber boots.

"Those do not look like dancing shoes."

"You're right. See if they fit." He sat on his bumper, pulled off his black loafers, and replaced them with winter boots.

Iris sat beside him, the cold biting through her dress. The boots were a size or so too big, but they would work.

"Why do you have women's mud boots in your trunk?"

"They were Whitney's. She left them at my place. I've been meaning to donate them, but haven't gotten around to it."

Iris stood and drew her coat tighter. The night was clear and cold. The air tasted fresh. It burned when she drew in a deep breath.

Jack took her hand and guided her toward the woods.

"Where are we going?" she asked.

"They plowed a path for the sleigh rides today." He looked back at her and smiled. His teeth were the only light in his face. He led her through the woods. She heard the faint sound of running water.

"Is there a stream?"

"Yes. Just keep hold of my hand. We're going to cross a little bridge. Stay right behind me."

She followed him, watching her breath plume out and float into the leafless trees above them.

"A little further," he told her, tugging her along.

They stepped from beneath the trees onto the open shoreline. The cosmos shined above and the ice splintered beneath their feet as they walked on the frozen beach.

"It sounds like breaking glass," she murmured.

"It does," he said. "Look up. Winter stars." He tilted his face skyward. "I've never seen them brighter than right here."

Iris looked at a sky so enormous it was staggering. The stars dazzled against the black backdrop.

"Wow…" She stumbled a bit and Jack gripped her around the waist.

"Here, let's sit."

"On the ice?"

"I brought a blanket." He stretched the blanket out and Iris sat, cringing at the bite of cold through the fabric.

She lay back beside him and stared at the sky. Jack snaked his fingers through hers, brought them to his warm lips.

"I heard about your brother, Dylan." Iris didn't know why she spoke the words. They slipped from her mouth before her mind had fully grasped the impact they might have in the moment.

Jack said nothing and Iris considered shifting tack, changing the subject completely, pretending she hadn't made the comment.

"You've never mentioned him."

"No. I rarely do. He's gone. What more is there to say?"

Iris considered her own brother, Frankie. She'd talked about him the first evening they'd spent together. Frankie's death had so defined her she felt incapable of not sharing it. "I don't know. I told you about my life after Frankie died. I'm surprised you didn't mention Dylan then."

Jack sighed. "I'm very good at compartmentalizing, Iris. I wasn't holding back. I literally didn't think of him during that conversation. It's a skill I learned a long time ago. If I sit with all the terrible things that have happened to me, that have happened to victims, that have happened in the world, I can't be of service. I rarely think about Dylan. That's why I don't talk about him. I still love him, I still have memories of him, but I don't think about him and that's what works best for me."

Iris said nothing. It bothered her he hadn't told her about Dylan, but she didn't want to push him.

"Tomorrow is the anniversary of his death," Jack murmured. "He committed suicide out here on the peninsula."

"I'm sorry."

He gave her hand a squeeze, drew it to his chest, and let it rest there. She could feel the rise and fall of his breath through his coat.

"I found him..." Jack continued. "I found him hanging from a tree that we'd both climbed a thousand times. We came out here a lot when we were young. My father often had business here with the foundation. He'd let us loose, and we'd be all over these woods."

"It's a beautiful place."

He made a sound, a strangled sort of laugh. "There's no place on earth like it."

The silence stretched then. Iris had ceased feeling the cold. Her backside was numb. The sky above seeped further toward unseen horizons as if it were spilled ink crawling across a page. It might have merely been the cold, the struggle of her lungs to expand in the steadily dropping temperature, but Iris felt breathless.

Irisss... The sound, faint, drifted from the darkness.

Iris pulled away from Jack and squinted into the forest behind them.

"Did you hear that?" she asked.

32

—————

He blinked in the direction she stared, quiet. "No. What did you hear?"

She frowned and listened. Someone had called her name, not quite someone, a mingling of the wind and the water and the trees as if something had used nature itself to summon her.

The shadow man.

"Nothing. I don't know."

Jack sat up. His eyebrows pulled together, lips thin. "We should go back to the party," he said suddenly, standing and pulling Iris to her feet.

"We don't have to. I'm sure it was nothing."

He reached down, groped for the blanket and balled it up, tucking it under one arm. "No, we should. The temperature's dropping and… we probably shouldn't have come out here at all."

"Why not?" She followed him, his hand in hers, him guiding them back through a darkness he clearly knew by heart.

"Because it's dark and cold and… easy to get turned around out here."

They returned to his car and put on their party shoes. Jack led Iris to the side of Skelling Hall.

"We'll sneak in the back so we don't get caught talking to that group huddled by the door," Jack told her.

Iris spotted Jack's father in the group of men.

194

At the side of the house, Jack paused at an arched door tucked into the brick exterior. "This is the Skelling door."

"The Skelling door?"

"Yeah. Only our family has keys to this entrance. There are two. I have one and my great-grandmother has the other."

"Why you?"

"My father had it for a long time and then…" Jack shrugged. "He was no longer interested in coming out here once a month to meet with the foundation. I took over."

Iris watched him slide the skeleton key into the iron lock. The door swung in, revealing a dark room much simpler than the rest of the mansion. It had scarred wood floors and built-in shelves from floor to ceiling.

"This was the servants' entrance when my great-great-grandparents built it," Jack told her, locking the door behind him.

"They had servants?"

"Yes. In those days, you'd hardly show your face as a wealthy family without them. Their servants came with them from Quebec when they immigrated to Michigan."

Jack led her from the room into a larger hall and then into another room.

"This used to be the formal dining room. Now it's the boardroom for the foundation," Jack explained.

A long mahogany table ran the length of the room. Though there were no lights on, Iris spotted paperwork stacked in one corner. As they passed it, she glanced down and noticed a name: 'Brett Stephens.' She slowed and tried to read the print upside down.

Jack opened another door and light spilled in.

She had only a moment and no time to distinguish what the document was about, but another name popped out at her: 'Frankie Walsh.'

Iris stopped, eyes narrowing. She started to reach for the page.

"Iris?" Jack said. "Hurry. I don't want to get hell from my dad for coming in the back way."

She dropped her hand. The urge to demand Jack come back in the room, flip on the lights and look at the paper with her died on her lips. He was part of the Skelling Hall Foundation. He was the party who represented the original family.

She followed him and stepped into the great hall with its soaring ceilings and marble floors.

Music drifted from the ball room. People stood in clusters, talking and drinking. As they passed the grand staircase, Iris looked up, watching for the little boys she'd heard earlier that evening, but the hall at the top was quiet and still.

"What's upstairs?" she asked, trying to quell the jumble of emotions that had coursed through her at the sight of her brother's name.

Jack paused, eyes flickering to the stairway. He shuddered and urged her forward. "Rooms, bathrooms, the usual. There's a parlor filled with Felix and Angelique's old stuff—letters, books, photographs. The foundation has talked about hiring someone to sift through it, maybe donate some to the historical society here in Sault Ste Marie, but it's quite an undertaking."

"Why did the foundation pay off Brett Stephens' mother?" she asked, unable to completely ignore the part of her that needed answers.

He turned, as if surprised at the question, but before he could answer, a man grabbed both his shoulders and squeezed.

"Jack Skelling!" the red-faced man boomed. "There you are. I've been trying to get in touch with you. You must have snuck off with this beautiful woman you've brought tonight." The man extended his hand to Iris. "I'm Link Larson—your friendly neighborhood insurance guy. I have that life insurance paperwork all drawn up," Link told Jack. "You've just got to swing by the office and sign it."

Jack nodded, but his smile seemed forced. "Great. I'll put it on my calendar this week."

"You better." He gave Jack an elbow to the side. "You can never have too much insurance when you're a prosecutor." He guffawed.

Iris stared at him. "Do you sell a lot of policies by scaring people into thinking their profession puts them in mortal peril?"

The man grinned. "Well, life insurance only pays if you're dead." He laughed again, but Iris didn't laugh with him.

"Let's hope you're drunk and not just crude," Iris snapped. "Come on, Jack, let's grab a drink." She dragged him away.

Link's smile faded. Apparently, he hadn't realized his humor was in bad taste.

"What an asshole," Iris said, aware that her reaction to Link had less to do with his comment and more to do with her own frustration about the document she'd been unable to read.

Jack chuckled. "I'm sure he'll be pondering this exchange for days to come. You don't hold back, do you?"

"Hmph. I did hold back. If I told him what I really thought, it would have ruined all our nights. I think you should seriously consider getting your life insurance from someone who looks a little less joyful at the prospect of your untimely death."

"Oh, believe me, he'd rather I live a nice long life and pay premiums for ninety-five years and never collect a dime."

Iris stopped at the bar. "Skelling Santa Claus cocktails?" she asked Jack.

He frowned as if his better sense were telling him no, but he nodded. "Yeah, and then let's dance."

Iris woke naked except for one of Jack's t-shirts, head aching from the Skelling cocktails, which indeed packed a punch. Her mouth tasted bitter and felt sticky. She needed to pee. She pushed the blankets off, careful not to disturb Jack, who slept on his stomach beside her, his head turned away.

In the bathroom, Iris peed and grabbed a cup from beside the sink, filling it with water. It was tepid, but she drank two glasses before hazarding a look at her face. Dark smudges from her mascara ballooned beneath her eyes. Her hair hung frizzy and tangled.

As she gazed at her reflection, the glass fogged as if someone were breathing inches away from the surface, but rather than warmth, the temperature in the bathroom dropped. Iris shivered and took a step back from the mirror.

A faint whine disrupted the quiet, as if someone dragged their finger down the glass. The invisible finger formed the letter 'S' on the glass.

"Iris?" Jack spoke behind her.

Iris jumped and spun around.

Jack stood in the doorway, naked except for underwear, eyes half-lidded. Behind him stood Norlene, fuzzy, undulating and then gone.

Iris blinked, rubbed at her chest to encourage the air to flow back into her lungs. "I had to pee," she told him.

He nodded, eyes slipping closed. "Me too. Excuse me."

He slipped around her and into the bathroom. She turned, expecting him to notice the mirror, the letter written there, but the previously milky glass was clear.

33

"Time for my run," Jack told Iris.

She'd been watching him get ready, waiting for him to leave.

"Enjoy the cold," she told him.

Jack kissed her and walked out the door.

Iris climbed from the bed and walked to Jack's tuxedo, which he'd hung on a hanger the night before. She searched for the key to Skelling Hall, but his pockets were empty. She considered the apartment, wondering where Jack would put the key. It hadn't been on his key ring when he'd taken it from his pocket the night before.

Iris opened the double doors that led into Jack's closet. His clothes were neatly hung and arranged by color, mostly black and white.

She glanced toward the door, imagining what she'd say if Jack walked in and found her snooping in his closet. She hurried to the window and peered through the blinds. At the end of the block, Jack rounded a corner and disappeared.

Iris returned to the closet and quickly sifted through his jackets, checking pockets. They were empty. She moved to the table next to his bed, opened the single drawer. It contained reading glasses, a novel about litigation and a small wooden cross. She stared at the cross, finding it odd, much as she'd been surprised by the tiny gold cross he wore around his neck. She closed the drawer and continued searching, moving into the main apartment, checking the table, his bookshelf, windowsills, all the places someone might set a key.

198

No luck.

After twenty minutes, she gave up and got in the shower, washing away the previous night's alcohol-fueled sweat. As she dressed, Jack returned.

"I'll take a quick shower too and then run you home," he told her. "I have to attend the anniversary dinner for Dylan at my parents' this afternoon."

"That'd be great. Thanks."

I ris climbed into Jack's car. As she buckled her seat belt, she spotted the key to Skelling Hall in the cup holder.

Jack laid Iris's dress, which he'd placed inside a dry-cleaning bag, into the backseat. He started the car and pulled onto the road.

"How are you feeling about the dinner?" Iris asked, resting her hand next to the holder.

Jack stared straight ahead. "Fine."

Iris closed her fingers around the key, but left her hand in place for another moment, waiting until Jack turned his head to quickly slide the key into her coat pocket. "Don't want to talk about it?" she asked.

His jaw tightened. "Not really, no. I had too much to drink last night. An afternoon at my parents' is not appealing."

"I was wondering about Skelling Hall. Wednesdays and Saturdays are tour days. Is there anyone in the hall the rest of the week? Is Miles Fincher there every day?"

Jack shook his head, flicking on his blinker and turning. "No. He has Sundays and Mondays off. Tuesday, he makes sure everything is set for Wednesday's tour. Friday is usually a paperwork day for him."

"Is that his only job?"

"Yes. He's mostly retired, but he's been overseeing Skelling Hall for a long time."

"No one is there on Sundays and Mondays? What about clean-up for last night's party?"

"There will be a crew in there today cleaning. They'll wrap up by sundown, so five-ish, and then the place will be ready to open again Wednesday."

"Why sundown?"

"The foundation has certain rules put into place by Felix Skelling.

One of the rules, with the exception of La Fête de Noël, was no one at the house after dark."

"That's a strange rule."

"From what I've gathered, he was a strange man."

"But Brett Stephens was there after dark. That's when he disappeared."

Jack frowned, but didn't look at her. "He shouldn't have been."

"Why did the Skelling Foundation pay off his mother?"

Jack sighed. "They didn't pay her off. They settled. Their reasoning was two-part. One, they wanted to compensate her for her distress over these last weeks. Two, they didn't want her to continue talking badly about the foundation."

"You're part of the foundation, aren't you?"

"Yes." He looked at her sidelong. "Why do you ask?"

Iris fingered the key in her pocket. "No particular reason—just curious."

Jack pulled into Lola's driveway. "Thanks for accompanying me last night. I really enjoyed it," Jack told her.

"Me too." She leaned across the seat and kissed him goodbye, grabbed her dress from the backseat and jumped from his car.

~

I ris found her grandmother in the kitchen.

Lola turned and smiled. "How was the party, poppet?"

"It was interesting. Lots of dancing, too many cocktails. The decorations were amazing. You would have loved them."

"I've seen them. They do go all-out, don't they?"

"You've been to La Fête de Noël?"

"Oh, yes, many years ago. It was a lovely time."

"You and Grandpa?"

"Mmm-hmmm."

"Why did you stop going?"

Lola frowned. "I guess we stopped going after Frankie passed. We had some hard feelings with the Skellings, as I mentioned. But let's not talk of such sad things the morning after your fun night. I'm making cinnamon French toast. I thought you'd be hungry after all that dancing." She cleared her throat and then held her elbow up to her mouth, coughing into the crook of her arm.

Iris took a second look at her grandmother, noticed the dark circles beneath her eyes. Had she lost weight? Her already thin body appeared saggy suddenly, as if someone had merely thrown some skin over a skeleton.

How long had Lola looked this way? Looked her age? Like an eighty-eight-year-old woman? A little grimace crossed Lola's face as if she were in pain.

"Here, let me, Grandma. I'll finish the French toast. You sit down."

"Oh, you don't have to do that, poppet," Lola said, casting a worried glance towards the chair Iris usually sat in. "You like to have your coffee and look over your work in the morning."

Work. That was why Iris hadn't noticed Lola's growing exhaustion. She'd been too busy obsessing over work, missing people she'd never met, and Skelling Hall to pay any real attention to her grandmother.

"It's Sunday—no work for me," Iris insisted. "Sit down, okay? Let me make you breakfast for a change."

Lola sighed and sat down. She patted the flyaway hairs from her face. "I am a tad sleepy this morning. Kept tossin' and turnin' last night. I guess I was a little scared about you at Skelling Hall. I kept thinking… oh, never mind."

"What? What did you keep thinking?"

"That something bad might happen, that bad things happen there. Of course, nothing bad has happened there in nearly a hundred years, not since the Skelling boys vanished, but… this old brain gets funny thoughts sometimes."

"Why not go sit in the living room, hmm? Put your feet up."

Lola smiled and stood, swayed, again that flicker of pain in her expression. "You watch out, poppet. I might get used to you spoiling me."

She hobbled from the room. Iris turned back to the bowl of eggs and milk and cinnamon. She dropped a piece of French bread into the batter and then flopped it into the frying pan where it sizzled.

Iris finished the French toast, burned only two of the four slices, added butter and syrup and carried plates for her and Lola into the living room.

Lola had closed her eyes, but she opened them when Iris paused beside her.

"Breakfast is served. I put a few sliced bananas on there too. I know you like those."

"Aww, what would I do without you, poppet?"

Iris sat on the couch, balanced her plate on her knees and cut a piece of French toast. She'd taken the burnt pieces herself, and scraped a bit of black off one slice before popping it in her mouth. "How have you been feeling, Grandma? Okay?"

Lola chewed and smiled at her. "I am positively overflowing. Spilling over with gratitude that you're here with me."

"When's the last time you visited your doctor?"

Lola took another bite and tilted her head, thoughtful. "Last spring, if memory serves. I have my annual visit in April."

"Maybe you should go early, do a check-up."

Lola shook her head. "No need. What ails me isn't in the hands of a doctor. It's old age and if we're lucky, we all catch it."

Iris frowned. "Still, you have a cough."

"Which is why I'll have some tea with honey and cinnamon after breakfast and then take a midday nap."

~

After Lola was settled in her room upstairs, Iris grabbed the car keys and left the house.

She punched Beatrice Skelling's address into her GPS and followed the directions out of town, past the Skelling Peninsula to a tree-lined dirt road. The road dead-ended in a long, paved driveway.

Beatrice Skelling lived in an impressive brick home with a two-car garage. The woods had been cut away, leaving a large expanse of property surrounding the house.

Iris parked in the driveway and took the cement walkway to the front door. She rang the doorbell and waited.

The door opened and Florence, who'd traded jeans and a sweater for her charcoal suit from the night before, smiled out at her.

"Hello again," Florence greeted her, opening the door further. "Come in. Mother's in the sun room."

Iris followed Florence through the roomy house, which was decorated in warm tones. The floor was cherry-colored and covered in beige and cream rugs. Oil paintings, mostly of cats, hung from the walls.

Florence opened a sliding screen door, which led to a glass room overlooking the back of the property. The snow-capped trees glittered in the midday sun.

Beatrice sat in an upholstered rocking chair. She too no longer wore her fancy dress, but instead a canary-yellow sweatsuit. Her face had been cleaned of the previous night's elaborate makeup. A black cat dozed in her lap.

She tilted her head as Florence and Iris walked in.

"Mom, Iris is here. Do you remember Iris from last night's La Fête de Noël?"

The woman ran her knobby fingers over the cat. "Oh, yes, I remember. My mother, Angelique Skelling, grew irises, the very dark ones. She called them the color of Russian violets. My father insisted the color was eggplant. They loved to tease each other. Well, my father loved to tease my mother, anyway."

Florence squatted beside Beatrice, stroking the cat. "Would you like me to take Andre?"

"Oh, no." Beatrice scratched the cat's ears. "He is happy right here."

Florence stood up. "Make yourself comfortable, Iris. I'll bring in some tea. Or would you prefer coffee?"

"Tea would be wonderful. Thanks."

"And some butter tarts," Beatrice added.

"You just had breakfast," Florence reminded her.

"And now I am ready for tea and a butter tart."

"Okay. Would you like one as well?" Florence asked as Iris settled onto a small sofa opposite Beatrice.

Before Iris could speak, Beatrice answered for her. "Yes. She is our guest and has likely never had one."

"Sure, thanks," Iris told her.

Florence left, and Iris watched Beatrice petting her cat.

"His name is Andre?" Iris asked.

Beatrice's eyes drifted up to hers. They looked clearer than the night before. "Yes, this is Andre. Phillippe died last year. He was twenty-two years old. I've had many cats in my life and I have always named them after my beloved family who are gone. Mostly my brothers, but a few Felixes and Angeliques have graced these halls as well."

"You must miss them."

"Oh, yes. I have missed them for a very, very long time, but that will change soon enough. I sense the end is coming. Probably not this year, we have only days left, but next year, or the year after. The time is near."

Iris wasn't sure what to say. An apology didn't quite make sense, so she bypassed it and dove straight into what she wanted to ask the old woman.

"Last night you said that Native Americans told your father the Skelling Peninsula was cursed. You mentioned an evil spirit."

"The maji-manidoo," Beatrice said. "It was the Ojibwe tribe who originally occupied this land. A people far more"—she paused as if searching for the right word—"in tune with nature than our own. Superstitious is what white folks called them, and perhaps in some things that is true. But it is also true that they paid attention. They knew the world was filled with spirits, both good and evil ones, and when they came upon evil, they told the others and they agreed to stay away from that place. Their name for what we now call the Skelling Peninsula was Maji-manidoo."

"That was the name of the evil spirit or of the peninsula itself?"

"To them, it was all one and the same. My father had bought the land and hauled in materials. The natives approached him. 'Do not build your home here,' they warned him, but he suffered from what so many men did in those days, a single-minded drive to fulfill his dream, and his dream was to build the most spectacular mansion, a home for his family, on that peninsula. To swim in the river, to hunt in the woods.

"My mother, Angelique, was less certain. She'd come from a family who believed in white and black magic, good and evil, signs. A man died while building the house. The son of another worker vanished while playing in the woods. But they forged on, finished the house. My mother gave birth to us children and for a time, all was well. There were no tragedies, and then my mother grew anxious. Her mother had told her the year after a woman's thirty-first birthday, something significant always occurs.

"Two days after my mother's birthday, she walked into the study and discovered a crow perched on the back of my father's chair. Oh, she wailed about that bird. You see, her family believed if you find a bird in your home, someone is going to die. In the days after she saw that bird, my brothers and I were not permitted to leave the house. We whined constantly until finally a few weeks later, unable to stand our constant begging, she let us back out to play. More weeks passed, and it seemed as if the superstition were silly nonsense, and then..."

Andre stood, stretched, and jumped from Beatrice's lap. He crossed the room and hopped onto the little couch next to Iris, staring at her as if expecting she pet him. She ran her fingers down his glossy back.

Still Falling

"The boys went out to play in the woods and never came home."

34

Florence opened the door with one hand, a tray balanced on the other. "Having a nice chat?" She looked from Beatrice to Iris.

"Oh, yes, quite," Beatrice told her.

Florence moved the little table near Beatrice's chair so that it sat between Beatrice and Iris. She laid it with linen napkins, saucers with cups of tea, a bowl of sugar cubes, a pitcher of cream and two plates, each containing a pastry that resembled a tiny pecan pie.

"Have a bite," Beatrice encouraged Iris, pointing at the tart. "This is my mother's recipe. Florence makes them now. I did for years and years, but nowadays these fingers are stiffer than wooden planks."

"Need anything else?" Florence asked Beatrice.

"No, thank you, dear."

Iris lifted the flaky pastry to her lips. It was dense with a brown sugary filling. "It's delicious," she said. "My grandma would love these."

"You'll take some to her," Beatrice said.

"Thank you."

Andre jumped off the couch and walked to the screen door just as Florence opened it to walk out. He followed her from the room.

Beatrice lifted her tea shakily to her lips and took a sip. "Now where were we?"

"Your brothers disappeared."

"Oh, yes... Andre and Phillippe. My mother knew right away.

206

They'd been gone for a couple of hours, but she started to pace about the house, wringing her hands, demanding my father go look for them. He got angry with her, insisted she calm down, stop being hysterical. This would haunt him later that he did not heed her warning, search the woods when she asked, but how were they to know?"

"I can't imagine."

"I wanted to speak up, to say the dark man has taken the boys, the maji-manidoo, but it was as if someone had stolen my voice from my body. I hid and watched and knew deep in my belly that the most terrible thing that could ever be visited upon a family had come to stay with us."

Iris studied Beatrice. "The dark man… You believe he took your brothers?"

"Oh, yes. The Devil does not arrive in a mask with a pitchfork in hand, he comes as the thing you've wanted most your entire life. The secret thing you've never spoken out loud, the thing you've dreamed. For me, the shadow man whispered, he sang me to sleep, he told me stories. For Andre and Phillippe, it was something much more, something they could not turn away from. He did not have to take them. They went to him.

"I've always known what happened to the boys…" She traced her fingers along the deep lines in her face as if searching for something she'd lost there. "I talked to the shadow man, sat on the shoreline and heard his voice like water whispering over the stones."

"Did you ever tell anyone?"

"Oh, no, the dark man forbade it. He sent me a dream one afternoon as I dozed on the banks of the river. In the dream I was a grown woman and I had a boy of my own, an angel of a child, and in my dream my boy followed the shadow man into the forest and into his cave and I knew when he slipped into that dark maw he'd never walk out again. The maji-manidoo was telling me that if I told anyone what happened to Andre and Phillippe, he would take my son.

"I woke up in tears. I was inconsolable for days. My mother sat at my bedside and fed me toutière and sang me *À la claire fontaine*, which was my favorite song. I wanted so much to tell her. Her grief had taken over our lives. We all were grieving, but for my mother…" Beatrice wound her fingers together and held them beneath her chin. "It was as if someone had snuffed out the light within her. And I had not realized how much her light lit us all. With my brothers gone, Skelling Hall became the saddest place in the entire world. Once a place filled with magic, with possibility, now it held only darkness."

"I understand," Iris breathed, for she too had watched her home transform into a tomb, a place of silence and shadows, devoid of the life that had once imbued it.

"You've seen him, the dark man. That's why you are here." Beatrice trained her eyes on Iris.

"Yes. I saw him chasing the young man who recently vanished from Skelling Hall—Brett Stephens."

Beatrice lifted her tea cup and sipped. She set the saucer on the little plate. "I once saw the maji-manidoo chase a boy."

Iris sat up straighter. "You did?"

"It happened when a man and his sons came to take my mother away. Her body, that is. She had died and her family from Quebec had come and they were all staying in the hall. It was so dark and I could barely breathe inside that house. I took to spending every moment from dawn until dusk outside.

"I heard the maji-manidoo whispering that day. I would not acknowledge him anymore. I was angry he had taken my brothers and now too he had robbed me of my mother by stealing that which she most loved. I believe he was calling to one of those boys, trying to lure him into the forest, but..." She squinted at her hands, rotated a large pearl ring. "The boy seemed to sense the dark man and he was not bewitched as my brothers had been. The boy became very agitated, jumping at each sound. He dropped his corner of my mother's casket. His father slapped him and he picked it up and continued carrying it to the wagon. They'd barely pushed it in and the boy took off like a shot."

Iris squeezed the cushion in her seat, riveted by Beatrice's story. Beatrice adjusted in her chair and the blanket on her lap slid to the floor. Iris bent forward and grabbed it. Something hit the floor with a ping. She looked down to see Jack's key to Skelling Hall had fallen from the pocket of her coat. She scooped it up and slid it back into her jacket before grabbing Beatrice's blanket and returning it to her lap.

"Thank you, dear," Beatrice told her. "I'd never seen a boy run so fast, and there, just behind him"—Beatrice held her fingers out, pointing, as if the window offered her a glimpse into that long-ago moment —"was the maji-manidoo. It streaked after that boy, more man than I'd ever seen it, but seven feet tall and so very black. It looked as if an oil spill had stood up and walked off the river. The boy ran and the dark man chased him and then the boy's father hopped in that wagon and jerked the reins and went after his son.

"I believe the father sensed that trouble had come for his son and, though he couldn't see it, he had to save him. He raced down the road and the older brother reached out, grabbed the younger boy and pulled him into the buggy. They sped off like the Devil was chasing them, and he was."

Iris released the cushion and leaned back, letting out the breath she held. "The boy got away?"

"Yep. He did, and people in town were already whispering about our house. After that, those whispers turned into a hullabaloo. People said Skelling Hall was haunted, that my father had made a deal with the Devil—that was how he'd come into his money, and now the Devil was taking his due. 'Stay away,' they said, and the people did. We still had each other, my father and I, and we had the domestiques who'd come with my parents from Quebec. They were a couple, Melina and Norbert—and they were like family.

"My father had always been a cheerful man. He had many friends and he and my mother threw parties. Their favorite was La Fête de Noël. But after the town turned against us, he shut himself into his room. He wrote and wrote. He walked about muttering to himself and then he started to go into the woods."

Florence appeared at the sliding door. "Everything going okay in here?"

"All is well, Florence. Leave us be," Beatrice told her.

Florence nodded, gave Iris a tight smile, and walked away.

"My daughter-in-law is very protective of me. She has me on a schedule of feedings and naps as if I am a newborn baby." Beatrice laughed. "I don't mind. Florence and Abel never had their own children. They tried, but it wasn't meant to be. Now Maddox, that is Jack's grandfather, my younger son, had children, so I was given grandchildren." She paused. "Now where was I?"

"Your father had started to go into the woods."

"Oh, yes, the woods. He sensed the boys were there, hidden somewhere, and he searched. He painted X's on the trees, so he could see where he'd been. Sometimes he dug holes, sometimes he hacked away bushes and vegetation. He'd go into the woods at dawn and not return until nightfall. It was winter when the men took him to the institution. Norbert summoned a doctor who had to drive several hours because the local doctor refused to come to Skelling Hall. The doctor declared my father crazy that afternoon and by the following day men had arrived to take him away."

"That must have been very traumatic for you."

Beatrice nodded. "It was, but Melina and Norbert did their best to shelter me. My father was not insane, not entirely anyway. He wrote to his lawyer, and he began the process of setting up the foundation. He wanted us out right away. He'd given Norbert strict instructions when he left, and Norbert took the money my father had left for him and he bought a house for us. Days after my father was taken, we left Skelling Hall. I did not see the hall again for two years."

"Did you ever tell your father about the dark man?"

"No. I believed in the dream the dark man had sent me and I lived in terror of it coming true. Then later, when my father went into the asylum, I realized he'd been speaking of this entity, writing about it, drawing pictures of it. I read his journals. He had realized the natives had been right all along."

"And in the years since? Have you talked about it?"

"Oh, yes. Our family is aware of this being. The foundation is aware. Most of them consider it foolishness. Maddox, my younger son, was aware of the maji-manidoo. He and I spoke at length about it. Maddox had felt it, had almost gone to it as a boy. From that moment forth, I never allowed him to visit Skelling Hall. I remembered the dream the dark man had given me, and I knew I must never allow Maddox to go back there. For a long time, he did not.

"It was my other son, Abel, who started La Fête de Noël. I'd told him stories of the grand parties from when we were children. He wanted to bring life back to Skelling Hall. I tried to discourage him, but he was representing our place in the foundation. He did most of it without my awareness and, truth be told, when I visited Skelling Hall after Abel had begun the renovations to open it for tours, I was astonished. It was just as I remembered it, and so many good years swam back to me. I thought that yes, we should go there. We should honor this place my father so loved. Perhaps that was a terrible mistake."

"Why did your father put the hall into a foundation? Why not outright sell it?"

"He never explained his reasons, but I've read his journals. He feared what might befall anyone who moved there. He had built that place, you see. He had been the one to strip away the trees and dig into the land and erect that magnificent house. He thought he might have even unleashed the being that stalked the peninsula, though I'm sure it had been there long before we arrived. The natives had told him as much.

"He could not stand to tear it down, but he did not want to put anyone else in jeopardy. I don't believe he ever intended it to be what it is today, a place that people tour. He never intended for the Christmas parties to begin again. He hoped it would be a museum, one that no one ever visited. Perhaps he imagined the land would gradually take it back. That someday the floors would split and trees would grow up inside of it, that the water would creep up the shore and erode it into the river. I cannot say for certain what he intended to become of Skelling Hall."

Iris said nothing. Her butter tart sat mostly uneaten; her tea had grown cold. A year ago, she would have written off Beatrice's statements as the rantings of an old woman, a woman whose life had been so filled with mystery and tragedy she'd gradually gone as insane as her father.

"You can read them, my father's journals," Beatrice went on. "Take the grand stairway to the second floor, turn left. At the end of the hall is the upstairs parlor. There's a bookcase. The journals are on the third shelf from the top. You might find other things too, interesting things."

"I thought the upstairs was closed to the public?"

Beatrice's eyes flicked to the coat pocket where Iris had tucked the Skelling key. Warmth crept into Iris's face. "I'm sure you could find a way. You said your last name is Walsh?"

"Yes."

"You're Lola Walsh's grandchild? The girl child."

"Yes."

Beatrice nodded. "I thought so. I need to rest now, but tonight is as good a night as any. Stay out of the woods, though."

"If it lures people into the woods…"

"I never wanted to go to him the way my brothers did. If he calls, don't listen. Get in your car and drive like your life depends on it. Anyone who follows the shadow man is lost forever. None of those boys will ever be found."

35

Iris stared at the looming structure of Skelling Hall. It was dark, save for two exterior light posts and a single light above the door to the entrance.

She had no intention of going in, of getting out of her car. With the heat blasting, the music on low, some twangy country song, Iris felt perfectly safe.

Beatrice's stories coursed through her mind. What more could she learn by going in? Worse still, what could she do about any of it? If Brett and Norlene had been taken by the maji-manidoo, what could Iris possibly do to prove it? To stop it?

All of her excuses didn't matter. Iris had to know why Frankie's name had been on the document in the boardroom.

"Three, two, one," she murmured and, in a quick motion, she turned off her car, swung the door open and jumped out. She jogged around the side of the huge house, her boots crunching in the hard snow, and found the door Jack had used days before. She shoved the key in, wiggled it and tried the knob.

It didn't turn.

In the forest behind her, a twig snapped. Iris didn't look. She gritted her teeth, shook the key more and shimmied the knob.

It still didn't turn, and another sound arose behind her, a whistle in the trees, a murmuring.

Irisss… it hissed.

She held her breath, jerked the key harder now, heart crashing against her ribs.

It clicked, and she twisted the knob hard and fell through the opening into the servants' entryway. She shoved the door closed and lurched away, then stopped and looked back. The door was unlocked. She had to put the skeleton back in the lock to secure it. She didn't want to. She wanted to get away from the door and whatever lurked beyond it.

"Three, two, one," she muttered again, bolstered less by her count-down than an urge to get out of the room and into some safer part of the house. She thrust the key in and it turned, locked in one go.

Something scratched against the door.

Irisss… She heard the call, muted, nothing more than the wind whining from the lake, but some strange part of her wanted to open the door and follow the voice, follow it into the forest, see what it might reveal.

She backed away, bumped her hip against the waist-high counter and turned, fumbled through the swinging wood door that led into the long hallway that cut a path to the once-dining room, now-boardroom.

The long table stretched in the darkness. Iris took out her cell phone and turned on the flashlight app, aiming it at the pile of paperwork she'd seen at the party. She prayed the document with Frankie's name hadn't been moved.

Papers still sat in the corner and as she crept toward them, she feared the one on top would be something different—a flyer, a tour guide—but no… she saw Brett's name and then, further down the page, Frankie Walsh's. Beneath his name, another she recognized: Duncan Stewart.

Her hands trembled as she pulled the paper off the top of the stack and leaned closer to read it.

Skelling Hall Foundation

Board Meeting Minutes (December 2014)

Open Issues

Urgent: The recent disappearance of Brett Stephens.

Board member G. Lovells presented this board with the recently accepted settlement with Bonnie Stephens in the sum of $5,000. Board is satisfied with decision.

Board member F. Skelling highlighted the potential press firestorm if the Stephens settlement had not been made. She also pointed out the potential for additional attention on Skelling Hall regarding previous individuals (i.e. Andre and Phillippe Skelling, Franklin Walsh and Duncan Stewart, and Norlene Weaver.) Board member J. Skelling does not believe Weaver's disappearance is connected to Skelling Hall.

Board discussed further actions to reduce negative publicity, including charitable donations and free tours for all schoolchildren in Chippewa County.

Other Issues

Budget: Need to factor in additional expenses for roof repair on the northwest corner in the spring.

Beatrice Skelling: Board member F. Skelling presented a recording of Beatrice Skelling describing yet again the unfavorable goings-on at Skelling Hall in the past. She specifically insisted to F. Skelling that her dying wish as the rightful heir to the Skelling estate was that Skelling Hall be closed for good. F. Skelling reminded Beatrice that the hall is not in her control and only the board can make such a decision.

It is the decision of the board members here today that rather than close the hall further precautions will be made to protect any visitors and staff, including a locked gate at the entrance to the Skelling Peninsula, which will be locked and secured any time Miles Fincher is not on the premises.

I ris returned the paper to the stack. Apparently, Beatrice Skelling had spoken to others about the hall's disturbing past. The board didn't seem at all surprised by the revelations. But why had they added Frankie's and Duncan's names to the list of disappearances and tragedies at Skelling Hall? Shallows Bay was several miles away from the peninsula.

Had the boys actually set off from the shore at Skelling Hall? No. Andy had said the boat they'd taken was always moored at Shallows Bay. It didn't make sense, but her skin prickled each time she looked at the paper and saw her brother's name there.

She'd spent the night before with Jack. He'd said nothing about the board meeting that he'd clearly attended where her brother's name had come up. Was it merely that Jack's friendship with the boys associated Skelling Hall with their disappearance?

Iris sifted through the stack of papers beneath, but found only receipts from vendors regarding the Christmas party.

She stood and paced away from the table. The light from her cell phone shone a large circle on the rounded plaster ceiling.

Beatrice had spoken of Felix's journals, his letters, all stored upstairs at Skelling Hall.

Iris held her phone out as she left the boardroom and walked through the grand hall to the large curved staircase. She walked up slowly, listening, expecting to see the ghost children she'd encountered previously at the house. No laughter rang out, no pattering feet. The silence in the house made her uneasy.

She ducked beneath the velvet rope closing off the second floor.

Turn left, Beatrice had said.

Iris followed the directions and stepped into an enormous room with soaring ceilings, tall windows, and antique furniture. A large bookcase stood along one wall. Iris went to it. She saw the old journals, leather-bound. Felix had crudely carved each year into their spines.

Iris pulled one free and opened it. The pages were thin and flimsy. She feared ripping the pages by simply touching them. The earliest journal showed a date of 1905, before Skelling Hall had even been built. The boys had vanished in 1932.

Iris took out a journal dated 1932 and shined her phone on the pages. The writing was hard to read. Some letters crowded so close together they overlapped. There were no dates, and the entries were interspersed with images of a dark figure gliding through trees. On other pages, Felix had drawn portraits of his two sons. They were lovely pictures, sketches of their innocent faces.

She slid it back on the shelf and selected another dated 1934.

Iris read one of Felix Skelling's entries.

Angelique is in further decline. Next month marks the two-year anniversary of the vanishings of our boys. I fear she will not live to see it. What will become of us, of my darling Beatrice, when Angelique is gone?

Iris flipped further into the journal. Many of the pages had little more than a few scribbled sentences. She paused at a longer entry.

I have come to believe Skelling Hall is a sort of capsule for the shadow man. I fear if we burn it or tear it down, of which I've longed to do both, we may release this malevolent spirit to do as he pleases.

Giiwedin, the Ojibwe elder, is sure that the shadow man he calls the maji-manidoo inhabits the land itself and we cannot rid ourselves of him. We can only move away from this place and do our best to ensure it is never occupied again.

Giiwedin believes the maji-manidoo is as old as the land itself. The gnarled trees have heard his call, but he has longed for human ears, for someone he might reach. The trees cannot pull up their twisted roots and follow him, you see, but people can. Curious little boys wandering in the woods.

Giiwedin told me a story of their final encounter with the maji-manidoo. A group of young Ojibwe men, four in all, canoed to the peninsula hunting for a large bull (male moose) one of them had spotted in the forest days before. They did not return to camp that evening and Giiwedin and other men from the tribe went to find them. Their boat rested on the shore, but the young men were gone. A smell of scorched meat hung in the air and the forest seemed to laugh at them as they searched for their young men.

A fear fell over the group. Giiwedin and his party returned to camp and that night he had a bawaajigan, a dream. A prophetic dream, he told me. In this dream he woke one morning to find all of the boys and young men had gone. The children and babies were crying and the women were walking about, perplexed. The air was filled with the scent of charred meat. A clear path of the boys' footprints led from their camp through the forest toward the peninsula. It appeared as if they'd all woken in the night, stood and walked into the forest. But in the middle of the peninsula, the footprints disappeared as if the boys had grown wings and taken to the skies.

He gathered his people together and told them the peninsula was forbidden. They must never go there again. He believed the moose had been conjured by a maji-manidoo to lure their young men to their deaths.

I wept when he told me this story. I wept for Andre and Phillippe, for my own arrogance in building this place. I ignored the warning of the Ojibwe and I have paid with my sons.

36

Iris set the journal aside. She felt nauseous. Her palms had grown sweaty as she read the story and she wiped them on her thighs. She wanted out of Skelling Hall. She wanted to be in Lola's car, speeding down the peninsula road back toward the big pink house full of games and warmth and laughter.

Iris returned the journal to the shelf and walked quickly down the hall. She wanted to run, to leap the stairs three at a time, crash out of the house and sprint across the parking lot.

Instead, she forced herself to walk slowly, to not risk plummeting head-first to the marble floor below. She clutched the banister, slid her hands along the smooth surface and focused on putting one foot in front of another.

Outside snow fell and the frigid air helped draw her back to her senses. She smelled river and pine forest and tilted her face up and inhaled.

It had only been a story, a story of another time, and she didn't have to believe it if she didn't want to. Frankie had drowned and Brett had gotten high and succumbed to the elements and Norlene had… well, she'd left to start a new life. Simple, uncomplicated explanations and Iris didn't believe a one of them.

She clicked the unlock button on the car.

A child giggled.

Iris paused. She was steps away from the safety of the front seat. She turned. The Skelling boys stood at the edge of the property. They wore their summer things, perhaps the same clothes they'd worn that final day.

"Hey!" Iris called out to them as if they might hear her, as if they were ordinary children oddly wearing shorts on this bitter cold northern Michigan night.

They laughed and the older one, Andre, ran into the trees. The younger Phillippe turned for a moment and his eyes met Iris'. It was as if he were truly there, looking at her as she looked at him, and before she could consider her next move she started towards him.

He ran into the woods after his brother, and Iris chased them both.

The snow felt thick and wet and blotted the forest before her. She held up her phone, the beam of light illuminating the snow-laden ground and trees feet in front of her. There were no footprints to follow, but she lunged ahead when she heard the boys' laughter.

Her lips stuck together. Iris licked them. They were chapped, scaly-feeling. She shoved her hands deep into the pockets of her coat, wished she'd grabbed gloves from her car, a hat and scarf.

On she went, ignoring the insistent voice that had begun with an urge to turn back and transformed into a high-pitched shriek that she was making a terrible mistake.

But what if... what if she could follow them? Follow them to the place where they'd gone that day, where Frankie and Duncan had perhaps gone as well, and then Norlene and finally Brett and how many others that the Skelling Foundation had never known existed at all? The Ojibewe people. How many had they lost to the maji-manidoo before they forbade their people from entering the peninsula?

Minutes passed, three, then five. Her legs ached. Her entire face, eyes too, burned from the cold.

She stopped, turned, taking the light with her, weaving the beam in a circle. Snow, constant falling snow in every direction. She had to go back. She turned and the sound found her. Not a giggle this time. A familiar voice.

"Iris..." It wasn't the voice of the shadow thing, an inhuman voice. It was Frankie. Frankie calling out to her.

"Frankie?" she yelled, but the wind whistling off the river snatched it away.

Iris tried to discern the direction from which it came and move toward it.

Stupid, idiotic, suicidal, moronic. Her rational brain besieged her with a string of insults, but her legs carried her on, her desperation to know what had become of her brother, of all of them, too tempting, so tempting she'd sooner freeze to death than turn away from the truth.

A head of her lay a hill and in it a cave.

Snow swirled in front of the black opening. Nothing about it felt good. Just the opposite. Goosebumps, not from the cold, prickled down her spine. The snow was falling like rain, heavy and wet. The wind off the water shook the branches of the leafless trees, and Iris's teeth chattered.

She pushed forward, ducking her head to fit into the cavern.

The cave was cold too, but the break from the wind was a relief. Iris squatted at the edge, not wanting to go deeper, unable to see beyond the first few feet. She had the sense it stretched far ahead of her, a yawning void she could not see. She pressed her back against the cold stone wall and pulled her hands from her pockets, blowing warm breath on her stiff fingers.

"Fuck..." she murmured, letting her eyes slip closed for an instant. She'd been stupid to trek off into the woods, to follow the ghosts of two children who'd vanished nearly a century before.

Iris bundled her coat higher, edging away from the fear floating like a soft mist at her ankles. She would not let it creep up, invade her senses, render her panicked and useless.

Her thoughts drifted to Andy, to Jack and then to Norlene. Each face passed through her mind and slipped away and again and again she came back to a vision of the maji-manidoo. He was in the cave nearby, sensing her as she sensed him.

Iris sank further down the wall. She barely felt the icy ground beneath her butt, pulled her knees close and buried her face in them. Fear seized her, paralyzed her.

The shadow-man was near. For a moment, though her face was pressed firmly into her pants, she smelled something rancid. A smell that reminded her of once finding a dead woodchuck beneath the porch at her childhood home. She'd crawled under the deck to retrieve her Frisbee and the smell had made her gag. When she'd locked eyes on the carcass, white maggots had been wriggling between its sharp teeth.

The smell overpowered her and she squeezed her knees closer, sure if she opened her eyes the shadow thing would be grinning at her with a giant mouthful of pointed teeth and maggots.

"Irisss..." The voice whispered her name—the sound of sifting stones on the beach, wind in the trees, and something coarser like a knife slicing through an aluminum can.

Iris pulled her hands from her pockets and pressed them to her ears.

The whisper stopped, but another voice replaced it. Frankie's voice calling out to her.

"Iris, come and see... you won't believe it."

Iris didn't move. She couldn't trust the voice. Frankie was long dead. The Skelling children were long dead. It was her and the maji-manidoo and nothing else.

Still when Frankie's voice called out again, she peeked from beneath her hands. No shadow man watched her. Iris lifted her head, stared into the darkness.

"Frankie?" she whispered, knowing it wasn't Frankie, couldn't be Frankie, but she wanted so badly for it to be him.

"Come and see, Iris..."

Her legs ached as she struggled back to her feet. Iris stared at the opening that led back into the gusting wind and shifting snow. She needed to go that way, to run like hell, but a wave of despair rolled over her when Frankie's voice called again.

"Iris... hurry... you'll miss it."

She turned and walked deeper into the cave.

37

Iris followed Frankie's voice further into the dark passage. She groped forward. "Frankie?"

The tunnel sloped down and curved. The temperature climbed, and she shrugged off her coat, let it fall to the dirt floor. She heard dripping and, though she no longer held her phone with the light illuminated, she could see the cave before her, the slimy stone walls and uneven ground.

How far could it descend? Surely not much further. They were on a peninsula and so close to St. Mary's River, but somehow it plunged down and down. Soon the only sound was that steady drip-drip of water from the cave ceiling. The cold had fled and been replaced by damp heat.

The air grew pungent, and Iris put the sleeve of her sweater against her nose.

"Iris… come see…" Frankie's voice, more urgent now.

There was a light up ahead, a flickering as if a fire burned in the cave. She walked toward it, hypnotized. Her legs no longer ached, nor did her hands or her face. She felt nothing at all, as if all sensation in her body had ceased. She searched for the feel of her breath as her lungs expanded, but even that seemed far off, a distant mechanism she couldn't tap into.

Before her, the ground dropped away. She was standing at the edge of a great cavern. The earth plummeted twenty feet or more and down in the center a fire raged.

A goliath of a man stood beside it. His form was indistinct, but she could see his head and face. He had wild dark hair, eyes black and shimmering in the firelight. He tilted his head back and laughed, mouth gaping open to reveal rows of pointed teeth. He was tall and taller still was his shadow that stretched behind him and rippled on the cave wall as if it were not attached to him, but moved of its own free will, jerking and twitching in an agitated dance.

Something turned in the center of the fire. Iris tried to make out the shape. It was meat roasting on a spit, but...

Not meat, not an animal carcass. Tatters of clothing hung from the roasting slab. A hunter's orange hat lay on the ground at one end of the spit. The hat that had belonged to Brett Stephens.

"Iris!" Lola shouted her name.

Iris whipped around and lost her footing. Her arms waved wildly, but there was nothing to grab hold of. She plunged over the edge into the cavern below.

~

I ris woke, not in the cave, but in the forest, the hard, frozen ground beneath her. She was blanketed in snow. It had stopped falling, and through the bare branches of the trees, she could see the dazzling cosmos. Winter stars, Jack had called them.

Her body was numb, her face rigid. She rolled to her side and sat up. Her body screamed in protest, her limbs unbending as she crawled first to hands and knees and then made it to her feet.

The dream was there, in her head, in her tissue. She tasted the smell of that burning flesh and bile rose in her throat. Iris staggered to a tree, braced one hand on it and hunched over, waiting to be sick. The nausea coiled back down. She straightened up, searched for the cave, but it was gone.

Stiff, sore, and bitterly cold, Iris trudged through the snow back toward Skelling Hall. The vision of the spit and the fire and the terrifying man floated up and flickered across her vision as she forged on, away from the cave that was both there and not.

She'd glimpsed the truth. She felt it, knew it in a way she'd known nothing before that moment with absolute certainty, and she knew as well, just as Beatrice had said, that none of the boys would ever be found. They'd followed something not of this world into a pit of hell and no search parties or tracking dogs or tenacious fathers would bring them back.

I ris arrived at Lola's house, shut off her car and climbed yet again into the frigid night. When she stepped through the doorway, she nearly collapsed with relief. The only sound was the soft rush of heat through the vents.

The lights were off, save the glow from the Christmas tree. Iris passed the living room and spotted her grandmother asleep in her rocking chair. "Good night, Grandma," she whispered, not wanting to wake her.

Iris slipped quietly up the stairs, peeled off her stiff clothes that smelled of smoke, and pulled on flannel pajamas. She climbed beneath the covers, but left the bedside lamp on.

She closed her eyes and drifted down.

I ris woke to the sound of Grandma Lola's slippers on the floor.

She tried to open her eyes, but her eyelids were heavy and sticky. She'd been dreaming, not the nightmare from the cave, but something much sweeter. Andy standing at the window of his little cabin watching the falling snow.

Light flashed, and Iris's eyes flew open. A winter storm was raging. Lightning blazed beyond the window and a growl of thunder followed.

"Grandma?" she murmured, seeing Lola then.

Lola stood in the doorway watching Iris. She didn't speak, just lifted a hand and blew her a kiss. Iris closed her eyes and sank back into sleep.

The morning loomed bright and clear. Iris had slept soundly despite the terrifying events of the night before. She stood and made her way to the kitchen.

"Do you want coffee, Grandma?" Iris called, opening a cupboard and getting her and her grandma's mugs out.

Lola didn't respond.

Iris walked to the doorway into the living room and started to ask again, then paused.

Lola sat in her rocking chair. Her eyes were closed, her lips planted in a half-smile. Something didn't look right about her grandmother. She appeared stiff.

"Grandma?" Iris spoke, but Lola didn't twitch, didn't begin her slow rocking.

Iris wanted to back away, return to the kitchen and make the coffee. Lola would smell it. She loved coffee. That would rouse her from the deep sleep she'd clearly slipped into, but even as the fantasy played out in her mind, Iris took the first tentative steps to her grandmother's side.

She pressed a hand against Lola's thin wrist. Her grandmother's arm was cold and unyielding. Trembling, she moved her fingers to Lola's throat, searched for a pulse, didn't find one.

A sob slipped from Iris's mouth and she shut her eyes, counted backwards—three, two, one.

She moved on wooden legs back to the kitchen, lifted her cell phone from the counter and dialed the police.

"911. State your emergency."

"My grandmother has died," Iris said, a shockwave rolling through her as her own words echoed in her head.

"Did she have an accident?"

"No, she's in her rocking chair. She must have... passed in her sleep."

"I see. Do you know if she had a DNR order?"

"I don't know. We never talked about that. She was eighty-eight years old."

"Okay, can you give me her name and address, please?"

"Lola Walsh," Iris told her and added the address. "It's the big pink house."

"We'll send paramedics and a police officer."

Iris ended the call and walked back into the living room. She pulled a chair close to her grandmother's and sat, slipping her hand into Lola's. The woman's fingers didn't bend or offer her usual return squeeze.

"Oh, Grandma..." she murmured.

It seemed impossible that this woman in the chair was Lola Walsh, her lively, loving grandmother. She wore the same pink housedress and fuzzy bunny slippers, but the essence of her was gone.

Iris wanted to scream. She could feel it bubbling. She wanted to grab the Christmas tree and toss it sideways on the floor. She imagined doing it, rampaging through the house and onto the front lawn, stomping the plastic candy canes and reindeer to bits.

It wouldn't change anything. It wouldn't make her grandma any less dead.

Loneliness surrounded Iris like cold, wet fog. It pressed in. Things that had seemed peaceful minutes earlier had become joyless in the thickening silence. Now the house was too quiet, forever quiet. Her grandmother's voice would never call down the hallway, her laughter drift in from the front porch. The sound of her board games as she moved puzzle pieces or tumbled Jenga towers, the shuffle of her slippers on the wood floor, the clatter of her baking in the kitchen—all gone.

A sob tumbled out and tears leaked from Iris's eyes. She clutched her grandmother's hand and watched as an ambulance and then a police car pulled to the curb in front of the house. Their lights were on, but their sirens were silent.

Three men walked to the front door, a deputy and two paramedics. Iris gingerly removed her hand from Lola's, though it made her chest constrict to let Lola's fingers go.

The paramedics performed their tests searching for any evidence of life, but all of them knew the woman had been dead for hours. Rigor mortis took hold of the body hours after death. She'd been gone since sometime in the night.

The deputy asked Iris routine questions, and then she watched as the paramedics wheeled Lola's body to the ambulance. They would deliver her to a nearby funeral home.

After they left, Iris plodded into the kitchen and pressed start on the coffee maker. It gurgled and spit brown water into the glass carafe.

She'd woken that morning oddly at peace despite her experience from the night before. Iris finally had answers, a horrible truth, but a truth just the same. She'd intended to tell Lola everything. But now the one woman she could confide it all to was gone.

Iris couldn't think of what she was supposed to do next, but she knew there was a list, people and places to call, details to attend to.

Someone knocked on the front door. She glanced toward the sound, but didn't move, couldn't will her feet to walk from the kitchen, pass by the living room and that empty rocking chair.

The knock came again, and then the sound of the door opening. "Iris?"

She recognized Andy's voice. She listened to his footsteps as he moved through the house. He appeared in the doorway. His forehead creased, his mouth turned down. "I'm so sorry. I just heard."

Iris said nothing, just leaned heavily against the counter. The ridge of it poked into her hip, gave her something to focus on so the other feelings couldn't get hold.

Andy entered the kitchen. He didn't try to hug her, which she was grateful for.

"Here," he said. "Just sit. I'll get your coffee." He guided her to a kitchen chair. He took Lola's mug and lifted the coffee pot.

"No." Iris stopped him. "Not that one. That one's mine." She pointed to the other mug, the one that read *Only the Strongest Women Become Lawyers*. Lola had bought it for her the previous summer.

Andy slid Lola's mug to the side and filled Iris's cup. "Cream or sugar?" he asked.

"No."

He nodded, started to hand it to her, then paused. "Some of that?" He pointed to a bottle of Baileys on top of the refrigerator.

She shouldn't. It wasn't even eight a.m. "Yeah," she said after a moment.

He grabbed the bottle and added a shot to Iris's coffee, slid it in front of her. It smelled sweet with the liqueur, like something Lola would have made—dessert coffee.

Iris massaged her breastbone, the tightness there. She took a sip of the coffee.

"Have you called anyone?" Andy asked.

She looked at him. "I know I need to, but... I can't think of who to call."

"Your dad."

"Oh, yeah... of course." She studied her coffee, tried not to imagine her father's voice when she broke the news. He'd feel guilty. He hadn't made it up to visit Lola the summer before.

"Also, the funeral home and Don Fraser."

"Why Don Fraser?"

"Don was your grandma's estate lawyer, right? Isn't that how you ended up at the firm? I'm sure he knows what funeral arrangements she made."

"You think she would have done that?"

"Yes. She was in her eighties. I'm sure she worked it all out with Don. Why don't I drive you there? To the firm. You can call your dad on the way."

"Okay. Let me go change."

Iris trudged up the stairs. She took off her pajamas and slid on a pair of dark jeans and a hooded pullover.

As Iris followed Andy from the house, Jack's Mercedes pulled to the curb.

38

———————

Jack got out in his jogging clothes. He barely glanced at Andy as he hurried up the walkway and grabbed Iris in a hug. She stiffened at the abruptness of the gesture and then her hardness cracked. Her tinfoil armor, as Lola had described it, couldn't hold up beneath the weight of this massive loss.

"Oh, Jack..." she murmured, pushing her face into his shoulder as tears seeped from her eyes.

He said nothing, just rubbed her back. When she looked up, her face growing raw in the cold morning, Andy had returned to his cruiser.

He gazed at her. "Call me if you need anything, Iris."

She lifted her hand in a limp wave.

Jack guided her back into the house.

"I have to call my dad," she murmured.

"Okay. Where's your phone?"

Iris patted her pockets, realized she'd never picked it up before leaving the house with Andy. "I don't know. In the kitchen, I think."

"I'll find it." Jack disappeared down the hall.

A memory of waking the night before drifted to the front of her mind. Her grandmother had been standing in the doorway. The woman had blown her a kiss and, as Iris examined the memory, she had the unnerving sense her grandmother had already been dead. She'd been paying Iris a final farewell.

"Oh, God..." she grumbled, rubbing at her face and fighting the onset of fresh tears. Why hadn't she woken Lola up when she'd gotten home? Why hadn't she checked to make sure her grandma was okay?

Jack returned with her phone. Iris's hands shook as she scrolled through the contacts and clicked the name 'Dad.'

He answered after two rings. "Good morning," he told her, cheerful, unaware of the bomb she was about to drop.

"Dad—" Her voice cracked. She took a deep breath and tried again. "Dad, Grandma Lola passed away last night."

His breath whooshed into the phone and then silence.

"She's dead?" he asked so quietly Iris barely heard him.

"Yes. She died in her sleep. The paramedics took her…"

"Lola passed last night," her father said, as if reaffirming a truth that didn't quite make sense. "I should come there, then? Right? That's what I should do. I'll drive up tonight."

"Yeah," Iris said, grateful that there would be someone else to help her navigate the days ahead.

"Are you okay, honey?" he asked.

"I'm okay." Was she okay? She wasn't sure. A numbness had settled over her, disbelief mingling with a desire to pretend nothing at all had changed.

"I have to go into work and wrap a few things up. I'll be there this evening."

"Okay. Thanks, Dad." She ended the call and slid the phone into her pocket. She felt the key to Skelling Hall and tensed, glancing at Jack as if he might somehow have laser vision into her pocket.

"Is he okay?" Jack asked.

"Yeah… Andy thought I should go to the Fraser Firm. Don handled my grandmother's estate and probably knows what arrangements she made."

"I'll take you."

"Do you have court today?"

"Nothing that another prosecutor can't handle."

"Good morning," Candace chirped as Iris walked into the front office at the Fraser Firm. She stood when she saw Jack trailing Iris. "And good morning to you, Prosecutor Skelling. Can I get you anything?"

"No, thank you."

Marv and Nina were standing in the hallway, talking. Marv looked up, slightly amused. "Better late than never, I guess," he said, tapping on his watch.

Nina's smile fell away at the look on Iris's face.

"Lola died last night," Iris told them.

Marv cringed. "Oh, damn… shoot. Put my foot in my mouth again. I'm sorry, Iris."

Nina walked to Iris and put her arms around her. "Oh, honey… that's terrible, just terrible. She was such a sweet woman."

Iris bit back the emotion circling, trying to take hold. "I came to talk to Don about her…" She couldn't finish the sentence, the words simply refused to come out.

"Her funeral arrangements," Jack cut in. "Is he in his office?"

Marv nodded. "Yeah, go on back."

Don Fraser was on the phone when Jack cracked open his door. Fraser held up a finger, eyes flitting from Jack to Iris and then back to Jack.

"Yosef, I'll call you back shortly. An appointment just arrived." He set his phone on the table. "Is everything okay?"

"Lola Walsh passed away last night," Jack explained.

Don frowned and steepled his fingers on the table. "I see. My condolences for your loss, Iris. Come have a seat."

They walked to the chairs facing Don's desk. Iris squeezed the wooden armrests as if she might transfer some of the pain into her chair.

"Are you comfortable discussing Lola's estate and end-of-life wishes with Jack present?"

"Yes," she mumbled.

"Okay then." Don stood and went to a file cabinet, opening a drawer and drawing out a gray file. He brought it to the desk and peeled back the cover. "Lola and your grandfather bought side-by-side burial plots at the Riverside Cemetery in 1978. She wanted to be buried there with him. She's already purchased the casket and paid for funeral arrangements at the Legacy Funeral Home. Moriarty Burbach is the owner and will have those details. Lola's name is already on the headstone in the cemetery. An engraver will add her date of death, which again Moriarty can take care of."

"She paid for it all ahead of time?"

Don smiled. "She was a woman who liked to be prepared. Lola came to me a few months ago with some changes to her will."

"A few months ago? Was she feeling ill?"

"No. I think her granddaughter moving up here spurred the change." He smiled at Iris. "Would you like to discuss that now, or would you prefer to wait for your father?"

"I don't know… maybe I should wait?" She shot a questioning glance at Jack.

"I'm sure Don can explain things now and then schedule an additional appointment with you and your father."

"By all means," Don said.

"Okay… go ahead," Iris murmured.

"It's pretty simple. Since her daughter passed many years ago, your father is the primary beneficiary and you are second. She left seventy-five percent of her moneys and investments to your father, the other twenty-five percent goes to you. She also wanted you to have her house."

Iris frowned. "But why? She knew I wasn't planning to stay up here."

Don shrugged. "She didn't specify and you don't have to stay if you choose not to. It's an asset like anything else. Sell it, rent it. The choice is yours and so is the house."

I ris sensed Jack's eyes on her as he parked in Lola's driveway—her driveway now.

Her throat constricted as she gazed at the pink house. She wanted so much for Lola to be inside. Iris yearned to walk in and hear Lola at her game table and inhale the scent of cookies. She wanted to sit in a chair while Lola brushed her hair and spill everything to her grandmother—all that had happened the night before, but not only that. All that had happened in her whole life that she'd squashed and buried and not spoken about.

A whimper escaped her and tears spilled down her face. She turned away from Jack and gripped the door handle.

Before she could leap out, Jack captured her hand and clutched it to his chest. "Iris… talk to me."

She couldn't. She clamped her teeth closed and shut her eyes.

He waited, said nothing.

A tornado of emotion ripped through her. She thought of all the years that had passed since Frankie had died, drowned, she had thought... but no. He hadn't drowned. The evil man in the cave had taken him. The maji-manidoo had lured him into the forest. That long-ago summer rose up in her mind, her fever dreams, nightmares that became waking realities. She'd never woken up. The nightmare had gone on and on.

"I think I just need to be alone," she told him. "Okay?"

"I get it. That's what I would want too."

"Thanks."

"I'll call you later," he told her.

She swallowed the thickness in her throat and stepped from the car.

In the house, Iris peeled off her winter clothes and went to Lola's room. She crawled into Lola's bed, heaped with blankets the color of bubblegum, and hugged one of her grandmother's pink frilly pillows. She cried herself to sleep.

~

The sound of knocking brought her back to the world. Iris blinked at the opposite wall where Lola's dresser was scattered with knick-knacks, all in varying shades of pink. Ceramic pigs, glass flamingos, kittens, bunnies, even a large pink elephant.

The knocking came again.

Iris pushed out of bed. The truth was there, the reminder of Lola's death that had momentarily slipped away as she slept. It descended upon her like a dark cloud.

She trudged from Lola's room and down the stairs. Andy was standing on the front porch. Iris opened the door.

He held up a paper bag. "I brought you some sandwiches. I figured cooking wouldn't be a top priority."

Iris started to thank him, but the words got stuck in her throat as her eye caught on Lola's pink mailbox painted with red hearts. Lola had called it her Valentine box.

A fresh stream of tears rushed down her cheeks. She shoved her hands over her face and squatted down, weeping. Her body doubled over as the loss of Lola stormed into her psyche and swept away the walls she'd been putting up for years.

Andy slipped into the house. He knelt beside her, rubbing her back. He said nothing, and after a while Iris slumped against him, the effort of holding herself up becoming too much.

When her crying subsided, he put an arm around her and helped her stand, guided her into the living room. Iris sat on the couch, staring at Lola's empty rocking chair.

"Do you want me to put a blanket over it?" Andy asked.

Iris shook her head, using her sleeves to wipe away her tears. It had hurt to cry, left her spent, but Iris also felt lighter, as if, for a while anyway, the cloud had dissipated.

"We can talk or I can sit here with you," Andy said. "Or if you want to be alone, I'll leave. Whatever you need, Iris, just say the word."

"Frankie and Duncan didn't drown," she whispered, surprising herself with the confession.

Andy leaned closer. "What did you say…?"

"They didn't drown. Something got them, something that lives on the Skelling Peninsula, that's been there for… I don't know, centuries, maybe longer."

"What are you saying? What thing? An animal?"

"I have to tell you something and it's going to sound crazy, but… I have to trust that you're going to believe me. All this time my grandma's been saying to be open, to have faith in what I'm seeing, but I resisted it. I have to stop fighting."

Andy sat in the pink striped chair, his eyes soft. He looked right in the chair, in Lola's house, as if he were as much a fixture as the antique white radiator affixed to one wall.

This was a man Iris could tell her secrets to and, she suspected, as improbable as they were, he would believe her.

"I lied to you about what I saw the night I wrecked my car."

"Okay."

"Just before the accident, I looked down the road that leads to Skelling Hall and I saw Brett Stephens. He was terrified and running away from something. I missed the curve and crashed."

"You saw Brett?"

"Yes, but… not only Brett. Something was chasing him. A figure was behind him, dark, more shadow than person. I only glimpsed it. Afterwards I thought I'd imagined it." Iris sighed and drew her hair over her shoulder, burying her hands in it.

"Maybe that's not the right place to start…" She kneaded her fingers together and squeezed. "My grandmother had this ability… she could see spirits."

"I know."

"You do?"

"Yes. Years ago, when I was… struggling after Harvey and Tom got murdered, your grandmother called me out of the blue. She said Harvey had been visiting her and telling her knock-knock jokes." Andy chuckled. "That was his thing. She said Harvey wanted me to go for it. She wasn't sure what he meant, but she wanted to pass the message along to me."

"Go for it?"

"Yeah. I'd been debating whether to enter the police academy. That was the nudge I needed."

"You believed her then?"

"Absolutely. And I believe you now, Iris. Whatever it is, I'll believe you."

Iris closed her eyes and remembered the man in the cave—the spit over the fire. She shuddered.

"I've been seeing the spirit of Norlene Weaver. I learned that Norlene might have gone to Skelling Hall to clean her last night alive. I kept sensing that Skelling Hall was the link between them, Brett and Norlene."

"Okay… but you said Frankie and Duncan didn't drown."

"I'll get to that. Yesterday I visited Beatrice Skelling. She told me all about this being, the maji-manidoo. Her family learned of it from the Ojibwe tribe in the early twentieth century. They warned Felix Skelling not to build his house on the peninsula. They said the land was cursed. They told Felix they'd lost boys and young men to this evil being."

"It's not a person?"

"No, it's… a spirit, I guess. A demon, maybe. I've seen him. He has spoken to me. He's been… watching me ever since the night I saw him chasing Brett. Last night I went to Skelling Hall. There was a document from a recent meeting of the Skelling Foundation. They listed Duncan and Frankie as tragedies that had occurred at Skelling Hall."

"But—"

"I know," Iris interrupted him. "I know they found the boat with their bags near Shallows Bay and I haven't gotten to the bottom of that yet, but that's not what happened to them. Last night, I followed the two Skelling boys who disappeared in 1932 into the forest."

"You went into the Skelling forest last night? It was practically a blizzard."

She smiled. "I can't believe the part that surprises you is the weather rather than my following two dead kids into the woods."

He tilted his head. "Good point, but I know how much you hate the snow."

"I followed them into the woods, but then I heard Frankie calling out for me. I found the cave of the maji-manidoo."

Andy frowned, the tiny crease appearing between his blond eyebrows. "Jack told us about a cave. That summer he was talking about it."

"I think the boys went to Skelling Hall that day and this being led them to his cave."

"And he killed them?"

Iris closed her eyes, wished she could expunge the memory of the fire, the smell, the hunter's orange hat. "Yes, he killed them and he killed Brett and I believe he got Norlene as well."

"Holy shit. Well, how do we find him? Their bodies must be in that cave."

"We can't find the cave. It's..." Iris tried to explain it, but it was a mystery even to her. "It's not of this world. It was almost like I stepped into another dimension, a world adjacent to this one. I don't ever want to go back there. No one should."

39

———

It was nearly seven p.m. when her father arrived at Lola's house. Andy had left an hour before. He was working an overnight shift, but he'd promised to call her the next day.

Iris's dad gave her a hug and then carried his bags upstairs before joining Iris in the kitchen. She cut up the sandwiches Andy had brought over and arranged them on plates.

Iris filled her dad in on what she'd learned from Lola's lawyer, Don Fraser. Afterwards, they ate in silence.

"What a nightmare," her father grumbled, surveying the interior of the enormous pink house. "Who will want to buy it?"

"A lot of people," Iris said. "This house is surprisingly popular. It's like a character all its own."

"Well, that's good at least. The sooner you sell it, the sooner you can get on with your life." A funny expression crossed his face and he turned to look behind him.

"What?" Iris asked.

"Weird, I just felt Lola's hand on my shoulder." He touched his shoulder. He took off his glasses and set them on the table. "Exhaustion catching up to me."

Iris wanted to tell him it wasn't exhaustion; it was Lola just stopping by.

"What do you think you'll do?" he asked.

Iris sighed and rubbed her face. She was tired and simultaneously

236

filled with nervous energy. "I'm not sure. I'd planned to stay for the summer. Here I am well into winter. The Fraser Firm has been great actually. I wonder if I should get a year under my belt, then start applying for firms down south."

"Still dreaming of warmer climates?"

Iris gestured at the window, at the snow blotting the world beyond. "It's hard not to." But even as she spoke the words, she didn't quite believe them. The thought of leaving Lola's house and Sault Ste Marie suddenly made her very sad.

"It's crossed my mind over the years, moving somewhere warm." He shrugged. "Wherever you go, there you are."

Iris's cell phone rang. Jack's name appeared on the screen.

"I'm going to take this, Dad," she said, standing and leaving the room.

"Hi," she answered.

"Hey, I just wanted to check in and see how you're doing."

"Better. Could you come pick me up?"

"Oh, sure, okay. Isn't your dad there?"

"Yes, but I'd like to talk."

"I can be there in ten minutes."

"Perfect, thanks."

I ris saw Jack's car pull into the driveway behind her dad's van. "I'm going out with a friend for a bit, Dad. I might be home late, so don't wait up."

Her dad was sitting in Lola's rocking chair flipping through one of her photo albums. He was misty-eyed when he looked at Iris. "Be safe out there, honey."

"I will."

She hurried to Jack's car and climbed into the passenger seat. He leaned over and kissed her cheek.

"How'd everything go today?" he asked.

"Okay. I mostly slept."

"Do you want to go to my apartment or-"

"I'd like to go to Skelling Hall," she cut in.

Jack was reversing down the driveway and pressed the brake, turning to look at her. "Skelling Hall? Why?"

"It's something I need to do and I don't want to talk about it until we get there. Can you just trust me on this?"

He looked uneasy, eyes darting back to Lola's house as if he wanted to ask her to get out, take a raincheck on their talk.

He sighed and shifted back into reverse. "Okay."

~

When they arrived at Skelling Hall, Iris didn't bother concealing that she had the key. She took it from her pocket and handed it to him.

He looked at it, puzzled.

"I grabbed it from your car yesterday and came here last night. I'll tell you everything inside."

They took the back way through the Skelling door, but unlike Iris venturing in the night before, Jack turned on lights rather than leaving them to navigate in darkness.

"Let's go upstairs," she told him.

He said little as she ascended the steps and walked to the parlor. As Jack switched on a lamp, Iris went to the bookshelf and extracted one of Felix's journals.

Jack watched her warily. He sat stiffly on a sofa. Iris walked the journal to him, opened it to a drawing of the maji-manidoo and handed it to him.

Jack studied the image and then closed the journal and rested it on his knees.

"Do you know what that is?" Iris asked.

In the corner of the room Norlene took shape. She walked across the parlor through the double French doors that led to the balcony and plunged over the side. Iris forced her gaze back to Jack.

"It's the dark spirit that Felix Skelling believed haunted this peninsula," he said, avoiding her eyes.

"What happened to Frankie and Duncan, Jack? And Brett and Norlene? Do you know? Have you always known and been part of covering it up?" Iris watched him, searched his expression for the truth.

"My father once told me he rarely visited Skelling Hall anymore because it felt like a ruin to him, a place void of happiness. The nostalgia had been stripped away when Dylan killed himself here. But not for me. The beauty of this place remained, the draw, something in my blood that led me into these woods thousands of times. The maji-manidoo drove Felix mad, he took Andre and Phillippe…"

Jack looked at her, his eyes troubled. "And yes… he took Frankie and Duncan too. They rode their bikes to the peninsula that day. I met them here at Skelling Hall. I showed them these journals." He gazed at the book. "And then we went in search of it—the maji-manidoo and the cave. I never thought… I never thought he would take them."

"What happened?"

Jack shook his head. "I don't know. I heard him, calling out to me. I wanted to go to him so badly. I kept asking them, 'Do you hear him? Can you hear him?' And they couldn't, but then we found the cave and we went inside and…" He flipped through the pages of the book and then set it aside on the couch, leaning forward, hands braced on his knees. "I woke up by the lake and they were gone. I was alone. I smelled like woodsmoke and my face and hands were sooty. I don't know what happened, Iris. I swear to you that I don't."

He stood and paced to the French doors, looked out. Norlene appeared again, shuddering through the doors and pitching over the rail. Jack turned away, stared at the carpet.

"I ran back here to the house. Miles called my dad and… that's how it started. My father was furious that I'd invited them here, put them at risk. He and my grandfather, Maddox, and my grandfather's brother, Abel, searched the peninsula, but they knew they'd never find them.

"My dad made me tell them where they might have gone if they hadn't come here. 'Fishing at Shallows Bay,' I said, because we did that all the time. They planted the bikes and Frankie and Duncan's backpacks, pushed the boat away from the shore. It was so easy. It's sickening how easy it was."

Iris sat heavily in a high-backed chair. She'd known already, in her gut she'd known, but hearing the details brought a new layer of horror to the truth. "How could you do that? How could your father do that?"

"My father thought… or at least he said… it was more humane. If they planted the bags and the bikes, it would look like Frankie and Duncan drowned. The families would have an answer. Our family had a legacy of the damage that comes with not knowing. My great-great-grandmother died from it. It caused my great-great-grandfather to go insane. My grandfather, Maddox, struggled with it the most. He hated the lie, but he agreed that the truth was too complicated, too… unbelievable—that there was no way to tell it."

Iris watched again as Norlene appeared, swept through the door and fell over the rail.

"How could you all leave this place open? Invite people here knowing that thing exists? That he kills people?"

Jack frowned. "I don't have a reasonable explanation. Beatrice has been trying to shut this place for years. For the men in our family... there's... it's like a compulsion, a need to resist its demise, its ruin."

"It has to be shut down. The doors locked and the key thrown away."

"You're right. Enough is enough." He walked to Iris and took her hands, his eyes searching hers. "Please forgive me."

Iris stared back at him, unsure of what to say. She was angry and yet when she imagined the position he'd been in that long-ago day with Frankie and Duncan, she could hardly blame him. He'd been a child and the men in his family had left him little choice.

"Okay... I don't know where we go from here, but I understand, Jack. I hate it, but I understand."

Norlene appeared again, rushed through Jack and Iris and through the French doors, plunged over the side.

Jack shivered.

Had he felt the ghost?

"Let's get out of here, okay?"

"Yeah," she agreed.

Jack returned to the couch, bent over and picked up the journal. Something fell from the pocket of his coat, landed on the carpet.

Iris frowned and stepped closer to the gold lion's head cufflink on the floor. Jack too stared down at it. Between them the silence stretched.

40

Iris turned and bolted for the door. Jack was faster. He beat her there, shoved it closed and stood in front of it.

"It was you that day. You broke into Norlene's apartment. You pushed me."

"It's not what you think," he told her. "I didn't mean to hurt you at the apartment. I panicked. I'd gone there because Norlene took the cufflinks from my car months ago. When you said you went to her place… I couldn't stop thinking about those goddamn cufflinks. They had belonged to my grandfather, Maddox."

Iris reached into the pocket of her coat, felt her cell phone. She had to call the police. Her mind whirred and her body tensed with the fight or flight response. Jack was bigger than her, stronger. Flight was the only option.

"It's okay," he whispered. "I always knew it would come to this. I did. And the truth is I've wanted to tell. I wanted to so bad, but… cowardice or self-preservation… something held me back. But now you know and it's okay."

When he opened his eyes, tears spilled over his cheeks. "We had an affair, but I didn't hurt her. Norlene was so lonely. Came from a broken home. Being an informant was the first thing that had ever made her feel important. At first, I kept her at arm's length, but she started calling me all the time. She had tips, she had theories.

"I was with Whitney then. She warned me that Norlene wanted

241

more than a working relationship, she told me to stop meeting her, to stop taking the calls, but this was the case that could launch my career, everything I'd worked my entire life for." He wiped his cheeks and gazed at a spot in the corner of the room.

Iris turned to look and there she stood, Norlene, with those dark, vacant eyes that were fixed on Jack and yet seeing nothing at all.

"The first night... that I slept with her, I'd lost a trial that day. I was furious and I drank too much. I ran into her leaving the bar, which... I don't know. I think she probably planned it that way. She'd started following me. I'd see her in odd places, places I knew she'd never normally be. I was walking to my car and she popped out of this alleyway and hurried up to me. Sober Jack would have done the right thing and walked home, but..." He shook his head.

"I don't even remember what she said that night, how I ended up in her car, but I remember crying. I was humiliated over what had happened in court, worried about talking to my father."

Iris still clutched in her phone in her pocket, but she'd loosened her grip. The smart thing would be to hit numbers, dial anyone and yell for help.

He rubbed his temples. "And then... we were in the woods. She'd driven us out of town parked on an old logging road and she started to kiss me. I didn't stop her. We... had sex that night. And once I'd opened that door, I couldn't seem to close it. It happened four more times, always during my low points. It was like she knew when I'd be vulnerable to her."

He tore his eyes from the ghost of Norlene.

"Can you see her?" Iris asked.

He ignored the question almost as if he'd forgotten Iris was there at all. "I know this sounds like a cop-out, like I'm playing the victim. I'm not. In the ten-thousand-foot view, I'm the bad guy here at every level. I had the power, the money, the status, and she was dazzled by it. The one thing she had, the thing she'd relied on her whole life, was... her body. It was the only thing men ever seemed to want her for and I used her that way too. I did."

"What happened to her?" Iris murmured.

"I didn't hurt her," he repeated. "She said she was pregnant. She threatened to tell everyone. She wanted me to be with her. I tried to avoid her, but she started calling all night long. She'd scream at my girl-friend to put me on the phone. She said if I didn't meet her, she'd refuse to testify or, worse, she'd get up on the stand and tell everyone I'd been screwing her and I'd left her broke and pregnant.

"One night I… I told her I'd pick her up and we could talk. I brought her here to Skelling Hall."

"Why here?"

He looked at the floor. "I don't know. I felt… that old familiar pull. I had this sense like… that's what I needed to do, that if I brought her here it would all click into place. We came in the hall and she got… kind of giddy. She started saying crazy things. Saying we could live in this house someday and raise our children.

"I lost it. I screamed in her face. I told her I hated her, that I wished I'd never met her. I don't remember everything I said, but… it was cruel. She started to cry and she ran out of the house and then… she was gone."

"Did you go after her?"

Jack hung his head. "No. I left. I got in my car and drove away."

"Jack… how could you do that? If she was pregnant…"

He stepped away from the door, opened it. "I've never regretted anything more in my life than the choices I made that night."

Iris eyed the door. She could walk out. He was letting her go, but he'd driven them there. She couldn't leave without him. "You think he got her then? The maji-manidoo."

"I don't know if he got her. I wondered if she walked into the river. If I'd driven her to… to take her own life."

Iris closed her eyes, her head growing heavier. The previous twenty-four hours had been the longest of her life. She wanted them to be over. "Can you take me home now?"

Jack nodded. "Yes. I'll take you home."

41

They climbed into Jack's car. He dropped his cell phone in the cup holder, slid his key in the ignition and started it. He stared straight ahead through the windshield.

"Damn..." he muttered. "I left the light on upstairs. I'll be right back."

Jack climbed from the car. Iris was alone in his Mercedes, keys in the ignition. She could climb in the driver's seat and race away, but she didn't.

She cranked the heat, put her numb fingers in front of the still-cool air pumping from the vents.

Beside her something shuddered. She turned as Norlene materialized in the driver's seat, the spot Jack had vacated only moments before. Her eyes were white and foggy as if someone had cut a piece of dirty ice and shoved them into the sockets. She was solid, as real as she'd ever been for Iris, and sopping wet. Hair oozed in rivulets over her shoulders. She opened her mouth and dirty river water spewed out.

Iris flinched, but no wetness touched her. Norlene had vanished. The dark leather seat sat empty.

In the cup-holder Jack's phone lit up. His voice emerged from the phone as one of his recordings started playing.

·   ·   ·

A*ugust 18*
They called me the golden boy. In college they said I was the darling of the teachers. I never went joy-riding, never snuck beers from the bottom drawer of the fridge like Neal did in high school, never took a hit from a single joint at a school party. I always did the right thing, the straight thing. And sometimes I paid for it. Sometimes the names weren't so flattering. They called me a goodie-two-shoes, narc, brown-noser. But it never mattered. I had a singular vision for my life. I am walking in those shoes now. The shoes I imagined twenty years ago as a boy watching Grandpa Maddox slam his gavel on the wooden pew.

I spent thirty-five years of my life pristine, not a single smudge on my record.

And then I met Norlene Weaver and now I see her everywhere. She's peering from windows, hovering behind trees, she's drifting beside me down the sidewalk, she's muttering in my ear when I try to sleep at night, sliding her icy fingers down my spine. In the past five days, I can count the hours I've slept on two hands. I've fallen from grace. I'm still falling.

Is it her spirit? Or is my own conscience haunting me?

Today she appeared behind me in the bathroom mirror at the courthouse. Her ghost, if that's what it is, did not look like her. She looked dead. Her face was bloated, her eyes bloodshot and bulging from the pale puffy flesh, her tongue stuck out slightly as it had when I rowed her into the lake, weighted her body and dropped her over the side.

Jack's voice broke in the recording as if he'd begun to cry.

I've never sobbed as hard as I did that night. It was everything I could do not to throw up, but I could think of nothing but DNA, evidence. I cleaned the stone walkway where she'd landed, but people don't realize how hard it is to clean up the scene of a crime, a murder.

Good investigators say there's always a trace. Any forensic team agrees. It doesn't have to be murder. Brush against someone in the subway and a trace contact occurs. Each degree of intimacy adds more depth to that contact—sex and murder perhaps being the deepest you can go. The exchange of bodily fluids, the closeness, breath and sweat and skin cells, semen, saliva... so much to leave behind and in the heat of the moment no one can wipe it all clean.

I tried to do it all, as much as I could anyway after I sat for an hour and stared in stunned disbelief at her ruined body. I understood then that I'd destroyed both of our lives. I even felt a pang of jealousy looking at her because she at least was free from this body and this life and this world and all the horrors yet to come.

I've devoted my life to studying murderers. They are loathsome-unforgiveable-monsters. I must now count myself among them.

It's only a matter of time. How long until I break? Until I drive to the sheriff's office and turn myself in? I cannot imagine going on this way.

How do they do it? These killers who live on as if nothing happened?

My entire life has now been reduced to one terrible night. Nothing else matters before the moment when I ended her life and my own in one screaming rage. I shoved her. I shoved her off the balcony knowing she would die and the baby inside her, whether real or imaginary, would die as well.

And I might as well have walked into the woods, followed the whispers of the maji-manidoo, because never had he called to me so urgently. I know now he is the Devil for it was he nudging me all through that night. Whispering on the warm summer breeze, hissing through the shifting stones at the river's edge.

Or maybe this is me again copping out, looking for someone to blame as I've watched so many defendants do. 'It's because my mother didn't love me, my father beat me,' they say. I have no such excuse. 'It was the dark man, your honor, the maji-manidoo, as my great-grandmother calls him, putting evil thoughts in my head.'

Jack choked out a harsh laugh.

Even now I am sealing my own fate, putting this confession here in this digital world. It's almost as if I want to be caught.

The recording ended and the screen went dark.

In Skelling Hall the light that had illuminated the second floor extinguished.

Jack was coming.

Iris found the door handle, yanked it, flung the door open and leapt out. She ran down the driveway beneath the dark canopy of trees as the front door of Skelling Hall slammed behind her.

Her feet pounded the snow-packed ground and she heard Jack giving chase, his footfalls heavy.

"Iris!" He shouted her name.

She didn't turn back, but ran harder, blood thrumming in her ears. How far did the peninsula road stretch? Less than a mile, but what would she find at the end except more deserted road?

Iris remembered the story Parker Stephens had told about finding Brett's footprints, how they'd vanished as if a giant bird had swooped down and plucked him from the earth. She shot a frightened glance toward the sky, but saw only the glittering stars.

"Please, God, Iris, please..." Jack's voice, pleading, cut through her terror, her urgency.

She'd gained ground. Her breath whistled through her teeth. He was further back. He was a runner. He could easily catch her and yet he was falling behind, giving up.

Iris slowed and turned to look at him.

He took a halting step toward her, held up both his hands. "Please don't run away from me. Please hear me."

Iris stood and watched him. She wanted to refuse him, to turn and run until her feet met the blacktop of the road and pray someone drove by that she could flag down.

The wind grew louder. It shook the trees on either side of the road. It howled in Iris's ears and she could no longer hear Jack Skelling. She watched him drop to his knees.

And then a whisper in the trees, but it wasn't her name that emerged.

Jack...

In the forest something shifted, a being darker than the night itself. It moved quickly, darting in and out of the trees like a wolf stalking a rabbit.

Jack raised his arms and closed his eyes.

"No..." She took a step toward him, watched the shadow roll out from the woods like a wave of black smoke. It surrounded Jack.

"Jack..."

From the road behind her she heard the sound of a siren. Flashing red and blue lights shone through the trees.

The cruiser slammed on its brakes. Andy leapt out and ran to where Iris stood.

They watched as road before them filled with a black fog, the wind roared and the trees clawed at one another.

"Come on," Andy said. He grabbed Iris's hand and pulled her back toward the car.

"No, wait..." She watched as the black dissipated. The wind calmed.

The road lay empty before them.

EPILOGUE

Iris stepped into the county jail and handed the guard her driver's license.

"I'll buzz you through," he told her.

She stood in the hall, one door locked behind her, waiting for the guard to release the door at the opposite end. A buzzer sounded and she stepped through.

Searchers had found Jack Skelling on the shore of the St. Mary's River the morning after their harrowing night at Skelling Hall. He'd been disoriented and cold, but alive. He'd insisted the sheriff read him his Miranda rights and arrest him on the spot. He was guilty, he'd told him, of the murder of Norlene Weaver.

Iris followed a guard to a heavy gray door. The guard opened it and she walked through.

"Hit the button when you want out," he told her, gesturing at a red button next to the door.

"Thanks."

Jack sat at a wooden table, his ankles cuffed to the legs, his wrists cuffed in front of him. He wore state-issued scrubs, but his hair had been neatly trimmed and his face was clean-shaven.

"Hi," he said. "It's good to see you."

Iris sat in the chair across from him, surprised at how good he looked, almost better than he had on the outside, younger, more at ease.

"How are you? How is this place?" she asked.

He smiled. "It's not great, but…" He shrugged. "I'm happy to be here. An odd thing to say, I know, but… I deserve to pay for what I did. I've always believed in justice. I swore an oath to uphold it, not because of the job but because of what runs through me, what I know to be true. Norlene…"

"You shouldn't talk about that now." Iris flicked her eyes to the camera mounted in the corner.

"I've confessed to everything, Iris," he said. "I told the detectives every single moment beginning with my first interview with Norlene. I'm pleading guilty. I've given them instructions on how to find her body. It's over. There's nothing more to hide. I wish I could have told you all this that night under the stars. I wanted to. I had this urge to and I wish I'd done it then. I wish I'd leaned into you and told you everything, but I didn't because for the first time since killing Norlene, I felt happy. I thought maybe I could go on, live with what I'd done. Turns out I couldn't."

"I'm sorry you're here," Iris told him and she was.

"I'm not," he said. "I've accepted my fate. I made choices, these are the consequences." He smiled. "Was it Andy who showed up that night at Skelling Hall? Your savior?"

Iris smiled, nodded. "Yes."

"How did he know to go there. Did you tell him?"

"No. He was on patrol and…" A bubble of emotion floated into her throat and for a moment she couldn't say it without crying. She swallowed and went on. "He heard Lola. He said it was like she was sitting in the back of his patrol car. She said 'Skelling Hall.'" That was it and he came."

Jack smiled and closed his eyes, let loose a long sigh. "He's one of the good ones."

"Why didn't the shadow-man take you, Jack?" Iris asked. "The maji-manidoo."

Jack sighed and interlaced his fingers on the table. "I've wondered that myself. The truth is I don't know, but Skelling Hall is closed. It won't reopen. After this… what I did there, that place won't ever reopen. And it's time to let it go, to let the maji-manidoo starve."

I ris knocked on Willow's door. The woman opened it wearing a hideous sweater adorned with dangling Christmas ornaments.

Willow beamed when she saw Iris. "Oh, Iris. Perfect timing. We're having our ugly sweater Christmas party. Come in and have some eggnog."

Iris smiled, tempted to decline, but instead allowed the woman to draw her into the house.

The table was crowded with casserole dishes, plates of deviled eggs and trays of Christmas cookies.

A tall, thick man wearing a sweater several sizes too small depicting Rudolph the Red-Nosed Reindeer walked into the kitchen.

"Iris, this is my Kurt. Kurt, this is the lovely Iris," Willow introduced them.

Iris shook the man's meaty hand.

"I'm real pleased to meet you, Iris," Kurt told her. "We can't thank you enough for helping us find out what happened to Norlene." His face fell and he wrapped a comforting arm around Willow's shoulders. "We were hoping for better news, but…"

Willow teared up and then forced a smile. "Kurt, get Iris some eggnog. We're playing Pictionary in there, Iris. You've got to join us."

From the other room people shouted guesses as someone drew on a whiteboard.

"I really appreciate your calling and telling me what happened. I know there's still a long road ahead, but… at least now we know," Willow said.

Iris pulled an envelope from her bag. "Jack Skelling wrote you a letter. He asked me to deliver it. I want you to know he made a full confession and the sheriff's office intends to send divers in to search for Norlene's body in the next few days, weather permitting."

Willow took the envelope and stared at it, the lines in her face deepening.

"Save it for later. Sometime when you and Kurt are alone."

Willow swallowed thickly and nodded. She walked the envelope to a drawer and slid it inside.

"Will you join us?" she asked Iris, her expression hopeful.

Iris glanced again at the room of partygoers. "Sure. I used to play Pictionary with my grandma and her friends. I've missed it."

Christmas Day

Outside the pink house snow fell. The fat, fluffy kind, Lola had called it, and for the first time that winter, Iris saw that it was, in fact, beautiful.

Not bothering to put on a coat, she walked out the door and into the front yard. She opened her mouth and caught snowflakes with her tongue as she'd done as a girl when the snow cast the world in shades of magic. She remembered the toys dazzling in the department store window, the glossy Christmas catalogue she and Frankie marked with red pens, the glitter of their Christmas tree when she snuck downstairs at night for a drink of water. Most of all she remembered Christmas mornings when all of them still existed together in one world: her mother, Frankie, Lola, her father and Iris.

The memories of those simple days, those days of magic, made Iris' chest hurt. She put one hand over Lola's pink sweatshirt. The slow throb was there, the pulsing that reminded her that she was still here. For her mother, Frankie and Lola too, their hearts had ceased, the beating was gone.

She'd taken such a simple thing for granted.

Andy's jeep turned onto the street and slowed to a stop in front of the house. He rolled down the window.

"Merry Christmas," he told her. He held up a tinfoil-covered dish. "I made biscuits and gravy."

She walked to him. "Merry Christmas to you. Sounds delicious. I have one thing I'd like to do first though." She walked around and climbed into his passenger seat.

He kissed her. "What do you want to do?"

"I want to get a cat."

He smiled and cocked an eyebrow. "I don't think the animal shelter is open today."

"That's okay. I know where we can find one."

That night Iris and Andy shared Lola's bed with her new cat, Frankie.

Iris woke in the night. The bed was covered in flowers, daisy-like with pale purple petals—asters. They were scattered across Frankie the cat and in Andy's hair. Iris sat up and touched one, lifted it to her nose and inhaled. It smelled like summer, like dirt and lake and grass. Through the window, she saw snow falling.

The door creaked. Iris turned as a figure stepped from the bedroom. She gazed at the back of a young woman, hair swishing over the top of her gold dress.

"Norlene," she called out, and the sound pulled her from sleep, rang hollow in the silent bedroom. Andy grumbled in his sleep, but didn't wake.

The snow didn't blow outside her window. It was full night and still too dark to see. The asters were gone from her bedspread, but the scent of spring lingered in the air.

Shadows danced on the ceiling from the dim amber light in the hall. The curtains shifted, blown by the heat from the floor vents. Iris looked at the doorway, half expected to see Norlene there stepping from the room, heading toward something wonderful in that glittering gold dress, a party perhaps.

But Norlene was gone.

THE TRUE STORY THAT INSPIRED STILL FALLING

On June 8th, 1989, a twenty-eight-year-old woman from Pikeville, Kentucky, disappeared. For the previous two years, the woman had worked as a drug informant with a local FBI agent. When she vanished, investigators had a range of theories, including that she'd simply taken off or been murdered by her ex-husband or a criminal she'd helped the FBI convict.

The truth was far more chilling.

In 1990, nearly a year after the woman had vanished, the FBI agent she'd worked with as an informant confessed to her murder. He revealed that he and the young woman had been having an affair and she claimed to be pregnant with his child. He was married with children and feared the revelation would ruin his marriage and tarnish his career as an FBI agent.

He ultimately led investigators to her body and admitted that during an argument, he'd strangled her to death. He later dumped her body in an isolated mountain area.

He was the first FBI agent ever to be convicted of murder.

For more information on the true story that inspired Still Falling, visit www.jrericksonauthor.com.

ALSO BY J.R. ERICKSON

The Troubled Spirits Series

Dark River Inn

Helme House

Darkness Stirring

Ashwood's Girls

Still Falling

Flowers in Her Bones

Or dive into the completed eight-book stand-alone paranormal series:

The Northern Michigan Asylum Series.

Do you believe in ghosts?

ACKNOWLEDGMENTS

Many thanks to the people who made this book possible. Thank you to Team Miblart for the beautiful cover. Thank you to RJ Locksley for copy editing Still Falling. Many thanks to Will St. John for beta reading the original manuscript, and to Emily H., Josie T. and Saundra W., for finding those final pesky typos that slip in. Thank you to my amazing Advanced Reader Team. Lastly, and most of all, thank you to my family and friends for always supporting and encouraging me on this journey.

ABOUT THE AUTHOR

J.R. Erickson, also known as Jacki Riegle, is an indie author who writes ghost stories. She is the author of the Troubled Spirits Series, which blends true crime with paranormal murder mysteries. Her Northern Michigan Asylum Series are stand-alone paranormal novels inspired by a real former asylum in Traverse City.

These days, Jacki passes the time in the Traverse City area with her excavator husband, her wild little boy, and her three kitties.

To find out more about J.R. Erickson, visit her website at www.jrericksonauthor.com.